FINDIN<

Annette Keen

© Annette Keen, 2017

Published by Sunbird Publishing

All rights reserved. No part of this book may be reproduced, adapted, stored in a retrieval system or transmitted by any means, electronic, mechanical, photocopying, or otherwise without the prior written permission of the author.

The rights of Annette Keen to be identified as the author of this work have been asserted in accordance with the Copyright, Designs and Patents Act 1988.

A CIP catalogue record for this book is available from the British Library.

ISBN 978-0-9574080-8-1

Cover design by Strumpet Design

Prepared and printed by:

York Publishing Services Ltd
64 Hallfield Road
Layerthorpe
York YO31 7ZQ

Tel: 01904 431213

Website: www.yps-publishing.co.uk

For all the lovely people I've shared a yoga studio with, especially my teachers: Lynne, Eva, Penelope and Mala.

Namaste

Annette would like to thank:
First and always, Andy and Pam, for your love, support and encouragement.
Andy for being my computer wizard too!

Lyn, Sue, Jenny K and Jenny J for reading sections of the manuscript and offering suggestions and advice when I could no longer see the wood for the trees. I would never have completed it without you lot cheering me on.

Special, huge thanks to Sue at Strumpet Design for turning my doodle into such brilliant cover artwork.

The team at YPS for your helpful, straightforward approach to getting this book published.

And all my other friends and family for believing in me.

FINDING BELLA

THE PHOTOGRAPH

It's black and white (but in reality mostly grey), a bit dog-eared around the edges, and the young woman in the centre of the shot is smiling. Not too broadly, it's not a carefree, happy to the brim sort of smile, but it's a smile all the same. She's very pretty, in a printed summer dress that shows off her figure, with a nipped in waistline and narrow belt, short, puffy sleeves and a V neckline. The fabric of the dress, mid-grey in this photo, makes a marked contrast against her pale skin. She's got dark, wavy hair, and there's a flower tucked behind her ear.

The girl has her right hand trailing across the top of a stone container of flowers, indeterminate in their drab greyness. A few feet behind her a pair of French doors stand open and there's just a suggestion of someone else there, inside the room, merging into receding layers of blackness.

* * *

That afternoon, when Douglas took the photograph, was the kind of July day that we like to think is the essence of that time of year: brilliant sunshine, cloudless blue sky, a garden full of flowers, bees and butterflies.

The flowers in the stone container were begonias and nasturtiums – an explosion of orange and red, with white alyssum tumbling over the top and sides. Tucked into the girl's auburn hair was one of the orange begonia heads from the container, and the stalk left standing did not go unnoticed later by the gardener, who tutted as he got his secateurs to the base of the plant and nipped it off. He picked up the flower head (subsequently abandoned on the paving slab), and added it to the basket he was slowly filling up with weeds and dead flower heads. The dress the girl wore that day was in a green and blue printed cotton, with a white belt at the waist.

There was a gramophone playing in the dining room behind her, and the sound of Fred Astaire singing "I'm Putting All My Eggs in One Basket" drifted out into the garden, lay across the still air, and floated off over the Purbeck Hills. Douglas had been lucky to get the record, one of several brought back from America by an old school chum long before they would be available in England.

The shutter clicked, and she called out to him.

'There's a wasp hovering over your left ear, Douglas! Careful, or you'll get stung.'

He brushed a hand across his ear, swatting the wasp away.

'One more photograph, then we'll be finished out here,' he said, shifting the tripod slightly and lining her up in the viewfinder again.

The girl sighed, then planted the smile back on her face.

It was the summer of 1936.

The casual onlooker might think that these were people who had it all. And maybe they did, but only for a little over two months longer.

LINDSAY

Nobody likes being unemployed. At least nobody I know, and I wasn't liking it much either.

OK, the first couple of weeks felt like being on holiday, but after that it started to get worrying, to put it mildly, and when I took a closer look at my savings account I stopped enjoying the freedom to do whatever I liked and started to twitch.

Skip-loads of advice came my way, some from people who'd never been unemployed in their entire lives, although curiously this was generally more helpful than the things one or two previously out-of-work friends had to say. I wasted hours in the Job Centre being grilled by snappy adolescents (well they seemed like adolescents from my fifty-two year old perspective), who contradicted each other constantly with the information they gave me. I attended a free course where I was able to update my CV, which didn't take long as I had been a loyal employee and my employment history only covered half a page. I had mock interviews at the town's Job Club. I scoured the local paper each week and applied for every job that it was even remotely possible I might be able to do, as well as some that I definitely couldn't, on the basis that nobody's born being able to drive a fork-lift truck. I dropped my shiny new CV plus covering letter into every local office I walked past. I enquired about work in all the High Street shops.

I got two replies to all this leg-work and they were both negative.

I started to buy Lottery tickets.

I cut right down on meeting up with friends if food and drink establishments were involved – as they almost always were.

Time moved on and nothing changed.

I stopped buying Lottery tickets.

Gradually, I gave up more and more of life's little luxuries. The only exception to this was my once a week yoga class, which I was determined to keep going, partly because I knew it was good for me, partly because as my social life dwindled this was just about the only thing left, and partly because Gary and Rufus always insisted on a coffee and scone afterwards in the café downstairs, a treat which they would never let me buy.

One day after class, when they offered to pay me each week to clean their already immaculate house, I wept. And then I accepted, as graciously as I could whilst blowing my nose.

CAROLINE

'I don't want to do it.'

'Why ever not? The viewing public will watch your voyage of discovery and take you to their hearts.'

'Can't you get me on *'Strictly'*?'

'I've tried, Caroline, really I have. To be honest they only want soap stars or singers from girl-bands. And you're not thin enough.'

'But I'd lose weight, everyone does. They've had people fatter than me before who've lost loads of weight. And they've had comedians too.'

'Only really fat ones. The trouble is you're not fat enough.'

'Make your mind up! Anyway I could work on getting fatter, that's easy.'

'Listen, I can't get you on *'Strictly'*. Or *'I'm a Celebrity'* or that cooking one.'

'Well that's good, because I can't cook.'

'Why don't you want to do *'Touching My Roots'*? It's a lovely show. It'll give your career just the boost it needs. Viewers will empathise.'

'My family were the dullest people you could ever meet, that's why. I come from mind-numbingly boring stock. People will switch off in their thousands and then even Radio 4 will drop me.'

'That's nonsense. They always find an ancestor of interest in every family. Why should yours be any different? The researchers turn up the most amazing things.'

'I don't want them going on about my parents.'

'Then say so. They'll want to look much further back than that anyway. You just tell them your parents are a no-go area for the programme.'

'Mmm.'

'So you'll do it?'

(A long sigh.)

'Oh, I suppose so.'

'Great, I'll go back to them. Good decision Caroline.'

'Mmm.'

A man asks a yoga teacher, "Can you teach me
to do the splits?"
"How flexible are you?" the teacher asks.
"I can't make Tuesdays," the man says.

THE YOGA STUDIO

Once, many years ago, Lindsay Walton was married
to a rather handsome boy called Simon. They were
both far too young and because of that neither listened
to their parents telling them they were too young and
fundamentally unsuited. They saved their money, got a
mortgage on a tiny house then proceeded to fill it with
second hand furniture and a load of kitchen equipment
bought in charity shops, most of which they never used.
They held parties there for their friends, and argued a
lot. When Lindsay and Simon divorced two years later
and sold the little house they found it had managed
to drop in value, and so neither of them got anything
much out of the exercise except a desire to forget all
about married life and a determination never to repeat
the exercise.

Lindsay has been very successful in this, and now
she can hardly remember her brief marriage at all.
Through all the years since she's been celebrating her
single status by doing whatever she feels like doing,
especially those things she knows Simon would have
scoffed at, and for a long time yoga has filled that slot
perfectly. The Friday lunchtime class fitted neatly into
her working day but nowadays of course, the timing
is no longer a consideration. No matter, she's hooked,

and she's become an integral part of the class in the same way that it is now a part of her.

When she arrives at the studio one unremarkable Friday she finds that Deirdre has, as usual, beaten her to it and is already lying on her mat with her legs up in the air.

Deirdre takes her yoga very seriously.

'We've got a new student today,' says Janey, in the soft, wispy voice that sends them off to sleep so easily during relaxation. Lindsay glances into the studio again, but before she can look more closely her attention is caught by the sight of Deirdre, who is now in Tree posture, balancing on one leg with her arms up over her head. Lindsay focuses steadily on her and is delighted to detect a wobble.

'She's a language student,' says Janey. 'From Thailand.'

Lindsay pulls her dark hair back into a tight ponytail and secures it with an elastic band. Great, she thinks. What this class really needs is a teeny-tiny double-jointed Asian girl to show the rest of us up.

It's called Yoga for Beginners, but strictly speaking none of them are. They've all been coming to Janey's class for ages, although most of them still can't do advanced postures and possibly never will – except for Deirdre of course and now, undoubtedly, the Thai girl.

Lindsay pays Janey her money, noticing as she does so that she's now got less than a pound left in her purse. But tomorrow is her cleaning day at Gary and Rufus' place, and they always pay her cash – far more than the value of the cleaning she does there because the place is already spotless. She slips off her shoes and walks into the studio.

'Morning Deirdre,' she says as she pads past her and goes across to her usual place.

Deirdre breathes out – whoosh – lowers her arms and starts to shake them. Her head is down and her hair forms a curtain all around her face. She acknowledges Lindsay with a barely audible 'hello'. The Thai girl is lying on her mat, seemingly asleep, with a blanket over her and just the top of her jet black hair poking out above it. Other people start to arrive. Janey takes up her position at the head of the class, everyone lies down and silence descends.

'Just take a few minutes now to arrive on your mat, and let's start with some deep breaths...' says Janey, and just as they're breathing in the front door rattles and there is a scuffling outside in the reception area. Two pairs of shoes hit the floor in a series of thuds, followed by the metallic clank of a belt buckle.

'Sorry everyone, are we late?' Rufus walks the length of the studio and plonks himself down next to Lindsay, while Gary tiptoes in more discreetly behind him and takes the only other available space – between Deirdre and the new girl. Lindsay opens one eye and smiles. Ha – serves you right for being late, she thinks, but then the Thai girl throws off her blanket to reveal rather a lot of puppy fat, and from then on she spends most of the session giggling silently behind her hand. So Gary is not challenged by being next to her after all, although Deirdre is a different matter altogether.

Janey gets them all back on course.

'Now, just relax and take a deep breath in through the nostrils, and then sigh it out through the mouth...'

* * *

Later, seated in their usual corner in Cappuccino Blues, Lindsay cradles her coffee cup in both hands and laughs loudly at one of Rufus' funny stories. They're the only three from yoga who go down for a coffee afterwards, which is a shame because it would be nice to get to know some of the others from the class. But although Gary has often suggested it, they just gather up their things, say goodbye, and file out quietly as if they're unable to break free of the spell Janey has woven around them.

'Anyway, petal,' says Gary, 'has anything come up yet, job-wise?'

Lindsay shakes her head. 'Nothing at all,' she says, 'but I'm still trying.'

'Had you thought about voluntary work?' asks Rufus.

'I was rather hoping to earn something, actually.'

'But it might be a way in to something better, you never know.'

Lindsay thinks of charity shops and shudders. 'I wouldn't want to handle other people's old clothes,' she says, wrinkling her nose. 'Those places all smell the same to me.'

'OK, there are plenty of other things. What about an apprenticeship?'

'I think I'm too old for that.'

'Avon Calling?'

'Is that still going? I thought they packed up years ago – I never see their catalogues around these days.'

'Well,' says Gary, 'something will come up soon. You just have to keep looking.'

She looks constantly. But the longer this goes on the harder it is to keep the momentum going.

* * *

On Wednesday morning Lindsay lets herself into Gary and Rufus' house. It's a big, modern detached house with beautiful décor and stunning pieces of artwork that they've collected on their many travels since they both took early retirement. They have an eye for colour and detail, and Lindsay thinks their house is more tasteful than those featured in the up-market magazines she flicks through in the dentist's waiting room.

Gary and Rufus always make themselves scarce on cleaning days so that they won't, as they put it, get under her feet, but this isn't the real reason at all. This weekly shift in their normal relationship is still a little awkward for all of them, and face-to-face contact is therefore best avoided while Lindsay has a duster in her hand. So they are in a routine now of visiting Gary's mum every Wednesday morning, which seems to suit everyone.

When she first started cleaning for them their instructions were to do 'whatever needs doing', which has always been tricky because they keep their house so clean and tidy that strictly speaking nothing needs doing. But she can't take their money for sitting around reading a book, so she cleans the kitchen sink, the bathrooms and toilets, vacuums the hallway and polishes the ornate mirror above the lounge fireplace. Sometimes there's washing on the airer in the utility room, so she'll do a bit of ironing, and after they've had one of their frequent dinner parties she unloads the dishwasher and puts the things away. They always leave her money in an envelope on the kitchen table, alongside a note telling her what they've left her for lunch – a salad in the fridge or something in the microwave. Gary and Rufus are the best mates she's ever had.

The local paper, folded on the kitchen table, catches her eye with its shouty headline about parking issues. She pulls it towards her, and starts thumbing through:

craft fairs, retirement dos, fund-raising events, local political sniping, the letters page. It's all very predictable, as are the job adverts. Care workers, (no, something Lindsay really could not bring herself to apply for), telesales (she's tried, over and over again but there must be something about her attitude that puts people off hiring her), restaurant kitchen help (never even had replies to those), on and on and boringly on. There isn't a single job there that she'd want to do, but there are a few that she will apply for nonetheless. She notes the contact details then glances at the facing page of obituaries.

Quite often she'll recognise a surname; an elderly relative of some kid she was at school with, or someone she once worked with. This week she's shocked to see that Sylvia Horton has died. The Hortons lived next door to her parents when Lindsay and her brothers were growing up, and the two couples were quite good friends at the time. As her mother hasn't said anything to Lindsay about Sylvia she obviously doesn't know she's died. Lindsay picks up her mobile phone and calls her mum.

'Sylvia? No I didn't know. Oh, poor old thing,' says Lindsay's mum Kaye, who at eighty one, is four years older than Sylvia was. 'To be honest I hadn't seen much of her in recent years – once they moved out of the road we didn't really keep in close contact. Poor Trevor, I must get in touch.'

'You'll find that difficult, he's already dead according to Sylvia's obituary. Gillian must have put it in the paper because I don't think her brothers stayed around here, did they?'

'Peter went to Australia years ago but I don't know where Matt ended up.' Kaye sighs. 'Sylvia always seemed so – well, tireless. Worked up till she was almost seventy, and even then she didn't just stay at home and knit, but went out and got herself a voluntary job up at Stonegrove. Funny that, I couldn't wait to retire...'

Kaye natters on, but even while Lindsay's putting the right responses in the right places (hopefully), she's thinking along a parallel line.

Stonegrove Hall. Where there might now be a volunteer vacancy... hmm.

STONEGROVE HALL

A Day Out for all the Family!
Visit Stonegrove Hall, built for Victorian entrepreneur
Hector Stanton in 1859 and the home of the Stanton
family ever since.
Experience life both Upstairs and Downstairs with our
interactive audio-visual displays, costume collections
and family portraits.
Trace the Stanton family history going back more
than 150 years as you walk through the rooms they
continue to use to this day.
Visit the Log Cabin, a play-house enjoyed by
generations of Stanton children.
Enjoy the year-round colour of the planting scheme in
our fabulous gardens – group tours can be arranged
by prior request.

Refreshments are served in the Carriage Room
Restaurant and the Stables Tea Room, or enjoy a
picnic in the Long Meadow, overlooking the beautiful
Purbeck Hills.

Make a day of it! Bring your whole family and maybe
meet some of our family.

Open daily 11am – 5pm, March to November.
Adults: £11
Children 3 to 16 years: £6
Family Ticket: £30

Available for weddings and other private functions

For 'How to Find Us' see over.

Volunteering is the ultimate exercise in democracy.
You vote in elections once a year, but when you
volunteer, you vote every day about the kind of
community you want to live in.

Anon

YOGA

For once, Gary and Rufus are early and Deirdre isn't. When Lindsay arrives the boys are already sitting on their mats chatting, and there's no sign of any of the rest of the class. She takes a place alongside Rufus.

'Guess what?' she says.

They take a moment to think.

'You've got a job?' asks Gary, smiling broadly in expectation of a positive answer.

'Not exactly. But I've got a voluntary job.'

'Well done!' says Rufus, patting her shoulder. 'Good for you! Who knows what this might lead to. Where is it?'

'Stonegrove Hall. I'm going to be a room steward.'

Rufus whistles, and they both look suitably impressed.

'Several notches up from the charity shops,' says Gary. 'How did you swing that?'

So Lindsay starts telling them about Sylvia Horton's obituary, and how she rang the Hall straight away and was invited to go along and meet them – and then other people start arriving in the studio and Dierdre rushes in with only minutes to spare and huffs about, pulling her sweater off and getting her cushion and bolster organised on the mat.

'I'll tell you the rest later,' Lindsay whispers, and they all lie down, close their eyes, and wait for Janey to take her place and empty all the rubbish out of their minds.

* * *

'As this is a celebration,' says Gary, 'I thought we'd go completely mad and have Danish pastries.'

He brings three crisp, flaky pastries across to their table and then goes back to the counter for the coffees. The Gaggia machine in Cappuccino Blues hisses loudly and Sergiu, the young Romanian barista, who wears the tightest jeans Lindsay has ever seen on a man, calls over to them.

'Very big celebration when you have Danish and not usual scones!'

'Lindsay's got a job,' says Gary.

'Well, sort of...' Lindsay cuts in. 'Unpaid.'

'Not paid? You work for no money?'

Clearly the concept of voluntary work has not been trending in Romania. Sergiu looks at her in amazement, pauses in wiping down the counter and then shakes his head as he takes up his cloth again.

'So,' says Rufus. 'Tell us all about it.'

And Lindsay is eager to tell them the story, so it comes out all in a rush.

'Well, I was interviewed up at the Hall by Helena Croft, she's the daughter of the family and the last of them left standing if you don't count her mother, who I gather just drifts around the garden and is a bit dotty – oh, and Helena's kids but they don't live round here anyway. And yes, they were looking for more volunteers partly because of Sylvia dying and partly because one of the other room stewards is about to go off to New Zealand for two months to see her son, and partly because Reg, who is also a volunteer, isn't in the best of health and sometimes needs to take time off.'

The barista, leaning on the counter listening, throws his hands up in the air.

'Too fast!' he says. 'Please more slowly, who is He-le-nar?'

Rufus shushes him, then turns back to Lindsay.

'Carry on,' he says.

'And she liked me, probably because I'm younger than most of their volunteers, so even though there's a waiting list I seem to have leap-frogged over the rest. I'm going to be in the room next to Reg, which is the Theatre Room. It isn't a real theatre, just a room where the Stanton children in... oh, can't remember...'

Lindsay rummages in her bag, pulls out the Stonegrove Hall brochure and information leaflet that Helena Croft has given her and starts flicking through it.

'... yes here it is, in the late 1800s. The children liked to write and put on plays so the parents had a tiny stage with curtains constructed in this room and that's where they entertained their friends and family. One of the daughters actually went on to be an actress.'

Gary and Rufus are impressed, and say so.

'You've picked up a lot in a short time,' says Gary.

Lindsay taps the brochure.

'I've got to learn this,' she says. Gary reaches out a hand so he can have a flick through it, and ends up getting quite engrossed in the history of Stonegrove.

'But next week I'm just there to wander around and talk to the other room stewards so I get a feel for the place. Then bang, straight in, on duty, the following Monday. I'm going there two days a week, but she knows I'm also looking for paid work so it's a flexible arrangement.'

Lindsay stops and spoons some froth off the top of her cappuccino. Sensing that she's come to the end of her story, Sergiu smiles and applauds, even though he hasn't understood most of what she's said.

* * *

Stonegrove Hall – A Brief History

Built in 1859 for wealthy entrepreneur Hector Stanton (b. 1810), his wife Emily and their five children William (19), Harriet (17), Joseph (16) Anne (14) and Elizabeth (11), Stonegrove Hall was an expensive project – and was always intended to look expensive.

Hector made his considerable fortune from importing all sorts of goods via his own shipping line. He brought into the UK anything and everything that was needed at that time: guano for fertiliser, timber from Canada, pianos, ostrich feathers, parts for steam engines...

He wanted a home that would reflect his wealth and chose a site near Wareham in the Purbeck Hills of Dorset. The house he built there, Stonegrove Hall, was on an elevated plot of land overlooking a river. The design of the house was typical mid-Victorian, with elements of the romantic Gothic revival style combined with Italianate flourishes, built using local Purbeck stone.

When Hector died in 1879 at the age of 69, the running of Stonegrove Hall passed to his son William, who lived there with his wife Jane, their three children and his mother. Changes were made to the building during this time, with electric lighting being added in 1887. William and Jane's two daughters married and moved away from Stonegrove, so the estate was left in the care of their son Walter, who assumed full responsibility for it when his father died in 1901, two months after the death of his wife.

Walter and Lydia had four children: William (d. aged 4), Charles, Mary and Sophia. It was while the children were small that an unused room on the bedroom floor was converted to the Theatre Room, as they used to enjoy writing and putting on their own plays for the enjoyment of their parents and friends. The room was equipped with a small stage and curtains, with just enough space 'backstage' for costume changes, and two rows of seats at the front. Sophia went on to become a renowned actress, her finest moment being when she appeared on stage in a supporting role to Dame Ellen Terry. The Theatre Room was not used as such by future generations of Stanton children, instead serving time as a store room mainly for sports equipment. It has now been restored and appears as it was when young Sophia Stanton took her first acting steps on its tiny stage.

During the First World War Stonegrove Hall was used as a rehabilitation unit for officers recovering from injuries gained at the front. During this time the family re-located to an apartment in London, returning in 1919 after extensive work had taken place to restore the original decorations in the rooms previously used as hospital wards.

When Charles and his young wife Cecilia, a beautiful American socialite, inherited Stonegrove Hall in 1921, major improvements were made to the upper floors of the Hall, and the young family of five moved upstairs to an apartment created from redundant servants' quarter. This had every modern convenience of the day. Mrs Stanton disliked the draughty, dusty rooms downstairs and made sure that her home on the third floor was the last word in 1920s interior design. Art Deco bathrooms were fitted, plus a labour-saving kitchen, and a lift was installed – which still works to this day. For entertaining, the show-piece rooms downstairs were still used, but Cecilia put in hand an ambitious programme of redecorating, and this is how they are seen today, as gorgeous as in their mid-20s heyday. As the children grew older they left their nursery bedrooms and moved back down to the bedroom floor of the house, leaving their parents upstairs.

In 1936, Douglas was killed in a motorcycle accident, never fully explained as he was an experienced rider and no other road users were involved. Stanton went into mourning for the beloved son and heir to the property, and his bedroom was closed up and left exactly as it had been on the fateful day. When Ruby inherited the house on the death of her mother in 1968 she opened up Douglas's bedroom to the public, and it has remained ever since as a memorial to a promising young life lost too soon.

For most of the second World War Stonegrove again served as a convalescent home for recovering servicemen. Only Ruby remained in residence, in the third floor flat of her childhood, and she continued to live there until her death in 2011, when the Hall passed to her younger sister.

Diana remains in an estate cottage, maintaining the lively interest she has always taken in the running of the gardens but having no great involvement in the house. Her only daughter Helena and her husband Anthony took over the running of Stonegrove Hall in 2012, and moved into Ruby's flat on the third floor – when another overhaul of the facilities and decoration there took place.

Their children have all married and moved away: James and Emma, Sonya and Chris, and Robert and Joanna are all frequent visitors to Stonegrove, along with James's daughters Chloe and Abigail, the 8th generation of Stanton children to enjoy the Hall and grounds.

Gary closes the guide book and passes it back to Lindsay.

'I had no idea about any of this,' he says. 'Shameful isn't it, to know so little about our local stately home.'

'Not exactly stately,' says Lindsay. 'It's surprising how homely it feels in there.'

'We should go on a visit, Rufus. We'll pick a day when Lindsay's on duty and grill her on her knowledge of the place.'

Lindsay pulls a face. 'Give me a chance to get a bit more familiar with it first.'

'Maybe we can help you to learn it,' says Rufus. 'Come over to our place and we'll have dinner first and then get stuck in to learning the facts. It'll be fun!'

'Will it? Well, OK if you're sure...'

REG

We're getting a new volunteer for the Theatre Room, replacing Sylvia on a Monday and Thursday. Nice young lady – well, she's young compared to the rest of us. Mrs Croft brought her round and introduced her to everyone on Monday, and she was bright as a button and so interested in everything it was a real pleasure to have her here.

Actually, it was quite useful too. Mr Croft had brought down a large trunk the other day – they'd found it in one of the attic rooms in Miss Ruby's old flat. Now that all the improvement work is almost finished and the Crofts are living there full time they keep unearthing stuff she'd tucked away. I've never been up there of course, but there must be a lot of storage space under those eaves and apparently Ruby was a hoarder so it's probably taking them an age to sort it all out. Anyway, this was full of things belonging to Douglas, so of course it came down to me as I'm in charge of his room, and I've been trying to find the time to go through it before and after opening times. Lindsay – that's the new girl – was a big help.

It was mostly full of old theatre programmes. Now that's interesting, because I didn't know he had such a fondness for the theatre and it's something else I can tell the visitors about him. And it ties in nicely with the Theatre Room next door, must have been something in the Stanton genes. Mrs Croft's going to get a small display cabinet to put most of the programmes in but a few can go out on his side table, next to the cup and saucer we keep there.

So Lindsay and I took the programmes out of the trunk, and underneath we found a dinner jacket – I think I might lay that out on the bed you know, as if he's just off to London for one of his theatre trips. And then there were various other bits and pieces, a couple of cameras, some road maps, a motorbike manual and several old records. I'm hoping the old wind-up gramophone in his room still works – we were going to give it a try but by then it was almost time to open the doors and let the visiting hoards in. I was thinking that I might have the records playing when visitors are here...

LINDSAY

It was great! I had such a good time today up at Stonegrove, just getting to know the place and the other volunteers. I thought at first it would be more use to me if I could work in the shop, or maybe the café, because I'd be learning things there that might get me a proper job, but the Theatre Room is so sweet and once I've learnt all the information I think I'll really enjoy being a room steward. Quite excited about it! Mum and Dad have said they'll come along on one of my days but I'm rather hoping they won't because Dad will be wheezing fit to drop by the time he gets up the stairs and makes it along the corridor.

Reg is next door, in the Douglas Memorial Room. He's a lovely man, so smartly turned out you'd think he was heading off to a business meeting. He's been very helpful to me too, and because he's been there for years there's not much he doesn't know about the place. I helped him sort out some old stuff that had belonged to Douglas, and it was really exciting because we didn't know what we'd dig out of that trunk next. It was busy today once the visitors started coming in and the kids are on Easter holidays this week so there were lots of families out for the day. That put an end to rummaging through Douglas's things. Reg is a real pro – once the visitors started arriving he was very brisk and businesslike. Loves to talk to them, you could tell.

Helena Croft always seems to be on the go and she's everywhere – I kept running into her as I was wandering about the place and in the end it got quite funny and I asked if she was stalking me. Wasn't sure how that would go down but she just laughed and said she thought it was the other way round.

She and her husband have recently moved back to the main house from their cottage on the estate. Her aunt had a flat on the top floor and since she died they've had it refurbished, but kept some of the best Art Deco features that some previous Stanton had installed. It all sounds lovely, I doubt if I'll ever get invited up there but I'd love to have a look round.

During the afternoon Reg pointed out Helena's mother, Diana Stanton-Lewis – she was out in the garden, pottering about with a huge hat jammed on her head and bright blue spotted Wellingtons, looking eccentric and very ancient and poking at things with her walking stick. She had George the gardener in tow, who looked cross as if he'd been dragged away from something else he was doing. He looks almost as old as her but surely he can't be. Reg doesn't have the answer to that one, but says George was working there when he started being a volunteer, that's almost fifteen years ago, and he didn't look any younger then. Must be all that time spent outdoors in all weathers.

It's largely thanks to Reg that I'm quickly getting to know a lot about this place. Diana Stanton-Lewis is the current owner of Stonegrove, she inherited it when her sister Ruby died a few years ago, but it seems that Helena and her husband had taken over the running of the place long before that. Reg says they've really turned it around in recent years, from a small time enterprise into a top local attraction.

Today was the first day for ages that I felt I was making a contribution to – well, anything really. Even though I wasn't actually on duty and didn't have a particular job to do it was good just to feel a part of what was going on. A couple of times people asked me where the restaurant was, or the Long Meadow, and even though I wasn't completely sure if I was sending them by the most direct route it was great that they obviously saw me as one of the team and didn't mistake me for just another visitor.

And that's odd, you know. I've lived around here all my life and yet I've never been inside Stonegrove Hall before. I wonder why not? I've been to craft fairs held outside in the grounds, and when I was a kid we used to bring picnics up here in the summer, but until today I had no idea what I was missing inside. It's a lovely house, I can understand why Reg is so attached to it.

'The pictures you will want TOMORROW – you must take TODAY!'

Advertisement for Kodak Verichrome Film, 1934

STONEGROVE HALL

Lindsay's second day at Stonegrove is full of surprises.

When she gets up to the first floor landing the sound of big band dance music is spilling out of the Douglas Memorial Room. Lindsay peers round the door to find that Reg has got the old gramophone working.

'It's not exactly hi-fi,' he says, 'but considering this is over eighty years old I don't think it sounds too bad.'

The gramophone is housed in an oak box, with a small cupboard underneath to store records. Reg has a duster in his hand, which he's been using to polish the wood and brass fittings. They stand together watching this miracle of 1930s technology and then the record starts to slow down and Reg winds the handle on the side until it gets back up to speed.

'Takes a bit of practice to know how much to wind it up,' he says, 'I haven't quite got the measure of it yet to last a whole record.'

Lindsay is impressed by Reg's devotion to his role here as room steward. He cares so much about getting it right that she feels a huge admiration for him and wonders if she'll be like this over the Theatre Room once she's got into the swing of it. Helena has told her there are some of the children's costumes tucked away behind the stage, and now Lindsay is starting to think about how she could display them to best effect.

Reg has got Douglas's tuxedo spread out on the bed, next to a couple of theatre programmes. She picks one up and flicks through it.

'You must feel as if you actually knew Douglas, working here for so long,' she says.

'Not really,' says Reg, which surprises her. 'I know a lot about him, but I've no idea what he was like as a man. His sisters both said he was the most marvellous chap, but then they would, wouldn't they? He died back in 1936 and his contemporaries must all be dead now as well, so I'll never know what anyone else thought of him.'

'Who's this?' Lindsay picks up a photo of a young woman from the bedside cabinet. She's very pretty, with a gorgeous figure, and she's got a flower in her hair.

'Ah, that's Bella.'

'And who was Bella?'

'I've absolutely no idea, a girlfriend I assume. I found it in the inside pocket of this jacket,' says Reg, indicating the tuxedo, 'and I thought I may as well put it out. I only know her name because it's on the back.'

Lindsay turns the photo over, and there it is. Written in a scrawly, artistic hand in black ink: *With love from Bella.* She looks more closely at it.

'I wonder if he took it, I mean he had those cameras so he must have been a keen photographer.'

'If he did then I'd say he was rather good for an amateur.'

'Do you think it was taken here?' she asks.

Reg looks over her shoulder at the photo.

'Quite possibly.'

'Would you mind if I took her downstairs Reg? I might be able to figure out exactly where she was standing when it was taken.'

'Be my guest,' says Reg, as he rubs his duster over another record, places it carefully on the turntable and then lowers the needle onto it.

Lindsay goes down the main staircase and out through the front door, saying hello to Marion on the front desk as she goes. Marion counts the visitors in, but because she thinks that it's more professional to do it discreetly, she holds the clicker behind her back. It makes Lindsay smile.

It's an overcast day, which probably means that numbers will be high. Several couples are making their way up the gravelled front drive from the car park as she turns around the side of the building, where George and a young lad are pulling up something in the borders. Lindsay hasn't had a chance to talk to George yet, and neither he nor the lad with him look up as she approaches, but she calls out what she hopes is a cheery greeting anyway. They both ignore her, although as Lindsay passes George cranks himself up to stand resting on his spade, and watches her walk away.

She hasn't quite got the layout of the Hall yet, so it's hard to know which window is which room, but as she gets to the back of the house she sees Helena coming the other way, looking business-like and country chic in a blue gilet, striped shirt and denim skirt, with her blonde and grey-streaked hair neatly pinned up.

'Hello!' she calls to Lindsay. 'Finding your way around?'

'Just about,' says Lindsay. 'I was trying to work out where this was taken.' She shows Helena the photo, and explains about Reg finding it in the jacket pocket.

'Oh, she's lovely isn't she? Well now, let's see...'

Helena looks along the length of the terrace, and back to the photo.

'I would say it was about there,' she says pointing to a spot near the second set of French doors. 'Unless those stone troughs have been moved about.'

Lindsay feels something furry brush against her leg and looks down. A large tabby and white cat is busy curling itself around her legs, stepping delicately over her feet, and looking up at her.

'Hello, who are you?' she says, bending down to stroke his head.

'That's Henry,' says Helena. 'There's always been a Henry here, for as long as I can remember. Except that we slipped up with the last one, who turned out to be a Henrietta.'

The cat follows them as they walk together to roughly where they think the photographer would have stood.

'Which room is that?'

'The dining room. We don't actually have those French doors open these days – might never get them closed again,' says Helena.

'Reg will be pleased to know we've identified the spot,' says Lindsay. 'Something else he can tell the visitors.'

Helena goes on her way and Henry is momentarily torn between which of them to stick to. In the end he remembers who feeds him and turns away from Lindsay, trotting along in Helena's wake.

Lindsay holds Bella's picture up in front of her, looks beyond it to the dining room, then back at the photo.

'Well there you are, Bella,' she says. 'Right back where you started.'

* * *

Marion is just explaining to some visitors where they should start their tour, when Lindsay goes back in through the front door. Helena has got there ahead of her.

'Lindsay – could you perhaps stay for an extra ten minutes after we close today? I just want to have a little word with all the volunteers,' she says. 'We'll meet in the Music Room, plenty of chairs there to save us all standing.'

'Sure – shall I tell the upstairs volunteers, save you the trouble of doing it?'

Helena lets her face fall into a sigh of relief as if Lindsay has taken a whole weight off her shoulders instead of just saving her the walk up two flights of stairs.

'Would you? Thanks *so* much. There should be five upstairs today.'

Later, as they all gather in the Music Room, Lindsay looks around at the assembled group. There are about twenty of them, but these are only the ones on duty that particular day. Must be a huge job, keeping track of them all, she thinks. And yet Helena knows everyone's name, which room the stewards usually work in, which of the ladies are from the shop and which from the cafés. However, it seems that the volunteers don't all know each other, and so there is already a quietness about the room when Helena starts to speak.

'I've got some rather exciting news for you! I'm sure some of you know the TV programme *'Touching My Roots'*?'

Helena looks around and several heads nod. Lindsay has seen the show a couple of times at her parents' house, although she wasn't aware it was still running. It strikes her as odd that anyone, celebrity or not, would want to drag their ancestors out in public, particularly since some of them have been quite seedy and in one much publicised episode downright criminal. Her mother would say it was just for the money, but it's hard to imagine they get paid much for doing a programme where they mostly just stand around with practised looks of amazement on their faces.

'Well, the production company have asked for permission to film here next month – I'll let you all have the dates once they've been confirmed.'

A ripple of interest runs through the volunteers. Helena consults the paper in her hand and pushes a few stray strands of hair back off her face and into a clip.

'It seems that they're researching the family tree of someone with a connection to Stonegrove, her great-aunt was one of the kitchen maids here between the wars.'

Reg nudges Lindsay and winks. She knows what he's thinking; that period is just right for them to want to film in the Douglas Memorial Room. She smiles back at him and nods, although she's actually wondering what a kitchen maid would have been doing up there in the first place.

Naughty Douglas, she thinks, and wonders how Reg would tackle a display of this aspect of his life; rumple up the bedspread and leave a trail of clothes on the floor?

'Their people will want to come in and have a good look round beforehand,' says Helena, 'and the film crew will probably be here for about three days in total, which means that some of you might not be on duty at all during that time. They say that only a very small percentage of what they film actually makes it into the programme, but we're sure to be in there somewhere. I'm a bit light on detail at the moment, but has anybody got any general questions?'

One of the ladies from the shop puts her hand up and Helena smiles encouragingly at her.

'Who's the celebrity?' she asks.

'Oh.' Helena refers to the sheet of paper she's carrying and flicks over to the back. 'Caroline van Dell,' she says. 'Isn't she on the radio? Comedienne?'

She looks around vaguely and one or two people nod in agreement. Lindsay has heard Caroline on quiz shows, and a picture that was in the Radio Times comes into her head; a petite woman with severe, white-blonde cropped hair, scarlet lips and outrageously big earrings.

'Nobody all that interesting then,' the shop lady remarks. 'I was hoping it might be someone a bit more glamorous.'

'Tom Conti!' one of the room stewards says.

'Alan Titchmarsh!' suggests another one, and there's a bit of laughter and banter.

The meeting breaks up in a light-hearted mood, and Lindsay goes off home thinking that she'll Google Caroline van Dell, just in case she gets to meet her. In the event, though, she forgets completely.

* * *

'Morning Reg, morning Bella.'

Lindsay breezes into Reg's room on her first real day as a Stonegrove Hall room steward, clutching her information folder. Bella smiles up from her new position on the mantelpiece and Reg raises an eyebrow.

'You're not going to read to them from that, are you?' he asks.

'Certainly not. I've learnt it off by heart and I've been practising all weekend on a couple of friends.'

Gary and Rufus were serious about helping her learn the Stonegrove history and together they nailed the details of the Theatre Room in a couple of sessions, with a lot of laughter and a bottle or two of wine to help things along. Keeping the folder nearby at all times is a belt and braces strategy, just in case her mind goes blank.

Reg laughs. 'I didn't mean it,' he says, 'I guessed you'd know it word for word by today. You won't even need to use most of the information, you'll find that the same questions come up all the time.'

It's a bright day, mid-April, but as the Douglas Memorial Room is at the back of the Hall and faces north-east, it won't get the benefit of the spring sunshine until later in the day. This location does the room no favours as it's dull to start with, full of big, heavy mahogany furniture and with dark blue drapes. Even the bedspread, which must have been quite vibrant once as it's a multi-coloured patchwork, has faded into dullness over the years. There are no ornaments, no bright splashes of colour, and were it not for Reg constantly on the look-out for personal items to display and anecdotes to tell the visitors, it would be a boring room to visit. Lindsay hopes the family appreciate his efforts.

The children have just gone back to school after the Easter holidays so the expected footfall is less than it was the previous week. In recognition of this, the kitchen has baked fewer scones and teacakes and the shop has only got one till open, but there are two parties expected during the afternoon, one full-size coach stuffed full of W.I. members, and a mini-bus bringing in mature foreign students. In Stonegrove terms though, this is going to be a quiet day.

However, Reg is standing by with his records, ready to evoke nostalgia for a period none of the visitors will be old enough to have lived through. The theatre programmes are sitting in a pile on the bureau, and as he talks to Lindsay he picks up the top two and arranges them on the bed next to Douglas's dinner jacket. He adds his watch (it's a Rolex, naturally, although it no longer works), placing it on the jacket along with a linen handkerchief, a silver cigarette case and a black fountain pen. He stands back to see how the arrangement looks, then steps forward again and moves the watch a couple of centimetres to the left.

'That's better,' he says, nodding with satisfaction. Lindsay can't see how it's better, but by now she has realised that Reg is a perfectionist where the Douglas Memorial Room is concerned.

'Helena said there are some children's costumes backstage in my room.'

'Are there? That's interesting, Sylvia never mentioned that. We'll have to get them out and display them on the stage.'

Lindsay's pleased that he's included himself in that enterprise, because she suspects this sort of thing won't be her forte, and Reg's unfailing eye for detail would be really useful.

Moving next door into the Theatre Room she puts her bag and folder down on the steward's table and starts straightening up the audience chairs. There are twenty in all, in two rows, but apparently on Christmases past the Stantons had to bring more chairs in to seat all their extended family and other visitors.

The chairs are mahogany, with padded seats covered in brown damask. Many of these are torn or the fabric has simply rotted away in places, but there is no rope barrier across this part of the room, only the stage itself, and so children often scramble up onto the chairs. Inevitably they've borne the brunt of Velcro shoe fastenings, buckles and sticky fingers – not to mention the passing of much time. The stage curtains are dark red velvet, always left open to show the empty space behind – empty that is except for a wicker trunk that once held costumes and props. The backcloth has been painted with sky, trees, a gate and a fence and Lindsay knows it was done quite recently by a couple of fifth-formers from the local secondary school on work experience. She won't say that, if asked. She'll just say that it's not the original.

A small console table against one wall displays a few pages of script, painstakingly written in a child's hand and now protected under glass, and the walls are covered with sepia photographs of solemn children dressed in elaborate costumes. Lindsay knows without referring to her folder which one is Sophia Stanton, the child who grew up to become an actress and whose proudest moment was when she played in a small supporting role to Dame Ellen Terry.

She checks her watch and takes a deep breath. It's a few minutes past eleven o'clock, and she knows that downstairs Marion will be standing in the front hall waiting for the first visitors, a clicker held inconspicuously behind her back.

Bang on cue, music floats through from the Douglas Memorial Room next door.

* * *

The room stewards take their breaks in rotation, providing cover for each other – or sometimes Helena will step in if she's not already busy. Reg comes into the Theatre Room to relieve Lindsay at two o'clock, and then stations himself on the landing between the two rooms.

In the Stables Tearoom the lunchtime rush is over

and the afternoon teas haven't started, so it's quiet. Lindsay recognises one of the ladies on duty from Helena's impromptu meeting of last week, and says hello to her.

'Had you ever heard of that so-called celebrity who's coming here?' she asks Lindsay as she pours her tea.

'Yes, I've heard her on the radio sometimes and one or two other people I asked say that she's quite well-known on the stand-up comedy circuit. She does Radio Four quizzes and comedy shows, that sort of thing.'

'Lesbian, is she?'

Lindsay is a bit taken aback.

'I don't know, what makes you say that?'

'I thought they usually were,' she replies, handing Lindsay a towering slice of chocolate cake which she hasn't ordered.

'On the house,' she says. 'It's one of the perks of being a volunteer here. The Stantons will get paid huge amounts for the filming,' she adds. 'I was here five or six years ago when the BBC were in for several weeks filming for a period drama. It was quite disruptive, but the family earned enough to pay for major repairs and that kept the place going.'

'It doesn't sound as if this will take too long, so maybe not such a big earner,' says Lindsay.

'Well. It's a pity we couldn't have had someone a bit more famous. I mean, apart from Radio Four listeners, who's ever heard of Caroline van Dell?'

CAROLINE

I warned them from the start that they were boring. This programme is not going to make riveting viewing for even the most ardent of my fans. So far all they've come up with is a couple of bachelor great-uncles on my Dad's side who owned a dairy and had a milk round in Bournemouth in the 1920s, and a great-aunt on my Mum's side who was a kitchen maid at Stonegrove Hall. The rest of them seem to have made a career out of not having a career. Talk about keeping a low profile. So, my filming schedule so far consists of:

A visit to Bournemouth, to follow the route of the 1920s milk round.

A visit to Stonegrove Hall, to find out what a kitchen maid's workload was like in the 1930s.

And then a visit to Gran's for a conversation with her about the family – but I need to talk to her first and tell her not to get side-tracked onto Mum and Dad. She can go backwards in generations, but not forwards.

It's going to be a disaster.

I should never have let Polly talk me into this, how she can think this will be a career boost I can't imagine. What's the use of an agent if they can't get the best possible exposure for their clients? I suppose the money's not bad, but if this programme goes tits up then I might just as well go stacking shelves in the Pound Shop.

I bet she could have got me on 'Strictly' if she'd really tried. Cow.

What on earth was Douglas thinking of? The parents are not impressed.

Ruby Stanton's diary, June 20th, 1936

STONEGROVE HALL

'Morning Reg, morning... oh, where have you put Bella?'

Lindsay arrives on the Thursday before filming is due to start, to find film technicians wandering about all over the Hall. Helena has told the production company that the house must remain open to the public as far as possible, and now with half an hour to go until opening time there's been a lot going on involving gaffer tape and cables. The technical crew are now adjourning to the Stables Tearoom to discuss the implications, or maybe just for a coffee and a skive.

'Bella's attendance at this particular party was not required,' says Reg, stiffly. 'Mrs Stanton-Lewis decreed it so.'

It's easy to see that Reg feels undermined in what he considers to be his domain, and Lindsay thinks that's completely understandable.

'Why?'

He shrugs. 'Who knows? An old lady's whim?'

'What did you do with the photo?'

Reg opens a drawer in the bureau. 'It's here. I couldn't just throw her away, could I?'

Lindsay is upset by this development. Firstly for Reg, who works so hard for Stonegrove in his quiet way, but also because she's grown to like having Bella around. She's a little bright spot in Douglas's rather austere room, and she lends a bit of humanity to him. For some reason, in spite of Reg's best efforts, Lindsay hasn't taken much to Douglas.

* * *

Often, on a warm day, Reg takes his lunch out into the grounds and heads for George's potting shed at the back of the kitchen garden, where visitors never go. He's been doing this for about twelve of the fifteen years he's been a volunteer at Stonegrove, and George is in the habit of putting out a couple of old wooden chairs from the shed when he thinks Reg might turn up. They don't know each other well, in spite of all those years of sharing lunch breaks, but there's an easy camaraderie between them which doesn't require much in the way of conversation and that suits them both just fine.

On this particular Thursday the sun is shining and in a sheltered spot it's very pleasant indeed. The chairs are already out at the side of the potting shed, George has got a brew going and Henry the cat is curled up nearby in a patch of sun. He opens one eye as Reg approaches but he lost interest in Reg years ago so he makes no attempt to move any closer. Henry knows a cat lover when he sees one.

'Afternoon, George.'

'Ah.. tea's coming.'

George makes builder's tea, strong and very dark, and it comes in big old chipped mugs. It reminds Reg of his National Service days. There's a bag of sugar with a spoon stuck in it, encrusted with a thick build-up of sugar crystals. Reg doesn't normally take sugar in tea but he's learnt that with George's brew, it's quite a good idea to spoon some into the mug.

They unwrap their sandwiches and eat in silence. Sometimes a bird flies down onto the patch next to them, and is rewarded with a bit of crust. There have been days when a rabbit has popped up nearby, thinking that the silence meant there were no humans about. When this happens George might swear at it or throw a stone or both, depending on how bad a time the rabbits have been giving him recently in the vegetable garden. Once a crow landed in the space between them and hardly had time to squawk before George lobbed a handful of gravel at it, most of which went over Reg's shoes.

After five minutes or so George pipes up.

'New volunteer up there?' he says, jerking his head towards the house.

Reg nods. 'Nice girl,' he says. 'Interested in people. The Stantons, Douglas.'

'Ah.'

A thrush lands near Reg's feet and he breaks off a bit of bread and throws it down. The thrush is joined by another, and then another. They watch the birds in silence as they hop about picking up crumbs. Henry starts to get interested but then yawns as though these days bird catching is really too much of an effort.

'Saw her with Mrs Croft the other day.'

George tops up Reg's mug from an old brown teapot. They finish their sandwiches and the sun warms them into a pleasantly comfortable state that's almost as cosy as if they were sitting in front of a log fire.

'Mrs Stanton-Lewis won't like that,' George says suddenly.

'Won't like what?'

'Her being interested in Douglas and the family.'

'Won't she?'

George shakes his head. 'Oh no.'

'Queer old bird,' says Reg.

'Ah.'

After another five minutes Reg checks his watch.

'Time to be getting back,' he says, brushing crumbs from his lap. 'Thanks for the tea.'

George collects up the mugs and puts them in the shed. He waves Reg off down the footpath and stands for a moment watching him go.

'She won't like that at all,' he mutters to himself.

* * *

It's the following day, and the yoga class is coming to an end. They've just come out of Downward Dog, which Gary hates with a passion.

'Well done, everyone,' says Janey. 'Come down onto your mats and into savasana.'

Gary exhales loudly, the *thank-goodness-for-that* sound that he usually makes at this point in the class. It's only because Rufus is keen on yoga that he comes each week, without him Gary would most probably give up and do something more to his liking.

They lose themselves a bit during relaxation, and then afterwards make their way downstairs to Cappuccino Blues.

'When does your filming start?' asks Rufus, taking coffee cups from Sergiu and passing them across to their table.

'Next Wednesday, so I won't be there at the start. I don't think they'll be coming up to our rooms anyway, much to Reg's disappointment. But apparently one day this week old Diana went right through the house like royalty on a state visit, checking up that everything was just so. She's a funny old girl. She had a bit of a flip-out when she saw the photo of Bella that I told you about, and Reg had to take it down and put it away in a drawer. Don't know why, but she made rather a scene apparently.'

'Ah, a jealous woman...' says Gary. 'Wants to keep the dead brother all to herself.'

'Do you think so?'

'Well, there must be some reason why she's disliked this Bella down through all those years, and jealousy is a very powerful emotion.' Gary splits his scone in half and starts spreading butter on it, then points his knife in the air suddenly. 'I bet you that was the old green-eyed monster rearing up.'

'I expect you're right, but maybe she was actually jealous of *him*, because she'd wanted Bella for herself,' says Rufus.

'Ooh,' says Lindsay. 'Interesting idea. Or maybe Bella was a trollop who seduced Douglas and stole his virginity.'

'Maybe not all the photos he took of Bella were as innocent as the one on the terrace,' says Gary through a mouthful of scone.

'Maybe she kill Bella,' says Sergiu, and they all turn round to look at him.

'You know, Sergiu,' says Rufus, 'your listening skills are really improving.'

Sergiu smiles a huge smile and looks very proud of himself.

'I give you free coffee refills today,' he says.

HELENA

It was just so unexpected. Mother got herself in a complete rage over that photograph, goodness only knows why but it was all very silly. And she was quite rude to poor old Reg, which was extremely unfair of her. I had a word with him later and I think I smoothed it all over – he's one of our longest serving and best volunteers and he really didn't deserve that tirade. We certainly don't want him leaving the Hall after all this time.

As Anthony said when I told him about it, if it weren't for the filming she wouldn't have even gone into the house, she hardly ever does these days. It's only the garden she's interested in and anything that happens in the house goes right over her head as a rule. So quite why this photo got her in such a state I have no idea. Poor Reg, he's such a dear, I hated to see her embarrass him like that.

Of course both her and Aunt Ruby were always hugely protective of their brother's reputation. I suppose this happens when people die young, they get placed on a pedestal and nobody will hear a bad word spoken about them. Anthony always said they'd have had him canonised if they could. But he was entitled to have girlfriends, surely? Even the saintly Douglas? And this one was so pretty.

Maybe that was the problem; they were jealous of her.

Anyway, the photograph's gone. Mother has forgotten all about it – as I knew she would. And Reg is back on side, even if his loyalty has been a little bit shaken.

I know the money we'll earn, plus the television exposure, will be worth a few difficult days but frankly I'll be glad when the filming is over and we can all get back to normal. I still remember how it was last time – I couldn't turn a corner without coming across girls with clipboards and feeling I was in the way in my own home...

'One shouldn't be unkind, but there's no reason to pretend to be friends either.'

Cecilia Stanton, to her daughters Ruby and Diana, June 1936

STONEGROVE HALL

The production people call Helena early on the Wednesday morning to tell her that the proposed filming schedule has been reduced from three days to two, and they won't now be there until the following day. She's a bit peeved about this, as she sees their expected income dwindle before her eyes, and it hardly seems worth it for all the upheaval.

Helena's husband, Anthony, is philosophical about the situation.

'One day less of them swarming all over the house,' he says. 'It'll all be over by the weekend darling, and then maybe your mother will stop prowling around like a tomcat marking out his territory.'

Since the incident over Bella's photo, Diana has taken to appearing in the house two or three times every day. She wanders in through the kitchen garden door then meanders around the rooms, her stick tapping on the wooden floors, ignoring the volunteers totally and moving things about – sometimes from one room to another. Occasionally she speaks to visitors, which alarms them a bit as she still has on her floppy gardening hat and canvas apron, although she has the sense to remove her Wellingtons and pad about in stockinged feet. Helena is not amused by this behaviour.

'I have tried to stop her,' she says, 'but you know how single-minded she can be.'

'Indeed I do,' Anthony mutters, as he dollops marmalade onto another piece of toast, then stops in mid-spread as a thought suddenly hits him. 'They won't want her for the filming, will they?'

'I've no idea, I don't even know if they'll want me. Communication hasn't been very good, to be honest. It was easier dealing with the BBC.'

'Well you would be an asset, my darling. Your mother will just make us look foolish.'

'I'll try to keep her away for the next couple of days. What we need is something to take her mind off it – I'll ring Emma, if she could come over tomorrow with Chloe and Abigail they would divert her attention.'

The Croft's eldest son, James, lives closest to Stonegrove, in Wimborne Minster, and his wife might be persuaded to drive over with their two-year-old twin daughters for a spot of granny-sitting. But Helena's left it a bit late so she leaves Anthony with his breakfast and newspaper, and goes straight off to make a grovelling phone call to her daughter-in-law.

* * *

The whole *'Touching My Roots'* circus arrives as expected early the following morning, long before Lindsay gets there. Trucks with equipment, and cars carrying crew, make-up people, liaison assistants and programme directors all scrunch up the front drive at around seven o'clock. Helena and Anthony stand ready to greet them and direct the vehicles to a section of the car park nearest to the house, which has been cordoned off specifically for them.

About half an hour later Caroline turns up with Jodie, the female presenter of *'Touching My Roots'*. As she climbs out of the car she gets her first sight of the rather grand front elevation of Stonegrove Hall, rising above her in Gothic splendour with an odd Italianate flourish here and there. If it were in red brick, she's thinking, it would make a great location for a horror film, but Stonegrove has a softer edge to it. Built of creamy-grey Purbeck stone, it presents an impressive but approachable face to the world.

And then she's caught off-guard momentarily, imagining how her great-aunt Elsie would have felt the very first day she arrived here as a fifteen-year-old in 1931, faced by this towering building, and newly separated from her family to go into service. Not, of course, that she would have approached the Hall up the carriage-drive as they have done today, but still...

It's the second time this has happened to Caroline, this pull of the past, something she is normally more successful at resisting. The other day in Bournemouth, as she stood outside the dry cleaning shop that used to be a dairy, and was handed photos of her great-uncles in their milkman's aprons and caps, she felt it then as well. But this time it's stronger and she feels herself getting sucked into something she can't recognise or put a name to.

As Caroline stands there gazing at the Hall, lost in thoughts of the past, Diana appears from nowhere and startles her by taking hold of her arm and hanging on.

'I know why you're here,' she says, 'and I don't like it.'

Caroline looks down to where Diana's knobbly old hand is gripping her wrist.

'Well that makes two of us,' she says, but before she can add anything further Anthony is at her side, apologising profusely, prising his mother-in-law off the celebrity arm, and guiding her to one side.

'Emma and the girls will be here soon,' he bellows at her. 'You'd better go home to meet them, hadn't you?'

Diana mishears and stares at him as if he's mad. 'Who?' she asks, cocking her best ear in his direction.

'EMMA,' Anthony roars, 'WITH. THE. TWINS.'

Diana seems to relax then, and lets him usher her away. As Caroline and Jodie stand and watch them go, Helena comes down the front steps and rushes forward with her hand held out.

'My mother,' she says grimly. 'Sorry about that.'

And then they go in and get started.

Caroline spends most of the time below stairs being shepherded about by Jodie, and followed by camera and sound engineers eager to capture every nuance of word and expression. They particularly like tears on 'Touching My Roots', the more the better, but they won't be getting any out of Caroline.

It's not uninteresting, seeing the old kitchens and food storage areas, although as great-aunt Elsie was only a kitchen maid there is a limit to what she did and therefore what they can show her that's relevant. They tour the whole area below stairs, getting a feel for the pecking order that existed there, and it very quickly becomes apparent that Elsie was firmly on the bottom rung.

Caroline looks at lead sinks, into which freezing cold water spluttered and gushed out of clanky old brass taps, and two vast copper boilers which would presumably have filled the room with steam. Then she's shown elaborate dinner menus from the early 1930s which comprised of many courses – and no plain cooking in sight, everything apparently fiddly and time-consuming to put together. They've already filmed a studio sequence, with the programme's expert pointing out the part Caroline's great-aunt would have had in preparing for these dinners, which seems to have consisted largely of peeling vegetables and washing up afterwards. Elsie would never have got as far as the dining room, not even to carry dishes up there. She probably never even saw it in all of the eight years she spent in Stonegrove.

'Of course when wartime rationing hit Stonegrove Hall...' Jodie's voice goes up a notch, she's doing her best to inject some drama into the piece, '...things were very different, but by that time Elsie had gone. In February of 1939, at the age of twenty-three, she married Thomas Carter, a local farm hand, and left Stonegrove. As far as we can tell, she never came back. Elsie's generation was the last to go 'into service' in large numbers, because once the second World War intervened, life – even in large country houses – was never quite the same again.'

Caroline's trying to run with this, she really is, but she can't help feeling that Elsie's contribution in the service of the Stanton family was so slight that she would hardly have been noticed or missed. Nobody has the remotest idea how Elsie viewed her job there, what she thought about these ridiculous seven or eight course dinners or the family and guests they were served to, and if Caroline is interested at all then these are the things she'd really like to know. But in a couple of days they are filming at her Granny Vera's house, and her hope is that Vera might have an insight into her big sister's time at Stonegrove.

After doing several re-takes, mostly due to technical difficulties with the lighting down in the kitchen and scullery areas, they break for lunch and Helena ushers Caroline, Jodie and the director over to the Carriage Room Restaurant.

'We'll do Jodie's introductory and closing pieces first thing this afternoon,' the director says to Caroline over lunch, 'so you can have a wander around if you like till later. I'll send someone to find you when we need you again.'

So she does wander around. She goes through the downstairs rooms, and up onto the first landing. She has a chat with Reg in the Douglas Memorial Room, and she pokes her head into the Theatre Room, but it's while Lindsay is on her lunch break so Reg follows her in and then tells her a bit about Sophia Stanton, and her one big acting experience with Dame Ellen Terry.

She doesn't go any further, because by then she's become a bit fed-up with the wealthy and privileged Stantons, who employed her great-aunt for eight years but wouldn't have known her from a cauliflower.

It's bright and sunny, and the garden beckons, so Caroline finds a bench in the sun and sits there alone with her thoughts and her little red notebook. This is the one she always carries, the place where she records all ideas that might turn into sketches or stand-up routines (supposing that she might actually do another Edinburgh Fringe, or be offered a crack at writing a sitcom) and today she finds she has quite a few observations about the day so far that she doesn't want to forget.

And some time later it's here, with her pencil scribbling away in the red notebook, that one of the runners finds her and rushes across the grass waving her hand and a folded sheet of paper.

LINDSAY

What a letdown! After Helena's big build-up I never even caught sight of Caroline van Dell, and the only time she ventured upstairs I was on my break. Typical. Reg said she was 'polite but distant'. This is not Reg's ideal visitor by any means, he likes them drooling with enthusiasm.

Filming finishes tomorrow – from the look on Helena's face when her mother put in an appearance this afternoon it can't come soon enough for her. Luckily the film crew were well away from her – Diana was making a rare visit upstairs, to the bedrooms on my floor, when Mr Croft caught up with her. She's getting to be a real nuisance these days, poking about and muttering to herself, but I think they're hoping that once all this is over she'll just go back to the garden and stay there.

I had a bright idea this morning. Caroline van Dell's great-aunt might have seen our Bella, or known about her, maybe said something about her and the family in her letters home. I thought if I ran into her I would just ask the question, but of course I didn't get the chance. So at lunchtime I wrote her a little note with my phone number and email, and then I asked one of the crew if they would make sure it got to Caroline.

If she could just have a word with the programme researchers – they must have gone through loads of paperwork and a lot of it probably gets tossed aside as being irrelevant, which of course any mention of Bella would be for this programme.

But not irrelevant to me. She's my mystery girl in the garden, and she must have a story or why else was Diana so put out when she saw her photo?

CAROLINE

Oh my God. I could see Jodie swallowing a yawn practically every ten seconds throughout today's filming. Poor thing, she was trying really hard to make Elsie sound interesting, but the truth of it is she was BORING.

Not her fault. Anybody who spends something like fifteen hours a day scrubbing and peeling vegetables, stoking up the range, stirring pans and then washing up piles of dirty dishes is entitled to be boring. As far as I could see the most interesting thing she did was to marry whatsisface and leave Stonegrove Hall for good. Even the Bournemouth milkmen were more interesting than her – at least they got out and talked to their customers. And poor old Elsie stuck it for EIGHT YEARS. Her brain must have been pulp by the time she escaped, she'd probably have married a carthorse if it meant she could get away from that kitchen.

Well, they can't say I didn't warn them.

I really can't see this programme being screened, in fact I hope it isn't because I'll be a laughing stock. Other people have fascinating ancestors who were brave or discovered things or led interesting lives, and the best I could come up with was a professional vegetable peeler and two milkmen. It's embarrassing.

The only good thing to have come out of this is that I got some decent ideas I can work on. The only bad thing is, I haven't got anything in the diary that would give me the chance to use any new material. I must speak to Polly as a matter of urgency – she needs to be ringing round, hassling, doing whatever it is that good agents do to get work for their clients. She needs to get me a big break. What wouldn't I give now for an unexpected phone call or email from a TV producer...

And this whole bloody disaster isn't over yet – tomorrow I've got to talk to Gran, thereby exposing yet another member of my boring family to the nation.

I must have been barking mad to agree to this.

A healthy, nutritious diet can help you look and feel your best, and is easier than you might think.

NHS Choices

CHRISTCHURCH

Caroline arrives back at her house in Christchurch, throws her bag down on a chair, hangs her jacket on the coat stand and goes through into the lounge where she flops down onto the sofa. Then the next thing she does is pick up the phone and call Polly.

'Today was the most embarrassing experience of my career – and I include in that the time I fell off the front of the stage at the Comic Relief showcase.'

Polly is unmoved. She's got other clients like Caroline, neurotics who need constant reassurance and think she's got nothing better to do than massage their egos.

'Well that's not what I heard. They're very pleased with how it's going so far.'

'You have to be joking! It was dreadful. Jodie struggled all day to find something – anything – to liven things up a bit.'

'Nonsense Caroline, just wait till they've edited the content and then I think you'll see the whole thing come together beautifully.'

Caroline rakes her fingers through her hair until it stands up on end.

'I'm going to remind you of those words when they decide not to air it.'

Then she puts the phone down.

Comfort food is needed. She goes to the kitchen, opens the fridge and finds that there's nothing much there as usual, which means she'll have to nip along to the corner shop.

Mr Jay Chowdhury, who knows Caroline's catering habits well by now, greets her warmly as she rushes in and grabs a basket.

'Delicious new cake range,' he says and points to some shelves near the back of the shop.

Caroline knows his advice is always worth taking, so she spends a few minutes checking out the selection, then goes for a coconut and lime fudge cake in a fancy box. On the way back to Mr Chowdhury at the till she adds a tin of custard, a bag of crisps and a packet of crumpets to her basket.

'Very good choice,' says Mr Chowdhury, who takes her money while at the same time wondering if she ever eats anything vaguely nourishing, because she certainly isn't buying it from him.

Caroline's wine rack, unlike her fridge, is usually quite well-stocked, and back at home she selects a bottle of South African red wine. It's a feast. Salt and vinegar crisps with the first glass of wine, then crumpets with mayonnaise, followed by the fudge cake and custard. A three-course supper, and just the kind she needs after the day she's had.

Before long she's gone through almost half a bottle of red wine. She checks the time and as it's too early for any gigs to have started she picks the phone up again and calls her friend Steve. He's never been shy of offloading his problems onto her, so she reckons it's about time it was her turn.

Steve is a cross-dressing performance poet. They met years ago at the Edinburgh Fringe, when they were both on their first time up there, and they clung together and became each other's confidence boosters, cheering loudly at their respective gigs. By the time she's finished telling him about 'Touching My Roots' he's laughing so much it'll be a wonder if his bra strap doesn't snap.

'It's not funny!' she yells at him.

'Are you kidding? It's fucking hilarious! You've got a whole stand-up routine right there!'

'I wasn't looking for a routine,' she says, although actually she was, and maybe this could work...

'Steve, help me a bit here. I need to salvage my career before it slides any further down the pan and hits the bottom. It's all very well saying "write a routine" but I need to have a reason to write another one. You know,' she adds sarcastically, 'a contract or something like that? I'm not getting enough work... and... and I can't do anything else. I'm thirty-four years old, with no partner, and a career that used to look promising and is just about to be dealt an almighty smack in the gob.'

'Oh, just camp it up a bit darling. When they do the after-location studio bit just be as funny as only you can – and it'll work. Don't take it all so seriously, just laugh at your family!'

Caroline is quiet for so long he's beginning to think she's hung up but eventually she replies in a tired little voice.

'I don't want to laugh at them, Steve. I want to be proud of them. I want them to be, you know, a bit special. I want them to have something to say that people will listen to and be interested in.'

Then Steve goes quiet, because now he can tell that she's really screwed up by this and what he's just said hasn't helped.

'It'll be fine sweetheart. There's nothing wrong with a family that worked hard all their lives. That's something you can be proud of.'

After they've talked a bit more (inevitably the conversation turns round quite swiftly to Steve) and she's put the phone down, Caroline knocks back the rest of the wine in her glass and wanders out of her lounge and across the hall to the small bedroom.

She switches the light on and stands in the doorway, gazing around for a moment before going across to an armchair on which assorted teddies and other soft toys are snuggled up together. She picks one of them up and hugs it to her chest, inhaling the dusty smell of its fur, before replacing it alongside the rest.. As she turns to leave the room her toe just clips a bicycle wheel, and she puts out a hand to stop it from falling sideways and knocking something else over. Then she flicks the light off, and closes the door softly behind her.

* * *

It's around 3am, and there it is again, the nightmare that won't leave her alone.

The three of them run, Caroline at the back shouting and urging them on but her feet are like lead and no matter how hard she tries she can't make any progress along the pavement. And then it comes: the squeal of tyres, a thump, thump, crump, glass breaking, an engine's roar. And in the middle of it all, herself, screaming...

Caroline awakes suddenly and sits bolt upright with a gasp. She's hot and sweaty, her pillow is wet and she's still crying. The bottom sheet is all rucked up and half the duvet is trailing on the floor so she must have been thrashing around a lot. Her head aches, partly from the wine and partly from an interrupted night's sleep and she knows without looking that her hair will be standing up in peaks, like an electrocuted cartoon character.

She sinks back on the bed for a moment and presses the heels of her hands into her eyes, as a last sob leaves her. Then she gets up slowly, smooths the sheet back into place and hauls the duvet up onto the bed. Her mouth is dry and tastes awful. When she looks in the bathroom mirror her hair is just as she expected it would be, and her eyes are red and puffy. A strong cup of coffee can only help, because there's no way she's going back to bed now, she's too afraid of having to go through it all again to attempt to get back to sleep.

Downstairs, sitting on the sofa with all the lights in the living room on full blast, she tries to untangle her thoughts and chase the dream away. She glances at the clock and does a quick calculation. In Boston, it will be about ten-thirty in the evening, still too early for her brother to be in bed.

She picks up the phone and stabs in his number. He answers on the fourth ring, and he already knows it's her because who else would be ringing him at that time of night?

'Mikey, could we just talk for a bit? I mean, if you're not in the middle of anything?'

'Sure. Bad dream again?' He looks across at his wife and mouths Caroline's name to her, then takes the phone into the study and closes the door behind him so that she won't be interrupted in the film they were watching.

'Yeah. Bad everything right now...'

* * *

Caroline's eighty-eight year old Granny Vera still lives in Poole, although she's no longer in the house

Caroline remembers from her childhood, but a nice, modern little warden-assisted flat. If it weren't for her dicky heart she'd have stayed put for a few more years, but getting up those stairs was making her wheezy and very short of breath, and it frightened her. Now she's all on one level, with a tiny patio area outside her French doors and alarm pulls in every room, and she feels secure.

When they go to film her it's just Caroline, Jodie, a cameraman and a sound man, but even so, they have a job fitting into the living room. Vera makes them all tea and hands round shortbread that she made herself.

Caroline has already warned her not to be sidetracked into talking about her daughter and son-in-law, Caroline's parents. This has had the effect of striking Vera dumb, as she's now afraid to say anything in case she puts her foot in it.

'What did great-aunt Elsie tell you about her days at Stonegrove?' Caroline asks.

Vera thinks for a bit, then shrugs, saying, 'Nothing much.'

There's a silence and Vera eventually realises that it's up to her to fill it.

'Well she was eleven years older than me, there were another four in between us two,' she says by way of excusing her inability to answer the question.

Caroline tries to prompt her.

'Well, was she happy there? Did she ever tell you how she felt about being in service, or what it was really like? No little bits of gossip?'

Vera puts her shortbread down and leans forward. Jodie leans in towards her, hoping something confidential, scandalous or just (please God) interesting is about to come her way.

'Her hands were rubbed red raw,' says Vera, and then straightens up. 'I remember the state of her hands very clearly. She could have done without that.'

Jodie leans back and glances across at Caroline, who is sitting up straight, her eyes big and round, looking intently at her gran. It's not going well, in fact it's going far worse than she had imagined it might.

'But she did the job for eight years – she must have made some comments about it when she came home to see you all,' says Caroline, finding it difficult to keep the impatience out of her voice.

Vera picks up her shortbread again, takes a bite and looks sideways at Caroline, as if fearing a trick question.

'Mum always said she hated it. Hated that nobody upstairs had a clue what went on to provide them with their meals. She said Elsie would have preferred to be cleaning upstairs than peeling those vegetables in cold water every single day.'

Caroline looks at Jodie, whose face is an impassive mask, and there's a silence.

'Well wouldn't you?' Vera asks defensively, to nobody in particular.

Jodie tries a different tack.

'What about your parents, Vera. Were they ever in service too?'

'Not that I know of. They never talked much about their younger days.'

Another silence develops. Vera can see now that she's let Caroline down and decides to have a go at redeeming herself.

'There's one thing I will say though...'

This time they all lean forward.

'Elsie could peel two pounds of spuds quicker than anyone else I ever knew.'

***

'I don't think there's much there that we can use,' Jodie says, when they get outside.

'No, I can see that. Sorry.'

'Never mind, we've got the researchers on it and they'll probably be able to dig up something else to work on. We might not make it now into the next season's schedule, though.'

Caroline can tell a brush-off when she hears one. She's partly relieved, and partly affronted.

'Not to worry,' she says brightly. 'I'm sure if they keep ferreting away at it we'll be able to pull it off in the end.'

But what she's really thinking is, please let this disaster be over soon.

HELENA

I'm beginning to realise what a find Lindsay is. She's always cheerful and nothing is too much trouble for her, plus she's very good with the visitors. We were lucky to get her before she was snapped up by one of those charity shops in town. For her sake, I hope she finds some paid work soon, but when she does it's going to be a dark day for us.

She came in an hour earlier than necessary yesterday and we got behind the little stage in the Theatre Room to sort out the boxes full of stuff that had been left there gathering dust for years. We found one or two children's costumes but they're quite tatty and threadbare – I think the moth may have got at them and considering they've been there for about a hundred years it's not surprising. Lindsay is very keen on displaying them, but I think we need to take some advice before we rush in and make matters even worse, so I'm going to contact the costume experts at the V&A.

There was some other stuff that we can put out though – various little props that the children used in their plays and more photos, including some of the stage in use with several little ones taking it very seriously. Also, surprisingly, a Ouija board. I'm not sure I would have recognised it as such but Lindsay knew straight away, and there was quite a bit of old sports equipment and yet another camera, all left there from when the room was just used for storage, I suppose.

And then, just when we thought we were done with discovering things, we pulled out a box full of old gramophone parts, many still in their original cardboard boxes. I remember Mother telling me that there was a time when Douglas was very keen on taking apart old gramophones and restoring them, and he worked on them in the Theatre Room because nobody bothered much about what went on in there. These must be the bits he had left over at the end. I'm sure I can find an enthusiast somewhere out there who can tell us more about them, and hopefully take them off our hands.

Luckily, when Douglas's enthusiasm turned to motorbikes he indulged that in the stables, not up here, or we'd be turning out fuel tanks and brake pads as well as all this other stuff.

Ruby has always loved the house at Stonegrove, but for me it's the gardens that will keep me here. Unfortunately Douglas was not greatly interested in either. If he had been, things might have turned out differently.

Letter from Diana Stanton to her cousin Elizabeth, April 1938

CHRISTCHURCH

Caroline wakes with a monster headache, due to lack of sleep and a bottle of red wine. Luckily, the morning is dry and bright and she decides a good, long walk might clear her head.

She has a quick shower, pulls on a pair of old jeans and a sweatshirt with frayed cuffs, and grabs a fleece as it's probably not as warm out there as it looks. At the front door she picks up her keys and phone, then goes back into the living room and rummages around in her bag for her constant companion, the little red notebook, and finally zips them all into her fleece pockets as she leaves the house.

She has a favourite route that she usually follows. It takes her out of the town, alongside some allotments, past the woods and onto a footpath across the common, before curving back through the other end of town. It's a circular route of about five miles, long enough to make her feel she's had a walk, short enough to get her back home in a reasonable amount of time.

She passes the allotments, where people are busy digging and planting but mostly just standing around chatting to each other. This reminds Caroline, like a sharp elbow digging her in the ribs, that she doesn't have too many people around here to chat to. Her friends, and Steve's a good example, are spread out all over the country. Her brother and his family live even further away, a seven hour flight from Heathrow. The people she works with at the BBC travel into London like she does, and then travel back home and away from her. She doesn't really know her neighbours. True, Granny Vera is not far away in Poole, but their relationship is not a chatty one – and will be even less so after the debacle of the television interview. So by way of compensation Caroline usually says a cheery hello to the gardeners on the other side of the wire fence when she walks past, and is pleasantly surprised today, as on most other days, to find that many of them reply. Her mood lightens.

With the allotments behind her the footpath takes her next across an old ironwork bridge that runs over what the locals still refer to as the 'new road', although it's been there for as long as anyone can remember, taking traffic out towards Southbourne. She's just on the start of the bridge when her mobile rings.

Caroline unzips the pocket of her fleece and fishes the phone out, but in her haste it slips through her fingers. She grabs at it as it starts to fall, and in doing so makes matters worse and tips it even further away. The ringtone continues jauntily until the answerphone kicks in, but by then the phone has hit the asphalt surface and skidded away from her towards the edge, where it comes to a sudden halt, right on the lip of the bridge.

Thank goodness, she thinks, bending down and stretching out a hand. But the decorative wrought iron railings holds her back, and the phone is just a bit too far away for her to reach.

As she squats there, holding on to the rail above her head, she realises that if she puts her shoulder out between the gaps in the ironwork she should then have inched just near enough to be able to close her hand around her mobile. Yes, that'll do it, she thinks and leans her shoulder, and then her head, forward and through.

And then, just as her hand comes into contact with the phone – which has started ringing again – there's an almighty commotion behind her and all of a sudden she's being grabbed and pulled at and the phone spins away from her and down onto the road, where a lorry drives over it.

Someone is shouting 'No, no, no!' and lots of hands seem to be tugging at her, and as she tries to turn around and fight them off, her head crashes up onto the iron railing immediately above it, she screams out in pain, and then faints.

* * *

The next thing Caroline knows there are people bending over her and she's got a headache considerably worse than the one she started the day with. She looks up into the face of a man in a dark green uniform. Someone nearby is crying. There's a lot of talking going on, several different voices all at the same time. The uniformed man lifts up two fingers, which is what Caroline would like to be doing right now, and asks her how many she can see. She tells him, but the word is thick in her mouth and on her lips, and she's feeling a bit sick. She drifts in and out of various bits of conversation, none of which she's involved in, before she feels herself being lifted onto a stretcher and then carried forward, swinging ever so gently, with the air brushing over her face.

And if it weren't for the sledgehammer that's bashing around in her head, it would be quite a pleasant sensation.

* * *

Lindsay is getting ready to head out for an evening at her parent's place. Kaye has asked her to go over for dinner, which generally means she and Peter have something they want to talk to her about. Experience flags this up in Lindsay's mind as one of two things: would she like to go back home to live, and save on expenses while she's out of work? (No, she wouldn't.) Would she help them through some bureaucratic obstacle course or other? She knows full well that they tend to get themselves worked up over official letters and all Lindsay has to do is translate into plain English and put everything back into perspective.

She's had an interesting day at Stonegrove today. Helena was away somewhere until just before closing time and therefore Anthony ventured out of the office for once and was more of a presence around the Hall. Lindsay found herself sharing a table with him in The Stables Tearoom on her lunch break, because he made a point of coming across with his tray to join her.

'Haven't had much of a chance to speak to you up till now,' he said, 'but Helena speaks very highly of you as a room steward.'

Lindsay found him remarkably easy to talk to and share a joke with.

Charming, in fact.

Nice, twinkly blue eyes.

A very attractive man...

Stop it, she told herself, and looked away from Anthony and out of the window, where Diana was tramping about in a flower bed with George, seemingly giving him instructions. Henry the cat padded across the flowerbed to join them, his tabby tail swishing as he gave Diana and her walking stick a wide berth.

'How long has George been here?' she asked. 'He seems very old to still be working.'

'God, yes, he's much too old, he should have been pensioned off years ago. Can't get him to stop working, that's the trouble. He's always been here, he was born here.'

'What, on the estate?'

'Yes, in the cottage he still lives in. His father was head gardener, and his mother was the cook, or was it the housekeeper? He just sort of took over from his dad.'

'Hasn't George got a son or grandson to take over from him? I've seen a couple of young lads in the gardens.'

'They're apprentices, he's supposedly training them up for when he retires but I can't imagine that ever happening because he's already left it too late to retire. I expect he'll just keel over in the herbaceous border one day,' Anthony said cheerfully, adding, 'No, no son to take over, or daughter if it comes to that.'

'He seems to get on well with your mother-in-law, I often see them together in the garden.'

Anthony laughed. 'Not sure I would say they were chums,' he said, 'it's more a case of tolerating each other because they both see themselves as the rightful custodians of the gardens. I think they've got a contest on to see who can last the longest at Stonegrove and they're both determined to win. George has probably got fifteen years on Diana, but my money's still on her. I suspect she'll see us all off,' he added.

As they looked out, Diana stomped a few feet away and pointed at something under a small tree. George, left standing alone in the centre of the flowerbed, turned his back on her, picked up his fork and carried on leisurely turning the soil over without a glance in her direction.

'As you can see,' said Anthony, 'he hangs on her every word.'

A little later Lindsay tore herself away from Anthony's entertaining company and went back to the Theatre Room, where she found Reg attempting to stop two small boys from climbing up onto the stage while their parents, oblivious, read the childishly-written script in the glass case.

Reg was relieved to see her, and she gathered up the small boys and took them by their hands back to the parents, who looked down at them with some surprise as if they'd completely forgotten about them. When the family had moved on she wandered across to the window, in time to see George walking past on the path below, making heavy weather of pushing a wheelbarrow full of compost. Diana was nowhere in sight.

Now, as she ponders her Stonegrove day, switches off her bedroom light and puts her coat on, the phone rings. She wonders about letting it go to answerphone, but then thinks Kaye might want her to pick something up on her way over.

'Is that Lindsay Walton?'

It's not a voice she recognises. Young, and weary.

'This is the Royal Bournemouth General Hospital.'

Lindsay thinks immediately of her parents, but she only spoke to Kaye a couple of hours ago and surely nothing life-threatening can have happened in that time? She swallows hard.

'Yes, it is.'

'We've got a Caroline van Dell in here, there's been a bit of an incident and Miss van Dell has sustained a nasty bang on the head.'

Lindsay frowns, struggling to make sense of what she's hearing.

'So... why are you phoning me?'

'Yours was the only number she had on her at the time she was brought in. We need someone to take her home and stay with her tonight.'

Lindsay remembers then the hastily scribbled note she asked one of the crew to give to Caroline.

'Well I can't do it, I'm just about to go out – plus I don't even know her. There must be someone else you can contact, a friend or neighbour? Family? I'm a complete stranger. Have you tried any of the contacts on her phone?'

'She didn't have a phone with her, just some keys, a notebook and your contact details on a piece of paper. Doctor won't let her go home on her own, someone needs to stay with her tonight.'

'Then keep her there.'

The voice sighs, the deep sigh of someone who is tired and has better things to do than have conversations like this.

'There are two issues here. One, we need the bed because there's been a major accident on the A338 and they're bringing them in to us. Two, Miss van Dell is kicking up a fuss and threatening to discharge herself.'

'Then let her – this is nothing at all to do with me.'

'Miss Walton, head injuries are tricky things. She's had a scan and everything appears to be OK, but it was a very nasty bang and the next twenty four hours will be critical. Also, and maybe I shouldn't be telling you this but.... well, there was some talk about a suicide attempt, although Miss van Dell is very clear about that, she says it was all a mistake.'

Lindsay runs a hand through her hair, pulls it back into a pony-tail and twists it around in her fingers. She thinks through her options.

'What if I just pick her up and take her home?'

'If we let her go then we need to know someone will stay overnight with her.'

There's a moment of silence, when Lindsay seriously considers slamming the phone down and rushing out of the door. But then she'd have it on her conscience all evening, and she still needs Caroline as a way of getting through to the researchers working on Stonegrove Hall. She picks up a pencil.

'OK, which ward is she in?'

* * *

It's almost an hour later when Lindsay arrives at the hospital, having first phoned her mum to cancel. Kaye was cross, dinner was almost ready to put on the table. Lindsay can only excuse herself by saying that a friend has been in an accident, but she knows it sounds thin and she can tell that Kaye is not convinced. Once she'd got her mother off the phone she threw a few things in a bag, and set off for the hospital.

It takes her a while to locate the correct ward, after a few false starts going up and down corridors that all look the same. The staff nurse on duty – not, she suspects, the one she spoke to – takes her along to the furthest bay and pulls back the curtains around the bed next to the window.

And they look at each other.

'Who are you?'

'Lindsay Walton. I've come to take you home.'

'Oh, have you now? I suppose you're with Social Services.'

'No, I'm the person they phoned to come and get you. I've got to stay with you overnight.'

'I don't understand – who phoned you?'

'The hospital. They found my contact details amongst your things, and phoned me.'

'But I've never heard of you, I don't know you at all...'

'No you don't, but I'm a volunteer at Stonegrove Hall. I sent you a note and it seems you had it on you when the er... the accident happened.'

'A note?'

'With my number on it. You didn't have a phone with you and...'

'A lorry drove over my phone when those idiots grabbed hold of me. It would have been OK if... well anyway. You're not staying at my place, I don't know you from Adam... Eve.'

'Listen, the only way they will let you go home is if someone takes you there, and then stays overnight. It's to make sure you're OK – head injuries are tricky, the nurse said so.'

'Oh, this is ridiculous!'

Caroline is not the only one losing her rag.

'Miss van Dell, I've just cancelled my evening out, driven here from Wareham, paid hugely to park my car, and now I'm offering to drive back to wherever the hell you live – all at my own expense, which is not easy for me as I'm out of work. You could be a bit more gracious about a situation that neither of us likes very much but we seem to be stuck with. Now, do you want to go or not?'

Caroline sits on the edge of the bed glowering at Lindsay. Then she picks up her red notebook and turns to the back cover. Tucked into the flap on the inside cover is a piece of paper. She takes it out and looks at it.

'Lindsay Walton,' she reads aloud.

'Yes. As I said.'

Caroline looks up at Lindsay. 'I hadn't even looked at it, I just put it in here when the runner gave it to me.'

'Well it's lucky you did, because otherwise you'd be stuck in hospital tonight.'

Lindsay picks up Caroline's fleece and holds it out to her. Caroline gets to her feet, a little unsteadily, takes hold of the fleece and pushes her arms into the sleeves.

'I'm sorry. My head hurts.'

'Mine too, as it happens. Come on.'

The ten mile drive back to Christchurch is quiet. Lindsay is still cross, Caroline is a little embarrassed, plus her head really does hurt and she's a bit frightened by it. Lindsay asks tersely for directions, Caroline gives them. When they reach her house – a bungalow as it turns out, in a street of similar properties on the edge of town – Lindsay pulls onto the front drive without waiting to be invited to do so.

Caroline goes ahead slowly, putting lights on and gesturing vaguely at the bathroom and the kitchen.

'I'll make a cup of tea,' says Lindsay, breezing forward into the kitchen. 'Go and sit down.'

And gradually, they both thaw out a bit and start, tentatively, to trust each other.

LINDSAY

That was just about the last thing I expected when I blundered into the wrong room.

Caroline has kept all her childhood toys, right up to her teenage years. I couldn't believe my eyes. Without even looking too closely I could see Care Bears, Cabbage Patch Kids, Barbie and Ken dolls, Beanie Babies, one of the genuine Tracey's Island models, not the sort that had been made to Blue Peter instructions when the shops ran out of them... She must have had the number one toy every Christmas. All seemingly in good condition, some still boxed.

And there were all the other usual things you'd expect a little girl to have – dolls, a pram, teddies and other soft toys, a pink scooter, dressing-up clothes, Disney videos... it was like a sub-branch of Hamleys in there.

I just stood and gawped. And then she came up behind me and said 'I suppose you think I'm a real saddo, keeping all this lot.'

I asked if she wanted to sit down and tell me about it, but she was looking quite pale and just said, 'Tomorrow. Not now.' So we went to bed.

I couldn't get to sleep for ages. I just kept thinking that it was all a bit weird, and wondering what I'd got myself into.

'My whole philosophy of Barbie was that, through the doll, the girl could be anything she wanted to be. Barbie always represented the fact that a woman has choices.'

Ruth Handler, Barbie creator

CHRISTCHURCH

Lindsay looks up to see Caroline standing in the kitchen doorway in her dressing gown. Without make-up and the trademark ridiculous earrings she looks younger, and vulnerable.

'How are you feeling this morning?'

'Better, thanks. Just a trace of a headache buzzing around, I only really notice it when I shake my head.'

'Ah, then don't.'

It's almost ten o'clock, and Lindsay has been up for over two hours. After conducting a quick inventory of edible food in the kitchen (which didn't take long), and throwing out all the stuff that's way out of date, she made a shopping list of essentials and found a plastic carrier bag in one of the drawers. So by the time Caroline puts in an appearance Lindsay's already been shopping and brought home a bagful of groceries from Mr Chowdhury's mini-mart at the end of the road. She's just another customer to him, making some basic purchases, but he'd be astonished if he knew such sensible food choices were all destined to end up in Caroline's kitchen.

Lindsay unloads everything onto the kitchen counter; eggs, tomatoes, mushrooms, wholemeal bread, tinned soup, salad, cheese... Caroline watches as each item comes out of the bag.

'Why don't you go and have a shower and then I'll make us some breakfast, well it'll be brunch now.'

'I'll give you the money for this, I don't expect you to pay for it. Obviously I never keep much food in the house because I'm away a lot.'

'Really?'

Lindsay reaches up, opens one of the kitchen cupboards and gestures towards the contents. It's crammed full of packets of biscuits, chocolate bars and cakes.

'I suppose this is what you usually live on. Don't you ever eat fruit or anything healthy?'

'Are you kidding? I love fruit. Only the other day I ate a whole chocolate orange...' But she's smiling as she says it, and in spite of herself Lindsay can't help but laugh as Caroline turns and walks up the hall towards the bathroom.

Half an hour later Caroline has discovered that banging her head has given her a huge appetite, as she wolfs down the unexpected treat of a cooked breakfast and then puts more bread in the toaster.

'Listen,' she says as they wait for it to pop up. 'I'm really sorry about the way I behaved yesterday. You've been more than kind to me and I don't know how to thank you for going to all this trouble. I'm a complete disaster, I know it. Anyway, you're off the hook now, you did what they asked and I wouldn't blame you if you walked away right this minute.'

The toast pops up with a clack.

'Can I finish my breakfast first?' says Lindsay, as she pours both of them another cup of tea.

'Oh yeah, sure. I just meant...'

'I know what you meant.' Lindsay takes a deep breath. 'Do you want to tell me what happened yesterday? At the hospital they said it might have been a suicide attempt...'

Caroline starts laughing, although Lindsay can't see what's funny about it. And so she explains about dropping her phone, and trying to reach it with half her upper body hanging over the edge of the bridge, and then how a couple of people who were probably out walking themselves got hold of the wrong end of the stick and dragged her back.

'So now I've lost my bloody mobile and all my contacts are in there. It's a disaster.'

'Not as big a disaster as if you'd followed the phone over the edge,' says Lindsay, who is on the side of the well-meaning walkers.

'There's no way I would have gone over the edge, I had enough trouble squeezing my shoulder and head through, never mind about the rest – we'll walk up there if you don't believe me and you can see for yourself.'

'That's not a bad idea,' says Lindsay, who's thinking that it's often easier to talk when you're walking alongside someone rather than facing them across a table. 'A bit of fresh air will do you good. I'll wash up first.'

'I'm not an invalid...' Caroline starts, then realises she's being spiky again and backtracks. 'Sorry, what I mean is, we'll do it together.'

* * *

It seems strange to Caroline to be following the exact same route as she was the day before, with all that's happened in between. She hopes the couple who pulled her back from the bridge aren't regular in their walking habits.

'Tell me about the toys,' says Lindsay, as they reach the allotments.

Caroline takes a deep breath.

'This isn't easy for me,' she says.

'OK, there's no rush.'

They walk a bit further on, but this time Caroline doesn't speak to the gardeners on the other side of the wire fence.

'When I was thirteen both my parents died,' she starts.

'Oh, I'm sorry. An accident?'

'Hardly. They were killed by a hit and run driver.'

'God, that's awful.' Lindsay stops walking. Caroline also stops and then turns to face her.

'And I was with them. I saw it all happen, and... well, there was obviously nothing I could do. I just stood there screaming and watched my Mum and Dad die on the roadside.'

Lindsay hooks her arm through Caroline's – a gesture that makes Caroline want to weep – and slowly gets her walking again.

'That's the saddest thing I've ever heard. I'm so sorry, it must have been absolutely terrifying for you. Who looked after you then? Foster parents?'

'Luckily, no. They let me stay in our house because my brother is eight years older than me, and he was still living at home, so I had an adult there to look after me. Also my Gran lived just a few doors away so she used to come in and clean the place up and cook for us. If Mike was away I went to stay at hers, or she and Grandad stayed over at our house. It worked OK. But that was more than twenty years ago, I doubt if

I'd get away with it today, Social Services would come barging in and mess everything up.'

Many questions come into Lindsay's mind and she's bursting to ask them, but she keeps it zipped so Caroline has the space to carry on if she wants to. But they are now approaching the bridge, and Caroline is sidetracked by her eagerness to show Lindsay the spot where yesterday's drama took place.

'See?' She points out the gap in the ironwork of the bridge. 'Nobody could fall from there – if I wanted to kill myself I could find a much easier way than trying to squeeze through an impossibly small opening like that. Actually, it would be a darn sight easier to just climb up over the top – you know I'm surprised nobody has done anything about that, it's dangerous leaving it like this.'

Lindsay is forced to acknowledge that a serious jumper would suss that out immediately.

'Your rescuers just rushed in without thinking. I suppose that's what you do when a situation appears to be dangerous.'

Caroline grumbles on for a bit about her mobile, and then they reach the other side of the bridge and the footpath leads them towards a clump of trees that mark the edge of a wooded area.

'Where's your brother now?' asks Lindsay, in an attempt to get Caroline back on track.

'He got a job that took him to the States, and now he lives in Boston. When he went I was about twenty-two, and we decided to sell the house in Poole. And then I moved here.' She pauses to pick up a flattened Coke can that has been abandoned on the path.

'It was only when I was clearing out the old house that I found all my old toys up in the loft. Mum hadn't thrown a thing away. I was a surprise late baby, when they probably thought they would never have another, and I freely admit I was spoilt. I suppose she couldn't bear to part with my toys as I grew out of them.'

'So you brought them with you to Christchurch?'

'I suppose I couldn't bear to part with them either. My childhood ended the day they were killed. Leaving our house – well it was a way of holding on to the times when I'd been happy, before it happened, when we were still a normal family.'

Lindsay would like to take Caroline's arm again, but isn't sure that she'd want her to.

'From the look of all those toys I'd say you'd been a lucky little girl. Your mum and dad obviously loved you to bits.'

A bird suddenly flaps up out of a tree, squawking noisily as it flies overhead, and then another one joins it. Lindsay is jolted back to the moment, and realises that up to then she hasn't been taking any notice at all of their surroundings. She watches the birds as they dive into another tree further ahead with a rustle of feathers and leaves.

'The police found the car quite soon afterwards, but they never found the driver. I used to think he would come back to get me too. Sometimes I still do.'

There doesn't seem to be much more to say just at that moment, and they fall silently into step as the path skirts the woods and heads off across the common.

'So why did you send me the note?' Caroline asks, suddenly.

'Oh. It was just an idea I had...' and Lindsay explains about Bella's photograph and the possibility that Caroline's great-aunt might have had some contact with her.

'Ha! Only if she had a tendency to hang around kitchen sinks,' she says. 'Or a weird fascination with potato peelings.'

'So, maybe not. But I also had another thought. The programme researchers might have turned up something about Bella and just dismissed it as having nothing to do with your programme. I sort of wondered if you could ask them.'

Lindsay is starting to feel a bit awkward about this. In the light of their previous conversation the idea of searching for information about a woman in a photograph, who nobody can identify, seems embarrassingly ridiculous. Caroline, however, is not in the least bit fazed by it and takes the whole thing completely seriously.

'I'm sure you're right, there must be loads of information that never gets used in these programmes. This is quite important to you, isn't it?'

'Not sure if I would say it was important, but it's a mystery that I'd rather like to solve. I've grown quite fond of Bella and I'd just like to know what happened to her.'

The footpath is turning back into town now, running into a cul-de-sac of neat houses. Caroline drops the squashed Coke can into the first rubbish bin they come to, and turns to Lindsay as they cross the road.

'I'll see what I can find out,' she says. 'I owe you one.'

Relaxation is a conscious endeavour that lies somewhere between effort and non-effort. To truly relax, you have to understand and practice the skill.

Yoga for Dummies

YOGA

'What's she like, Caroline van Dell?'

'She's OK, once she's loosened up a bit. Uses the word 'disaster' rather more than most people.'

Having just listened to Lindsay's account of the time they spent together Rufus finds this quite funny, and can't help laughing.

'With some justification from the sounds of it,' he says.

'She does seem to have been dogged by bad luck.'

Lindsay has left out the bit about Caroline's room of toys, and just mentioned that her parents died when she was young.

'She sounds like the archetypal image of a comedian,' says Gary, 'a tragic figure hiding behind comedy. You only have to think of Tony Hancock or Kenneth Williams.'

'I don't think she's depressive, although she's certainly got a sad background. That whole thing about a suicide attempt was ridiculous.'

'So she says,' says Gary.

'No, her version rings completely true. She couldn't possibly have fallen onto the road by getting through that gap, it's much too small. Anyway, she was OK by the time I left her, and she promised to have a word with the programme researchers.'

'Then I hope she follows it through. You were very good to her, Lin.'

'Actually, I quite enjoyed her company,' Lindsay says, because once they'd got used to each other they did seem to get on rather well.

Out in the reception area they can hear Janey registering a new student to the class as other regulars including Deirdre arrive and get settled on their mats.

Gary lies down and shuffles about a bit to get comfy. Rufus leans across to Lindsay and asks her in a whisper about her plans for the coming May Day bank holiday weekend.

'I'm up at the Hall most of the time,' she whispers back. 'Helena asked me to go in tomorrow and Sunday to help out generally, and Monday's my regular stewarding day anyway.'

'We're gardening if the weather's OK, but we thought we'd come up to see you on Monday.'

'Oh, good. There's a jazz band playing some of the time in the garden, and various things going on for kids – jugglers and stilt walkers and face-painting. Mum and Dad said they might come along on Monday too.'

Janey tiptoes in, lights a couple of candles, and Gary stage-whispers in a posh accent 'Do shut up, you two,' which makes Lindsay laugh, then they all settle down as Janey tells them to start counting their breathing in and out. Rufus yawns, Deirdre sighs her breath out extra loudly and Lindsay wriggles her feet under a folded blanket as the relaxation starts to wind them all down.

* * *

When Lindsay checks her phone after the class there's a message on there from Caroline. She rings back when they get into Cappuccino Blues, but the signal isn't good in there and the noise of the Gaggia makes it even more difficult to hear clearly, so she ends up standing outside in the doorway with a finger in one ear. Caroline repeats herself again.

'I'm really sorry, they didn't have anything on your Bella.'

'Well, thanks for trying anyway. It was always a long shot.'

'I might have another chat to Granny Vera though. She was completely useless when I was there with Jodie for the interview, but maybe away from the cameras she'll have more to say. It's another long shot, but I'm going to try it anyway.'

A police car zooms past with its blue light flashing and siren screeching. Lindsay lets it go before she replies.

'Ask her if she knows anything about Douglas Stanton, I think Bella was his girlfriend.'

'Ah, the man with his very own Memorial Room? OK, I'll have a go. How did he die exactly? Please don't tell me he was found in the billiard room with a length of lead piping at his side.'

'Motorcycle accident. It was one September night in 1936 and nobody knows exactly what happened but it seems there were no other vehicles involved.'

'There were no other vehicles in Dorset then, full stop.'

'Rubbish. There must have been the odd Daimler puttering up to the gates of Stonegrove Hall. Not to mention tractors and delivery vans.'

'Which would obviously have been driving about late at night. So that's another mystery, first Bella and now Douglas. Is there no end to the excitement you bring into my dull life?'

'That is the end.'

'I'll talk to you again when I've spoken to Granny Vera.'

An ambulance rushes past, siren wailing.

'Where on earth are you?' asks Caroline. 'It's very noisy there...'

Lindsay explains.

'Oh you do yoga? I know a great joke about yoga. Man asks a yoga teacher if he can teach him to do the splits and the teacher says, well how flexible are you? And the man...'

'I can't do Tuesdays,' says Lindsay. 'I've heard it before.'

'Oh. Well, never mind...' says Caroline, then rings off.

Lindsay returns to the warmth of Cappuccino Blues and reports back to Gary and Rufus.

'You can't say she's not trying,' says Rufus, 'but you've got to face the facts – maybe you'll never find out any more about Bella.'

'No, maybe I won't. It's intriguing though, and even if the story turns out to be boring it's tantalising that it's so close and I can't get at it. Diana knows, but I doubt if she's going to spill the beans, not to me at any rate.'

'She might to her daughter.'

'Possibly. Maybe you'll see Diana when you come up to the Hall – mad old biddy in Wellingtons,' says Lindsay, 'most probably stomping about in the flower beds.'

'I can't wait,' says Gary, stirring several spoonfuls of sugar into his coffee. 'This voluntary job has certainly broadened your horizons, you're meeting a wider cross-section of people than ever before. Until recently we were the most interesting people you knew.'

Rufus laughs.

'Now we're just the most normal,' he says.

Sergiu pauses in wiping down the counter and folds his arms.

'But what is the normal?' he asks, to nobody in particular.

Rufus puts his head in his hands.

'Oh God,' he says, 'now he's become a bloody philosopher. I liked it better when he couldn't understand a word we said.'

Sergiu laughs. 'I have good teacher,' he says. 'Many words learnt on the pillow.'

And then, as if on cue, the door opens and Deirdre pops her head round it.

'Erm, shall I come back later?' she asks Sergiu, and he waves a hand at her and says 'Sure, sure, later.'

At the table in the corner three pairs of eyes turn to look at Deirdre, but she's already gone.

I hate it here Mum, and I miss you all.
Can't I come home?

**Letter from Stonegrove Hall maid to her mother,
March 1935**

SHADY PINES

The following day Caroline rings Lindsay back.

'I've got a lead,' she says. 'It might be nothing but I thought I'd share it with you.'

Lindsay can't believe her luck. She's a bit surprised that Caroline should take so much interest in what is no more than a personal crusade, but it's gratifying that she's making good on her promise to return a favour.

'Go on,' she says.

'Well, even without a camera and mic shoved up her nose Granny Vera couldn't tell me any more about Elsie's time up at Stonegrove, BUT... ' Caroline pauses for effect.

'Yes – BUT... '

'One of Elsie's cousins, a couple of years younger than her, also worked at the Hall at the same time. Gran didn't mention her before on the basis of "you never asked me". She was an upstairs maid, so she probably cleaned out the fire grates and changed the beds. Maybe did a bit of dusting and took the rugs out to the garden for a good beating.'

'OK, I get the general picture.'

'So, what I'm saying is that she might have seen a bit more of what went on with the family. And – wait for it – she's still alive, in a care home in Wareham. Probably not too far from where you live, actually.'

'Good grief – how old is she?'

'Ninety-four, and seemingly still all there. I've been in touch with the home and we're going to visit her this afternoon.' Caroline can't keep a note of triumph out of her voice.

'We are? That's fantastic, well done Caroline. Odd that the television company didn't find her, though.'

'I suppose they didn't pick her up because her surname was different to Elsie's and they wouldn't necessarily have made the connection. I've not said anything to them yet, in case she's no more help than Granny Vera was. Anyway, *we've* got her now. So I'll see you at the Shady Pines in Drovers Road at 3pm.'

And she's gone.

This is all rather exciting, Lindsay thinks, a bit like detective work but without the sordid bits. Well, so far. She glances at her watch and calculates that she has plenty of time to drive over to Stonegrove, get Bella's picture out of the bureau in the Douglas Memorial Room, and then be back in time to meet Caroline.

* * *

At five minutes to three, Lindsay walks through the front gates of the Shady Pines Care Home, and Caroline drives in shortly afterwards. She's fluffed her hair up a bit and put on a neutral lipstick instead of her usual bright red, and discreet silver earrings.

Nothing about her to scare an old lady, Lindsay thinks, as long as she keeps the slightly hysterical edge out of that voice she usually uses on the radio.

They go in, and meet the manager.

'Betty's expecting you,' she says. 'It's so nice for our residents when they get different visitors,' and she leads them off along the corridors, past doors of different colours, until they stop outside one that's painted orange. Lindsay lets Caroline go in ahead of her.

'I'll get one of the girls to bring you some tea,' the manager says before she leaves them to it. 'And a vase for those,' she adds, pointing to the bunch of tulips Caroline has fetched along.

Betty is sitting in her chair and looks quite chirpy for a woman of her age. She's a tiny woman, with fine, white wavy hair. Her eyesight must still be pretty good because she's not wearing glasses, although there's a pair sitting on a magazine on her side table. She's got a lovely, bright smile and maybe because she knew she had visitors coming she's wearing a little bit of powder and lipstick. Lindsay's thinking that she'd like to look that good at ninety-four years old. But mobility is obviously an issue for Betty because there's a Zimmer frame standing by, and a wheelchair is folded up over in the corner next to the door.

It's quite a nice little room, walls painted a soft peach with flowery curtains and a matching bedspread that tone in with the colour. Several family photos are lined up in frames along the window ledge, and somebody has brought in a couple of bright polyanthus plants in ceramic pots, and placed them on the chest of drawers, next to the television. Betty's room is on the ground floor and overlooks the garden, so she's got a nice view of lawn and shrubs, plus there's a bird table right outside her window. As Lindsay looks out a couple of birds are hanging upside down on half a coconut shell and another is pecking up bits of bread and seeds from the platform. Below, on the grass, sits a ginger cat, looking up hopefully with its mouth twitching.

There aren't any other chairs in the room but there's a redundant footstool, which Caroline perches on, whilst Lindsay sits on the edge of the bed. Caroline takes hold of Betty's hands and explains who she is and how she's managed to find her. This takes some time as Betty's grasp of the family tree is a little shaky. She remembers Elsie, but can't place Vera and therefore has no knowledge of Caroline or her parents.

'Do you remember that you and Elsie were both working in Stonegrove Hall at the same time?' Caroline asks.

'Oh yes! She left shortly before me if I remember rightly, when she got married. We didn't see much of each other though, because she worked in the kitchen and I worked upstairs.'

'Yes, my Granny Vera told me that. It's about upstairs that we wanted to ask you, Betty. You see I was asked to go onto a television programme about tracing my ancestors...'

'Were you?' Betty is thrilled, if a little confused. 'Why did they ask you?'

So Caroline has to explain what she does.

'Are you one of those celebrities?'

'Well, yes I suppose so.'

'Do you know Des O'Connor?' asks Betty, smiling broadly.

'Erm, no, I'm afraid I've never met him.'

'Oh, he's always been a favourite of mine. What about Ken Dodd?'

'Sorry, our paths have never crossed.' Caroline doesn't want to get side-tracked so she presses on, even though it's obvious Betty is really more interested in finding out more about her celebrity status than talking about her long-distant career as an upstairs maid.

'Anyway', she says, hoping that Betty will stop wittering on about ancient television personalities and get her head around the topic in hand, 'they found out that Elsie had worked up at Stonegrove Hall but they didn't find you – I suppose because your surname was different to hers nobody realised that you were cousins and therefore you and I are related too. I only just found out when Granny Vera mentioned you. I suppose what you did was very different to what Elsie did?"

Bettty gets back on track, nods her head vigorously and flaps a hand.

'Upstairs or downstairs, being in service was very hard work, I can tell you that. So much cleaning and washing, and when the family had guests there was even more to do, what with making up all those beds and everything. Mr and Mrs Stanton moved out to a cottage on the estate leaving the girls up in the Hall – did you know that? It was after Mr Douglas died, not long before the war. I don't think Mrs Stanton could bear to be around his things all the time. She closed his room off and left it just as it was.'

They hadn't known that. Lindsay scribbles it into a notebook she's brought with her. Betty's memory of that period in her life seems quite sharp so Caroline edges a bit closer to where they want to be with her next question.

'Were you there when Douglas died?' she asks.

'Oh yes, my goodness that was a terrible business, broke poor Mrs Stanton's heart. Him and his motorcycles – always tinkering about with them in the stables. They said he had ten or more of them in bits and pieces, all being worked on at the same time. Not that I ever saw any of this, I was too busy in the house to go gallivanting up at the stables!' Betty laughs, shaking her head at the very idea. 'What about Jimmy Tarbuck?' she says suddenly.

Caroline grits her teeth. 'No I don't know any of these people, Betty. I think we probably work on different shows.'

Lindsay can see she needs to jump in now and keep Betty pointed in the right direction, as Caroline is obviously getting a bit impatient.

'Was there a lot of gallivanting going on up at Stonegrove?' she says, 'I mean, did any friends of Douglas or his sisters come visiting?'

'There were always visitors around. It would be an unusual weekend if nobody other than the family were there, especially in the summer. Not only friends of the young Stantons, some very important people came down to Stonegrove sometimes. Politicians and the like...' Her voice tails off and Lindsay decides this is the time to bring out her photo of Bella.

'Do you ever remember seeing this young lady there?'

She passes the photo across to Betty, who reaches across to the side table for her reading glasses to get a better look. She squints at it, moves the photo closer and then nods her head.

'I remember her. She was there a lot during the summer that Mr Douglas died, we used to see her about, wandering in and out of the gardens with him or on her own. Sometimes she had a friend with her, but usually she came on her own. We thought she was probably a girlfriend, he was often up in London and she used to come down on the train from London. The chauffeur usually picked her up from the station.' Betty takes her glasses off and puts them back on the magazine. 'Or sometimes Mr Douglas went himself. She used to be put in the blue bedroom in the first floor corridor,' Betty says, and Lindsay gets a mental picture of the corridor and presumes that the bedroom in question is further along from the Theatre Room, one of the rooms not open to the public.

'So she often stayed over at Stonegrove?'

Betty nods again. 'She was there the night he went off and killed himself,' she says.

Caroline looks across at Lindsay. There's a little tap at the door, which then swings open.

'Here we are then. Lovely to have special visitors, isn't it Betty?'

One of the staff has arrived with a tray of tea and biscuits, and organising this so that everyone has the milk, sugar and biscuits they each want takes a little while. By the time they get back to where they were Betty has lost the thread.

'So what do you think happened that night?' Caroline asks.

Betty breaks a Digestive in half and nibbles at the edge of it.

'What night, dear?' she asks.

'The night Douglas died,' says Lindsay.

'Oh that. Well, he went off and crashed his motorcycle.'

'Yes, but why would he go off in the middle of the night like that?'

Betty shrugs and takes a sip of tea.

'They said there'd been an argument,' she says.

'Oh? Who was arguing?' Caroline asks, leaning towards Betty.

'Mr Douglas, his sisters, her...' she replies, pointing towards the photo, her voice tailing off.

'Was that unusual?'

'Was what unusual?'

'Arguments – didn't they get on?'

'I don't really know, dear. I only remember about the row that night because after we heard he'd died someone said that might have had something to do with his riding off like that on his motorbike.'

'So you didn't actually hear this argument going on?' Caroline asks.

'I don't think so... '

They glance at each other. Lindsay's thinking that this has probably gone about as far as it can because Betty is clearly starting to flag now, but Caroline is like a terrier with a bone and she won't let it go.

'Did you find out what they were arguing about, Betty?'

'No! We weren't privy to things like that.'

'But there would have been gossip, surely.'

'Well maybe, but this was a long time ago...'

'Where were they when they were arguing?'

'I don't remember dear.'

'But somewhere where they could be heard?'

'I suppose so...'

'Caroline I think that's enough for now...' Lindsay tries to step in because she can see that Betty is wilting under interrogation. But Caroline ignores her.

'Someone obviously heard them and reported back downstairs...'

Betty leans her head back.

'I really don't know,' she says, wearily, closing her eyes.

'And it must have been quite some argument if...'

Lindsay gets to her feet.

'Betty, it's been lovely meeting you,' she says and reaches forward to take Betty's hands in hers, 'but I think we've taken up enough of your time.'

Caroline looks up sharply.

'Thank you for sharing your memories with us.' Lindsay grabs Caroline's bag from the floor and shoves it towards her. 'Maybe we can come and see you again another day, if you'd like that.'

Lindsay nudges Caroline to her feet and pushes her towards the door, where she turns to give Betty a little wave, with Caroline muttering angrily in her ear.

'There was broken glass in the conservatory next morning,' says Betty suddenly, as if it's just come back to her. Her eyebrows are lifted, her eyes opened wide, as though even she's astonished by what she's telling them. 'A window had been smashed, and there were pieces of glass all over one of the chairs and a table.'

They stop in their tracks and wait to see if Betty has any more to say. Her focus seems to shift for a moment but then she looks up at them standing in the doorway.

'Somebody had cut themselves too, I washed up blood from the floor. But Mrs Legg the housekeeper said we wasn't to talk of it again.'

LINDSAY

Caroline was furious that I cut short the visit to Betty, and I was furious with her. She was convinced we'd have got more out of her, but poor old thing, you could see she'd had enough. I think Caroline was being very aggressive in her approach, pushing Betty well beyond the point where she should have stopped. So we had a row when we got outside, and she just kept going on about 'her programme', and why couldn't I see how important this was for her career?

I've come to the conclusion she's not really the slightest bit interested in Bella, who's now been relegated to a walk-on part in an unfolding drama which she hopes to get the television company interested in. She's certainly gone far beyond '*Touching My Roots*', especially after Betty's parting shot about the blood. Now she thinks she's on the trail of a murder. Anyway, if she's determined to keep going with this she'll be on her own now because I'm having nothing more to do with it. I draw the line at harassing old ladies.

I'll have to talk to Helena and Anthony soon, before this gets out of hand and definitely before Caroline goes charging in there giving them the third degree. At the very least they ought to be fore-warned so they can be ready for her. But this weekend is the May Day bank holiday and it's going to be very busy with all hands to the pump, so I can't say anything till that's out of the way.

This is all my fault, I should have just left well alone. The Crofts will probably end up wishing I'd never found my way to Stonegrove.

CAROLINE

I couldn't believe it!

Just as we were starting to get close to something interesting bloody Lindsay comes over all brisk and pushes me out of the room! Another five minutes and I think I might actually have made a breakthrough with Betty. And I don't accept that she was exhausted, as Lindsay told me in no uncertain terms, she was just getting going. At her age the memory needs a bit of jogging and that's all I was trying to do.

It's all very well for Lindsay, she's just got an interest in someone she doesn't even know, but it's a bit different for me. My future career might hang on this. If there's one thing TV companies like it's a true-life drama, and with my family at the centre of it, and me being the one to uncover the story – well obviously there's tons of mileage in that.

Lindsay was really cross with me and stomped off, so it looks like I'm on my own now – as always.

I'll just have to go back to Betty and see what else she can come up with. Blood on the floor certainly came as a surprise, I wonder what that was all about? Perhaps Lindsay's Bella ended up under the herbaceous border...

Or maybe I should talk to the Croft family up at Stonegrove first, that Helena seemed quite approachable although I don't fancy having to interview the mad mother, Diana Stanton-Wotsit.

It strikes me they were all a bit deranged, that whole generation of Stantons. Probably a bit of inbreeding somewhere along the way.

Honestly, no wonder we had a war...

*'Don't you just love to dance? I do. I don't
understand how it is that some people can't dance at
all, not even a little waltz or a bit of Lindy Hop.'*

*'We aren't all made like you, you know.
Thank goodness.'*

Bella, with Ruby Stanton, August 1936

STONEGROVE HALL

Unusually for a bank holiday, the weather is gorgeous.
George and his apprentices have been busy and the
Stonegrove gardens look lovely, with jewel-coloured
tulips flowering in the borders, pink and white blossom
on the trees, and drifts of bluebells in the woodland
areas. The daffodils are mostly over, but a few late
ones are still in flower in shady patches under the trees,
cheerful little splashes of bright yellow. Stonegrove Hall
is looking its best for the expected droves of visitors.

And they do indeed turn up; families and couples
all out to enjoy the gardens in lovely weather and take
advantage of the other attractions that Helena and
Anthony have organised. The Hall is up to maximum
staffing levels over the weekend, and there's a buzz
about the place that Lindsay finds invigorating. She's
spent Saturday and Sunday as a woman-of-all-work,
and enjoyed doing a variety of different things, even
when it was just collecting trays of used crockery at the
restaurant or café. Both evenings she's been exhausted,
but in a good way. The bank holiday Monday is
probably going to be their busiest day of the weekend;

Lindsay will be back on her regular room steward duty then and she's been looking forward to it.

She's one of the first to arrive on Monday, but Reg has still beaten her to it and is already getting organised in Douglas's room when she pops her head around the door.

'Whoever was in here yesterday has made a right mess of these programmes,' he grumbles. Reg had left them nicely fanned out across the top of the bureau but this morning they're just in a haphazard pile and one of them has fallen to the floor and been left there. The patchwork bedspread is rucked up as if someone has sat on the side of the bed, and Douglas's watch has slipped off the tuxedo and now lies face down beside it.

'Can't get the right calibre of volunteer,' Lindsay says and smiles at him.

'I know I'm an old fuss-pot but I do like to see things presented properly,' he replies, grumpily. 'And Bella's disappeared.'

'Oh Reg, she hasn't, I've got her.'

He looks up, surprised. 'Have you? Whatever for?'

Lindsay doesn't want to say anything about visiting Betty, or the revelations she came out with, at least not until she's had a chance to talk to Helena.

'Oh... I'd been telling someone about her and I just wanted to show her the photo. You don't mind, do you?'

'She's not mine to mind about, but as long as you've got her I know she's in safe hands.'

'I'll put her back...'

'I know you will. If the other volunteers are going to mess things about like this she's probably safer with you anyway.'

101

Lindsay decides to leave Reg to it, hoping he'll settle down once he's got all the props set out again to his satisfaction. She goes into the Theatre Room and has hardly finished straightening the chairs when she hears someone coming along the corridor and next thing Helena's speaking to Reg next door in the Douglas Memorial Room.

'The band will be playing on the terrace on this side of the house, just warning you in case it's a little loud. You might want to keep your windows closed...'

Reg looks up from the pile of theatre programmes.

'Then I won't try to compete with the records today. You can have too much of a good thing.'

'Well I was hoping that when the band have their breaks you would take over with the records, Reg. It creates a really nice atmosphere for people as they walk into the house – such a good idea of yours.'

Lindsay can hear all of this going on from next door, and smiles to herself. Helena has definitely got the measure of Reg.

Helena leaves him to it, happier than when she found him, and goes next door to Lindsay.

'That's fine with me too, I heard you telling Reg. What time are they starting?'

'As soon as they're ready, although I don't think they're all here yet. Probably around eleven thirty.' Then Helena's mobile rings and she scurries off back to the office.

Just before eleven o'clock, Lindsay wanders into Reg's room to see how he's getting on, and it's clear that she needn't have worried about him. The room is now perfectly arranged again, and Reg is sitting on his steward's chair calmly reading a book and humming to himself.

'Doubt if there'll be much time to read today,' he says. He checks his watch then closes the book and puts it away in his briefcase. 'But I thought I may as well bring it, just in case it's a bit slack later on.'

Lindsay crosses the room and looks out of the window, onto the terrace below where the band are setting up. And what she sees certainly takes her by surprise.

'Good heavens,' she says, 'I had no idea!'

Reg joins her to see what she's looking at.

'Look, that's Anthony – did you know he was in the band?'

The man in question, who's carrying a clarinet, has turned away from them and is chatting to the double bass player.

'Are you sure?'

'Positive, wait till he turns round...'

And then he does, and it's definitely Anthony.

'Well I never!'

'Is this the first time the band have played here?'

'As far as I can recall.'

'Helena never said anything...'

Then the most extraordinary thing happens. A second Anthony steps out of the shadows, shakes the clarinet-playing Anthony by the hand and they have a man-hug.

'Twins!' Reg and Lindsay say together.

'Hence the little twin grand-daughters, it's in the family,' says Reg, who has now lost interest and moves away from the window.

But Lindsay hasn't lost interest, far from it. Another Anthony, just as attractive as the first – and she's not working for this one. The day takes on a new gloss.

* * *

Kaye and Peter arrive just before lunchtime. Peter wheezes and gasps his way into the Theatre Room and Lindsay makes him sit on her steward's chair until he's got his breath back. Kaye has seen it all before and shows little concern about Peter's condition, preferring instead to hear about Sophia Stanton and the other little actors as Lindsay talks her through the photographs and the play script in the glass case.

'... and there are some costumes but we can't put them out because they're too delicate. So Helena's talking to the conservation people at the V&A...'

Once Peter's had a rest he goes over to the window and looks out at the musicians below, now in full flow.

'They're getting quite a crowd down there,' he says, and Kaye joins him at the window. The band is playing swing music from the 1940s, and one adventurous couple has started jiving on the terrace alongside them.

'She'll ruin her shoes on those paving slabs,' says Kaye, but the dancing woman doesn't seem the least bit put off by this. The number comes to an end and the audience applaud both the band and the dancers, who take an extravagant bow. It's at that moment that Lindsay peers over her mother's shoulder and recognises them. It seems that surprises are the order of the day.

'Well, well! Who'd have thought it?' she says.

'Someone you know?' asks Kaye.

'Both of them, actually...'

It's the first time Lindsay has seen Deirdre in anything other than her yoga kit, but today she's looking rather glamorous in sparkly ballerina pumps and a full-skirted red and white polka dot dress, her hair tied back in a long ponytail that's swinging around her shoulders as she dances. Away from Cappuccino Blues, Sergiu seems to favour a different style of dress completely.

Gone are the tight, tight jeans and the narrow black tee-shirts that show off his pecs and biceps. In their place, he's wearing wide corded trousers with braces and a loose-fitting white shirt.

The music starts again and so do Deirdre and Sergiu, and Lindsay suddenly cottons on to the fact that their appearance is not by chance, they are clearly a planned part of the entertainment. Helena had never mentioned dancers – but then why would she? Neither Deirdre nor Sergiu had ever mentioned that they were dance partners – but she can count on one hand the number of times she's said more than a few words of small talk to Deirdre, and Sergiu was just... well, Sergiu. And it's no wonder he's got such well-defined muscles, and a good thing too, because now he's lifting Deirdre up and swinging her around and she's smiling broadly and looking quite un-Deirdre like. Lindsay hopes that Rufus and Gary turn up while all this is happening because if they don't see it for themselves they'll certainly never believe her.

* * *

It's two o'clock and the band are on their break. Kaye and Peter have gone home, and Lindsay is ready for a drink and a sandwich so as soon as Reg gets back she heads off to the café.

Deirdre and Sergiu are nowhere to be seen, but the musicians are grouped around one of the tables at the back of the Stables Tea Room. Lindsay takes her tray outside, sits in a lovely warm patch of sun and has only just got settled when she sees Gary and Rufus coming up the gravel path leading to the café. They haven't spotted her, and as she watches them it seems that Gary is dragging his feet a bit and definitely looking under the weather. She waves them across to join her.

'You OK Gary? Too much gardening yesterday?'

'It's probably the start of my hay fever,' he says, 'all this tree pollen around.'

'He usually gets it this time of year,' says Rufus, 'sneezing scheduled to start any minute now. They say the pollen count's really high at the moment and we're surrounded by it here with all these trees in blossom. Anyway, how's it been going? There seem to be plenty of people around at the moment.'

'Yeah, it's been great, very busy all weekend.'

Bang on cue, Gary sneezes.

'What did I tell you?' says Rufus.

They decide to get coffees before they start looking around, and as they go into the café and join the queue, so the musicians come out. And as if it were planned, it's at precisely this moment that Anthony comes round the corner and almost collides with them right in front of where Lindsay is sitting.

'Lindsay!' Anthony says, 'Have you met my brother Nick?'

'No, but I've heard him – you're playing right underneath my window,' she says, holding out her hand.

'I'm so sorry, you poor thing,' Nick says, 'I hope we didn't drive too many people away from you.'

'Lindsay's been our right hand woman this weekend,' says Anthony.

'I've enjoyed it, it's been great to see how all the different parts of this place work.'

'And then we turned up and spoilt it for you,' says Nick.

'No, you haven't at all, it's really nice to have the music – adds a bit of atmosphere. I know your two dancers, actually.'

'Do you? The band have only just started using

them but it seems to be working rather well. People obviously like them and that Lindy Hop thing they do is just right for this kind of music.'

Seen up close, the twins are not quite identical but they certainly share the same charm and the same startlingly blue eyes. Be careful, Lindsay thinks, you know nothing about this man. But then she thinks, oh what the hell, loosen up girl.

'I'm in the Theatre Room, I was looking down at you earlier on. I thought you were Anthony at first, then he turned up and I realised that you were twins.'

'Ah, you see Nick, it still works...'

'When we were kids we used to set people up all the time – I didn't realise we were still playing that game but my brother obviously hasn't lost his appetite for the double-take. You didn't pre-warn the staff then?' Nick asks Anthony.

'Well naturally I didn't want to get them over-excited – two of us at once, it's a lot for people to cope with, even the unflappable Lindsay.'

'Oh, I expect I'll manage,' Lindsay says, throwing Nick her best smile.

Just then Rufus and Gary arrive back with their tray of coffee and cakes. Realising they are Lindsay's friends, Anthony carries on into the café with the bag of coins they've asked for, and Nick turns to catch up with his fellow band members.

'OK, looks like we're back on. I might pop up later to see what they've done to the old Theatre Room,' he calls back, with a wave.

Yes please, she thinks, that would certainly be nice.

But before this thought can take a hold of her Rufus and Gary have to be regaled with the story of the dancing duo, which prompts a good deal of speculation.

'I thought Deirdre had a husband and young children?'

'Doesn't mean she can't dance.'

'No, but...'

'So do you think they're doing something other than dancing?'

'Don't know. He did make that comment the other day...'

'...about the pillow, yes I thought of that.'

'Might not be Deirdre's head on it though.'

'We must go and see them when the band are next on.'

'Oh yes, it would be rude not to.'

'Hope they won't mind us watching...'

'Why would they? It's a public place, and we are the public. They wouldn't be here if they didn't want people watching them.'

'Then that's settled. You'd better finish that flapjack, the music's started again.'

*Whatever your skills, there's a volunteer role for you
– as a first aider you will be part of a team that saves
lives and delivers care to people in need at public
events in your community.*

St. John Ambulance website

THE YOGA STUDIO

It's the end of the week and the yoga class are assembling, ready for an hour's stretching and deep relaxation. None of them had a chance to speak to Deirdre at the end of her dancing stint at Stonegrove, so Lindsay, Rufus and Gary have all been expecting to offer their congratulations before today's session. But Deirdre is late, slipping into the studio only just in time for Janey to start the class, and by then they're all flat on their backs with their eyes closed.

They've only just started the warm-up and Lindsay is beginning to get lost in her practice when she hears it for the first time, quite softly.

'Ouf'.

She looks to Gary on the mat to her left, and even though it's quite cool in the studio his face is running with sweat. She levers herself up onto her elbows, facing him sideways, and whispers his name.

'Gary?'

'Ouf.'

Janey pauses in mid-sentence and looks across.

'OUF. AAARGHghghghgh ...'

Gary clutches at his chest, the sound gurgling through his throat, then slumps back and suddenly everyone is aware of what's happening and the mood has completely changed.

Janey springs to her feet and grabs her phone. Rufus leaps up and kneels at Gary's side, one arm around him, shaking him, and shouting his name, although Gary won't know about it because his eyes have rolled back and he's stopped breathing. The other students are all standing, waiting, watching, and hoping someone who knows what they're doing will take the lead here, because although they've all seen the videos nobody feels confident enough that they can remember exactly what to do.

And someone does take the lead. Deirdre throws herself across the studio and straddles Gary, pushing Rufus out of the way as she does so. And then she gets to work, tipping Gary's head back, moving his tongue to the side, breathing into his mouth, pumping his chest, and repeating it over and over.

Nobody is panicking, except for Rufus, who's now in pieces. Lindsay has her arms around him, and were it not for him crying the studio would be eerily quiet. The only other sounds are Deirdre's breathing and her soft grunts and the thump thump thump as she pushes down on Gary's chest.

Janey speaks into the silence to say that the paramedics are on their way, then she runs downstairs so she can meet them and show them where to go. Sergiu, aware that something's up, exchanges a few words with her and then leaves his customers to join her vigil out on the pavement.

Up in the studio Deirdre keeps going.

Rufus keeps crying.

And nobody can take their eyes off Gary.

The paramedics take a long ten minutes to arrive, and Deirdre doesn't let up at all. As soon as they get into the room they take over, give Gary oxygen and an injection, and carry on with the resuscitation process, talking to him all the time even though everyone knows he probably can't hear them.

Deirdre falls into an exhausted heap on the floor, and Janey gives her a long hug, then she gently moves all but Rufus and Lindsay out of the studio and into the reception area. One by one, they silently drift off home, but Deirdre stays.

Eventually the paramedics start to get Gary ready to be stretchered into the ambulance. It's not easy getting him down the stairs, but they are careful and resolutely cheerful. When they get to the street entrance Sergiu is still hovering near the café door and he comes out as they go past and silently crosses himself. Lindsay sees it, and hopes Rufus hasn't.

The ambulance crew are prepared to let Rufus go with them, but Lindsay must follow them over there in her car. Her hands are shaking and her knees are like jelly, so she takes a deep breath and gathers herself because driving is the last thing she wants to do right at that moment. And this must be written across her face because one of the paramedics puts his hand on her shoulder.

'They'll be expecting us when we get there so he'll jump the queue,' he tells her, 'but remember we'll be on blues and twos so we're allowed to speed – you're not. Just take it easy and arrive safely.'

She watches as they load Gary in through the back doors and then Rufus climbs in after one of the crew members and the doors close on them. The blue lights start up and the ambulance pulls out into the traffic with its siren screeching.

Lindsay turns to Sergiu.

'Deirdre kept him alive till they got here. She was amazing.'

Sergiu nods, and turns to go back into Cappuccino Blues, and at just that moment Deirdre comes clattering down the stairs behind Lindsay with her own bag slung over her shoulder and Lindsay's held in her outstretched hand.

'Can I come with you?' she asks. 'I'd like to know Gary's OK.'

* * *

They're taking Gary to Poole hospital, and although it's less than ten miles away it seems as if they'll never get there. They catch every set of traffic lights, and more often than not they find themselves driving behind a learner driver. The paramedics advice to observe the speed limit isn't needed.

'How did you know to do that?' Lindsay asks Deirdre.

'Before we moved here I used to teach a dance class in our village hall, and there was a first aid group in straight after us,' she says. 'I got interested and ended up doing the course. And then for a while I volunteered with St John's.'

'Was this the first time you'd done it for real?'

'Yeah, and I hope I never have to again. It's very scary.'

'You were brilliant though, you kept your nerve and just got on with it.'

'That's what we were always told – keep focused on what you're doing. I wasn't even aware of the rest of you being in the room.'

'Rufus was in a real state,' says Lindsay.

'It's a frightening thing to witness, imagine how awful it must be when it's someone you love?'

Finally, they pull into the hospital car park and make their way across to the Accident and Emergency department, where they run into their ambulance crew coming out.

'He's on his way up to the Intensive Care Unit so he's in the best possible hands,' one of them says. 'You did a good job there,' he adds to Deirdre.

And then, quite unexpectedly, she bursts into tears.

* * *

And so Lindsay finds herself negotiating another set of corridors in another hospital, not so very long after she'd ended up in the Royal Bournemouth in search of Caroline, but this time with Deirdre at her side.

They sit outside the door to ICU, and wait. Rufus is in there, but Lindsay and Deirdre aren't allowed in and in a funny way they're glad about that. After half an hour or so Deirdre goes off and gets them each a cup of tea and a KitKat, which neither of them eats. Every time the doors open they look up. Nurses come out, doctors come out, visitors come out – but Rufus doesn't. Occasionally people go in and the doors swish quietly closed behind them.

Another hour goes by.

And then the door opens again and this time when they look up it's Rufus, and they're both on their feet and he's nodding and not being able to say much but they can tell from his face that Gary is still with them and if Rufus has left his side then he must be doing OK.

'Deirdre... what you did back there... I can't...'

Rufus puts his arms around Deirdre and pulls her into a bear hug. Her face disappears into his chest and then he stretches out his right arm and pulls Lindsay into the hug too and they stand together for long moments during which Lindsay hears herself repeating over and over, 'He's going to be OK, he's going to be OK.'

When they let go of each other and sit down Rufus explains what the medical team have been doing and how things are looking for Gary's recovery.

'He's hanging on in there and they're fairly pleased with his progress so far. "Stable" is the word everyone keeps using. Doesn't tell us much but I think it's all I'm going to get at the moment.'

'You'll stay here I suppose?' Lindsay asks.

Rufus nods. 'At least until tonight. Then if he's still the same I should probably go back home and try to sleep although I doubt if that'll be easy. I have to ring his mum, too. She'll want to come straight over I expect.'

'You must look after yourself – you won't be much good to Gary if you get worn out,' says Deirdre. 'You ought to have a drink and something to eat – what did I do with those KitKats?' she adds, rummaging about in her bag.

'I could murder a cup of tea,' he says and they decide they may as well go down to the cafeteria because there's nothing more they can achieve by sitting outside ICU any longer.

The tea is welcome but although Rufus attempts to get a cheese and ham sandwich down he abandons it after a few bites.

'I guess we'll have to make some life-style changes,' he says, 'diet and things. But that's nothing. I just want him back...'

Lindsay takes his hand in hers.

'He'll get all the care he needs here, and when he goes home he's lucky that he'll have you to look after him.'

'And you'll be surprised how many other people will rally round to help,' says Deirdre. 'Does Gary's mum live nearby?'

'This side of Dorchester, it takes us about half an hour to drive to her place. I should really call her now,' Rufus adds, taking his mobile from his pocket and pushing his chair away from the table. 'Back in a mo.'

Rufus heads for the corridor and Lindsay and Dierdre look at each other.

'Tough on him,' says Lindsay, with a sigh.

'Yeah. Are you going to stay on for a bit? Only I should get back home soon, my kids will think I've run off.'

'Oh, yes, of course. I'll give you a lift back to Wareham...'

'No need, I can easily get a bus, I'll just call them so they know what's happening.'

'Well, if you're sure? I'll probably stay till Gary's mum gets here, just to give Rufus some moral support.'

They both stand up. Suddenly, it feels a bit awkward.

'I'll be off then.'

'OK. See you next week at yoga.'

'Can I call you in the meantime – find out how he's getting on?'

'Oh, of course.' Lindsay rummages in her bag for a pen, writes her number on a serviette and hands it to Deirdre. 'Any time, whenever...'

'Right. OK.'

There's a bit of a silence and then Lindsay holds out her arms and gives Deirdre a hug.

'You saved his life,' she says, and Deirdre lets out a long sigh.

'I did my best,' she says, 'I just hope it was good enough.'

And then they step away from each other and as Deirdre picks up her bag two KitKats fall out of the front pocket.

'Take these,' she says as she heads for the door. 'You might be glad of them later.'

* * *

Gary's mum, Iris, arrives almost an hour after Deirdre has left. For most of that time Lindsay has sat on her own outside ICU, with Rufus just popping out for a break every so often. There's nothing at all that she can do, but she just doesn't want to leave him there on his own.

Iris looks at least ten years younger than her eighty-six years. She's come in a taxi, she tells Lindsay, and will go back to Wareham with Rufus when he's ready to go. Until then, she's prepared to sit it out in the hospital. She has with her an overnight bag, and a cool bag with sandwiches and cake in it.

'Never trust hospital catering,' she says, briskly. 'Half the time they haven't got what you want and in the middle of the night when you're hungry there'll be nothing available but chocolate bars from a machine.'

'You did well to get all this lot together at such short notice,' says Lindsay.

'My next door neighbour is a taxi driver,' says Iris. 'His wife came straight round and made the sandwiches while I packed a bag and we waited for him to get back from his previous call. Then as soon as he did I was ready to go.'

Not long after Iris has made herself comfortable Rufus joins them, and Lindsay decides it's time she left.

'Call me tomorrow morning,' she says, 'even if there's nothing much to tell.'

Outside in the car park it's still surprisingly warm, even though the afternoon is slipping into a still evening.

Who would have thought, thinks Lindsay, how this day would have ended up when we all set off this morning for yoga.

She walks wearily to her car and when she's inside switches her phone back on and finds two missed calls and one message, all from the same number, one that she doesn't recognise. When she checks the message she gets a pleasant little jolt of surprise to see who it's from.

Please call me. Nick, is all it says.

Douglas is a decent enough chap, but those sisters of his are just awful. And they make it perfectly clear that they can't stand me.
Bella's diary, July 1936

WAREHAM

It's tempting to call back straight away, but Lindsay exercises extreme restraint and waits until she's got home and taken her shoes and jacket off. It takes so long for Nick to answer that she's just getting ready to leave a message when suddenly his voice comes on the line and throws her completely.

'Oh, hello, sorry I kept missing you,' she says.

'Erm – who is this?'

How many women have you got messages out with? she thinks.

'It's Lindsay, Lindsay Walton. I had my phone switched off because I was in hospital. With a friend that is, I mean there's nothing wrong with me, I was there with him. He'd had a heart attack.' She pulls a face and thinks, oh just shut up.

'I see, well I'm sorry to hear about that. I hope he's doing OK?'

'I think so, it only happened this morning and – in fact Deirdre, you know Deirdre who...'

'Lindsay, I think we need to talk. I met Caroline van Dell this afternoon when I was up at the Hall...'

Lindsay's heart sinks. Caroline has got there before her, before she's had a chance to say anything to Helena and Anthony, and probably screwed up any prospects she might have had of remaining as a Stonegrove volunteer. Behind these thoughts she's aware that Nick is still talking.

'... obviously thought I was Anthony. Anyway I fobbed her off by saying I was too busy to talk at that moment and I'd have to phone her with a day when we could meet. She mentioned you, a couple of times.'

'I was planning to talk to Helena and Anthony about this on Monday when I'm there on room duty.'

'Well I haven't said anything to them, I thought I'd have a chat with you first and see if I could divert any potential trouble. She seemed a bit, erm, pumped up.'

'Yes, I imagine she would. Look Nick, I've just this minute got in but if you can give me half an hour I'll meet you somewhere, or you can come here? Or I'm around over the weekend.'

'I'm not, I go back to London first thing tomorrow morning. I'm guessing you live in Wareham? Shall we meet at the Black Bear – in about forty-five minutes?'

Lindsay, not knowing whether to be exhilarated or depressed by this turn of events, agrees. And then dashes around her flat in a frenzy for the next half hour.

* * *

Nick is already waiting in the bar when Lindsay arrives at the Black Bear, admittedly ten minutes later than they'd agreed due to changing her outfit three times. It's hard not to look frazzled, after the day she's had and is still having, but she takes a few deep breaths, strides in through the main entrance and hopes she looks more together than she feels.

He stands up as she heads towards him and is soon up at the bar buying drinks. It's years since Lindsay was in the Black Bear, and she glances around tentatively to see if there's anyone there she knows, an old school friend on a night out who might come waltzing over or someone working behind the bar who would know her. But there's not a single face she recognises, which comes as a relief.

'So,' he says, once they're settled, 'what's the story with Caroline? You seem a fairly unlikely pair.'

'Ha! You could say that. It's a long story in a short time frame, I've hardly known her five minutes but it's going to take me a lot longer than that to explain our connection.'

'OK, well I imagine if you've been at the hospital all day you haven't eaten...'

'Er, not really, just a sandwich in the cafeteria hours ago.'

Nick nods and looks around for one of the bar staff.

'Then I'm going to get us a table and you can tell me this long story over dinner.'

'Oh, I didn't bring my cards with me...'

Nick rolls his eyes. 'Then I'll just pay for mine and you'll have to wash up,' he says. 'Obviously I wasn't expecting you to pay, it was my idea.'

And so half an hour later, they've got a cosy window table and a bottle of Sauvignon Blanc on ice and Lindsay has got to the bit where she sends the note to Caroline via one of the runners.

'Very enterprising,' he says, as their starters arrive.

'I thought so too,' she says, 'but it rather backfired on me...'

Nick listens patiently as the story unfolds, providing just the right comments in all the right places so it's obvious he's taking it all in.

'So basically, you two are coming at this from completely different angles.'

'And looking for completely different outcomes. I can see that her career could do with perking up and if she can make something out of this that'll give her the boost she needs then good luck to her. But ...'

'But you don't like the way she's going about it.'

'No I don't, and not at my expense, or Helena and Anthony's either. I got Caroline started on this, but it was in all innocence and I don't want to be the scapegoat when the shit hits the fan.'

Nick smiles at her, it's a real heart-melting smile, and of course he can't help that.

'You like Stonegrove, don't you?'

Lindsay nods. 'This is the closest I've come to a proper job in a very long time, and I love being a volunteer there.'

'Well they certainly value you, I know that for a fact, and I wouldn't be too worried about telling Helena and Anthony exactly what you've just told me. They won't hold any of this against you, they're not like that.'

'But if Caroline makes the programme she wants to then it could reflect badly on Helena's family, and I'll feel responsible for putting her in that position. If she won't help Caroline it will look like she's got something to hide, and if she does then she'll just seem treacherous. She can't win.'

'Well, Caroline's waiting for a call from me, or at least Anthony, so she won't go barging in for a few days and by then you'll have had a chance to talk to them. Anthony will come up with a plan, he's very good at that sort of thing.'

'I hope you're right.'

Nick refills their glasses.

'I wonder what did happen that night,' he says. 'Ruby was a strange old girl, I wouldn't put much past her. And you've seen Diana, the other weird old bat of course?'

'Oh, don't you start...'

'Blood on the floor, remember...'

'Well let's see. That was just a nose bleed, Douglas got them all the time when he was over-excited.' Lindsay giggles and silently congratulates herself on having the good sense to leave the car at home and walk into town.

Nick leans forward. 'Oh yeah? Broken glass?'

'Diana tripped over her pearls and dropped her gin and tonic.'

'Raised voices?'

'Well obviously they had to speak up over the sound of the record player. Ruby was dancing the jitterbug and singing along to the Cab Calloway Orchestra at the top of her voice.'

'Ha! You've got an answer for everything, haven't you? Except this: what *did* happen to Bella? You can't answer that one.'

'No I can't, and that's the problem.'

They fall silent for a moment.

'Are you having a pudding?' asks Nick, passing a menu across to her. 'They do a great Death by Chocolate here. I believe the recipe's been in the Stanton family for generations.'

'Oh, stop it!'

'Look, if you can't figure out what happened to Bella how is Caroline going to do it? There's only one person who actually knows the truth and that's...'

'... Diana, yes I know. I wouldn't fancy Caroline's chances of tackling her.'

Lindsay reaches for her bag and fishes around in it for a moment.

'Here she is,' she says, putting the photograph on the table.

'Diana?'

'No of course not. Bella. This is the photo that started the whole thing off.'

Nick takes the photo and looks closely at it, then turns it over and reads Bella's scrawl on the back..

'Pretty girl,' he says. 'Lousy handwriting. Not privately educated, that's for sure.'

Lindsay looks up at him to see if he's joking, but he's obviously not.

'Well that's the first constructive thing anyone's said so far.'

'Yep. You need me on the case.'

That smile again. It's unnerving. Lovely, though...

'I'll bear that in mind.'

He gives the photo back to her. 'By the way, any news of your friend in hospital?'

Jolted back to reality, Lindsay hastily reaches for her phone and checks it. There's a text from Rufus. *Doing OK*, is all it says. Suddenly she feels bone-tired.

'He's keeping going, not too bad it seems. I really think I should go,' she says. 'It's been a hell of a day, I think it's just catching up with me now.'

It's only a fifteen minute walk back to her flat and Lindsay brushes aside Nick's offer to drive her home.

'No, it's really OK,' she says. 'I could do with the fresh air and thinking time. Thanks anyway. And thanks for dinner, it was lovely.'

He doesn't push it.

'I'll call you tomorrow,' he says, 'when you've hopefully had a good sleep, and you can think about how best to approach Helen and Anthony.'

And so they part, with not as much as a peck on the cheek.

Damn, Lindsay thinks. Obviously didn't play that one right.

But it doesn't really matter because she can't quite get her head around the idea of Nick, not while it's still so full of Gary and everything that happened earlier in the day. Even Caroline's taking a back seat at the moment, although that's a situation that will have to be faced up to very soon.

Ruby thinks she's common. I'm afraid I agree with her.

Diana Stanton's diary, July 2nd 1936

STONEGROVE HALL

Saturday starts dull, and then gets worse. The sky grows so dark it's as if there's been an eclipse of the sun, and then rain starts to splash on the ground, fat drops coming down hard in straight lines. Stair rods, Lindsay's gran used to say back in the days when most households had them and people knew what was meant. And so it continues, throughout the morning, and Lindsay can tell that this is a day when nobody will go out unless they absolutely have to.

Rufus and Iris have to of course, they will brave the weather to go to the hospital and most probably stay there all day. Lindsay imagines Iris packing up more sandwiches and cake, enough to last a week. Rufus' morning phone call to Lindsay didn't tell her much, just that Gary is stable and responding to treatment, which is probably all they can hope for at this early stage.

Nick phones her at around eleven, from London.

'I'm going up to Stonegrove today,' she says. 'It'll be quiet because of this torrential rain, so Helena and Anthony should have time to talk.'

'Well, good luck with that, I'm sure they'll be fine. And if they want to call me they've got my mobile number.'

'All I can do is just come straight out with it and tell them everything. I hope they don't show me the door.'

'They won't do that. They've got a lot of time for you and they'll see this for what it is. They certainly won't want to lose you. Call me later, let me know how it went.'

It comes as a surprise to Lindsay that Nick should be sufficiently interested to want an update. But then, she reasons, it's his family too, albeit through marriage. And like it or not, he's involved in Bella's story now.

The rain hasn't eased up one bit by half past eleven, and Lindsay decides it's as good a time as any to drive up to Stonegrove. She checks that Bella is still tucked safely into her handbag, gathers up waterproof jacket, car keys and umbrella, and sets off before she loses her nerve and finds an excuse to stay.

* * *

From the staff car park it's a short walk to the estate office entrance, but far enough in this weather to get wet. She shakes out her umbrella and adds it to the many already dripping into the stands inside the doorway, then hangs her waterproof up.

Helena's assistant Beverley is the only person in the office, although she's got company in the form of Henry the tabby, currently taking refuge from the rain. Lindsay is reluctant to interrupt her as she's got paperwork spread all over her desk, but she looks up and smiles encouragingly.

'Are Helena and Anthony around this morning?'

'They're around, not sure where right now. I think Helena was going over to the shop. Anthony was in here not five minutes ago, if you hang on he'll probably be back soon.'

The phone rings, and Beverley answers it. From his vantage point on the window ledge Henry yawns, stretches and looks round at Lindsay, who's already heading for the door. Not wanting to look as if she's listening in to Beverley's call she walks into the corridor and sees Anthony coming towards her carrying a cardboard box full of leaflets.

'You're two days early,' he says, 'but very welcome any day. I was just going to drop these off then grab a coffee – will you join me?'

'I was actually hoping to have a word with both you and Helena,' says Lindsay.

'In that case I'll just call and tell her to meet us in the Stables,' says Anthony as he deposits his box in a corner of the office and fishes his mobile out of his pocket.

They walk together down a maze of corridors to reach the closest exit to the tearoom and Lindsay is amazed at how little of the Hall she really knows well. Certainly without Anthony she'd never have found this route to the Stables.

'Dreadful weather,' he says, choosing a big umbrella from the selection next to the service door. 'We'll make a dash for it across the courtyard – here, take my arm.'

And off they go, dodging the worst puddles, although the way the rain is bouncing up there isn't much chance of arriving with dry feet even though they're only going a short distance.

Most of the tables are empty and there's every chance of them staying that way unless the weather bucks up some time soon, so it's easy enough to get settled down away from the door and the serving counter. By the time Anthony has brought the coffee over Lindsay looks up to see Helena arriving.

'Hello,' she says, unwrapping herself from her raincoat. 'This isn't the kind of day I'd expect to see a volunteer who didn't have to be here. Is everything OK?'

Lindsay smiles, but without much conviction.

'Please don't tell me you're leaving,' says Helena, her face falling. 'Have you got a job? Because if you have I'm really, really pleased for you, but...'

'No, it's not that. But without meaning to I seem to have got involved in something, and I'm afraid you and Stonegrove are going to get dragged into it now.'

Anthony raises an eyebrow and looks questioningly at Lindsay. It reminds her of Nick. Helena just looks perplexed, her mouth set in a straight line. Lindsay takes a deep breath and knows that now she's got started she's got to go through with it and tell them every last detail.

'It's about Caroline van Dell. And that picture of the girl we found in Douglas's suit – you remember, the one that upset your mother.'

Helena nods. 'You're telling us there's a connection between the two?'

'Kind of. It all started the day Caroline was filming here – no, it started before that because I was intrigued by the picture of Bella...'

Lindsay talks, Helena and Anthony listen. Then she gets to the bit where she sent the note to Caroline.

'That was enterprising,' says Anthony.

Lindsay looks at him in amazement. 'That's exactly what Nick said.'

The words are out of her mouth before she can stop them.

'Oh? What's this got to do with Nick?' asks Anthony.

'Ah, well you see Caroline mistook him for you – I'll get to that bit...'

Anthony smiles at her, sits back in his chair and folds his arms.

'Well I never,' he says. 'Welcome to the girlfriends and ex-wives club.'

'Anthony!' says Helena. 'Just let Lindsay tell her story.'

Anthony finishes his coffee and puts the cup down. He's still smiling. Lindsay can feel a blush creeping up her neck. She's wondering how many ex-wives there are.

'So, she got the note from one of the runners but didn't even read it at the time. And then two or three days later I got a call from the hospital...'

Lindsay's back on track with her story now, but she can't look Anthony in the eyes because she knows what he's thinking and although he's got it wrong she rather wishes he was right. It takes another round of coffees to bring Helena and Anthony up to the events of the previous day and Nick's surprise involvement.

'He said you could phone him if you wanted. He can tell you about meeting Caroline better than me.'

Helena leans forward. 'So on the basis of what this old lady told her Caroline is hoping to prove that one of my family finished Bella off that night in the conservatory – right?'

'And then turn the story into a TV documentary programme, yes.'

'And now I've got to make an appointment to see Caroline,' says Anthony. 'Well, that should be fun, thanks Nick.'

'I'm so sorry,' says Lindsay. 'This is all my fault.'

'No,' says Helena, 'it isn't. You couldn't have known how this would turn out.'

'If only I'd said something at the start before it got out of control...'

'Well, we are where we are. There's nothing... Lindsay?'

Anthony reaches across the table and takes her hand. Lindsay is mortified to realise that she's started crying.

'Sorry,' she says, diving into her pocket for a tissue, not finding one and then using a serviette to blot her eyes. 'Yesterday was just the most awful day, what with all this and...' and then she's off again telling them about Gary.

'Good grief woman, no wonder you're upset. Go home,' says Anthony, squeezing her hand. 'Go and visit your friend and then go home and have an early night. Don't even think about Stonegrove until you come in on Monday.'

'I can still come in then?'

'You'd jolly well better,' says Helena, 'we need you here. Look, this will all turn out to be a storm in a teacup. Whatever Caroline's hoping for there's nobody left who can tell her what really happened that night. It'll just remain a mystery and a good old mystery won't do us any harm at all.'

Anthony sits back and looks at Helena. 'Nobody left, except your mother...' he says.

'Yes, well I'll deal with her,' Helena replies, briskly.

CAROLINE

He's a bit of a charmer, that Anthony Croft.

"Come for lunch," he said. "It'll be our pleasure."

It might not be when he knows why I want to talk to them.

I told Steve yesterday about this lunch date, although I could tell he wasn't taking it entirely seriously when he offered to come along as my food-taster. I doubt if even the Crofts would do something as blatant as poisoning me over lunch in their own restaurant, although they might end up kicking me out before the pudding arrives... Steve's started referring to it as the day of the long dessert knives. He thinks I'm going to leave there with a fork sticking out of the top of my head.

I'm rather hoping I won't run into Lindsay when I'm up at Stonegrove, that would be awkward and in a funny way I feel disloyal to her doing this. There's also a part of me that would quite like to see Lindsay again, I've missed her common-sense input into my disaster of a life. For one thing there's no decent food left in my kitchen now.

If only I could have talked to Betty again, I might have been able to go in to this lunch meeting with something a bit more concrete. I do think they were being a bit over the top at the Shady Pines Home, not letting me in. I bet she never really said she didn't want me to visit again, I mean, we are family after all. Maybe what she meant was that she didn't want to see Lindsay again, and they've got confused between us.

I wonder if I could get Granny Vera to visit Betty? She might be able to wheedle something else out of her and the staff wouldn't stop her going in, just one old lady visiting another. Nothing sinister about that...

Weekends at Stonegrove are getting to be a bit of a bore. The ugly sisters won't even talk to me now and Douglas is getting more and more obsessed with his motorbikes. John can sometimes be fun though.

Letter from Bella to her friend Enid, August 1936

STONEGROVE HALL

Anthony has arranged for Caroline to have lunch at Stonegrove in a week's time.

'Let's keep her waiting for a bit,' he said to Helena, after making the phone call. 'No point in rushing into this.'

In truth, Anthony needs more time to figure out how to handle the situation. Caroline may well have hit on something here, he wouldn't be entirely surprised at anything Ruby and Diana did in their youth since he has always thought they were both as mad as a box of frogs. But Helena's convinced that whatever scenario Caroline's built up in her head she can't possibly have any proof. So the whole thing remains conjecture – or does it? As far as Anthony can see it's not inconceivable that in the time since they parted company Caroline might have uncovered something Lindsay doesn't know about.

But even that isn't really the problem, it's more a question of what she does with her suspicions, unsubstantiated as they appear to be. It looks as if she's after trial by television, which would certainly show the family up in a pretty bad light and, unlike Helena, Anthony doesn't believe in the maxim "no such thing as bad publicity". Some media revelations, he knows, can be very bad indeed. Anthony and Helena have worked their socks off to make Stonegrove a viable, growing business, and he's not sure either of them have got the strength left to fight off an aggressive media attack.

But in any case Helena has already decided it's time they became pro-active.

'I'm going to sit Mother down and talk to her,' she tells Anthony.

'Ha! You make it sound so easy,' he replies. 'What makes you think she'll talk to you? You two haven't got a particularly good track record in the communication department.'

'Yes, I know, but I can at least give it a try and see what sort of reaction I get.'

'I can tell you exactly what sort of reaction you'll get. She'll be furious and start throwing things about, and then she'll clam up.'

'Maybe, but maybe not. She might be glad to get it off her chest after all these years.'

'Oh, so you think there's been something on her chest? You believe there were unpleasant goings-on that night?

Helena sighs. 'I don't know. I think it's possible. Maybe we should assume the worst for the sake of argument, face her with it, and then let her talk her way out of it.'

Anthony leans back in his chair.

'Well that's a bold move,' he says.

'Anyway, I'm going to go across to her later today, but I need to see Lindsay first and get Bella's photo off her.'

'Bravo, Helena. D'you want me to come with you when you do the deed?'

'No, best I do it alone.'

Lindsay is talking to visitors in the Theatre Room when Helena appears in the doorway and then signals that she'll hang around in the corridor till they leave. Typically, they're the sort of visitors that want a natter so it's many minutes later when they move on, by which time Helena has spent the time having a good look at all the pictures hanging in the hallway, some of which she'd completely forgotten about.

There's a black and white photograph of Douglas, posing on the driveway surrounded by half a dozen motorcycles in varying stages of refurbishment. He's sitting astride another machine, gleaming and obviously road-worthy, grinning broadly and holding a cigarette. She's surprised Reg hasn't already swapped the photo with one of the local views hanging in his room. Then as she stands back and looks again she realises that there's a darker edging of wallpaper all around it. This is not the picture that was hanging there originally, perhaps not until quite recently.

Lindsay comes out of her room to find Helena peering behind the picture.

'How long has this been here?' she asks.

Lindsay takes a look at it. 'I don't remember seeing it there before,' she says, 'but then I don't remember looking at any of them all that closely.'

'No, me neither, not for years.'

Hearing their voices, Reg joins them in the corridor.

'I've never seen that before,' he says. 'If I had I'd have wanted to have it in there,' he adds, gesturing behind him to Douglas's room.

'How very odd,' says Helena. 'Maybe it came down with some of that other stuff we found in the loft. I'll ask Anthony what he knows about it.'

But she knows Anthony will be baffled. He doesn't have anything to do with the interior of the house, or the furnishings and fittings. There's a detailed inventory for insurance purposes though, and Beverley in the estate office will know where to find it.

Later, after Helena's got Bella's photo from Lindsay, she goes down into the office and Beverley locates the relevant pages of the inventory for her. The pictures in the corridor are listed in some detail even though none of them has any real value, but there's no mention of a photo of Douglas.

Helena takes the inventory upstairs and counts the pictures hanging on the corridor walls. There are fifteen, and there are fifteen on the inventory. One of them, and eventually she figures out which one, has been removed and replaced with the photo of Douglas and his motorcycles. The missing picture is a watercolour of nearby Maiden Castle by John Cecil Fellowes, an artist Helena has never heard of, although it turns out that there are three more paintings by him in the same corridor. It would be a mammoth task to find out if the Fellowes painting has been re-located somewhere else in the house, but Helena's not even going to try because for some reason she's got a hunch that it hasn't.

It's another mystery, and one she can do without as she's got quite enough on her plate already with Bella.

* * *

It's mid afternoon by the time Helena gets to her mother's cottage, one of four on the far side of the kitchen garden. Diana is sitting in her lounge with an incomplete jigsaw on the table in front of her. The television is on and the volume is deafening, so when Helena lets herself in and calls out to her mother Diana is completely unaware that she's there. It's not until Helena moves into her sight line that she looks up, startled.

'You should have knocked,' she bellows.

'I did,' Helena bellows back, then reaches across and turns the television off. Diana looks astonished.

'Whatever did you do that for?'

'I want to talk to you, and with that blaring out it's impossible.'

Diana carries on sifting through the jigsaw pieces in the box, suddenly pouncing on one and fitting it into a space.

'Aha!', she says, triumphantly. 'I've been looking for you. And you were hiding.'

'Mother,' Helena starts.

'And here's your neighbour!' says Diana with a laugh. But the second piece refuses to fit where she wants it to go and she throws it back into the box with a sigh.

'Mother, what do you know about this girl?'

Helena holds the photo of Bella in front of Diana, who looks at it, and then back at her box of jigsaw pieces.

'Her name is Bella,' says Helena.

'I know her name.'

'What happened to her?'

There's a long silence, broken only by the sound of Diana shifting the pieces around in the box.

'On the night Douglas died, what happened to Bella?'

Diana looks again at the photo, then pulls it from Helena's hand before she can stop her, and rips it in half. She tosses the two pieces on the floor and goes back to her jigsaw, peering first in the box and then at the table.

Helena doesn't make a move to pick up the two halves of the photo.

'You see, someone has been looking into how Douglas died that night. They've found out that Bella was here but it seems nobody actually knows what happened to her afterwards. They're beginning to think you and Aunt Ruby did something to get rid of her. Did you?'

Diana says nothing.

'I need to know, Mother. What happened to Bella?'

'I don't know,' Diana says slowly, 'and I don't care.'

'Is that the truth? You and Ruby didn't have anything to do with her disappearance?'

'It was all her fault, common little bitch.' Diana reaches forward and sweeps the half-completed jigsaw off the table, then throws the box of remaining pieces after it.

Helena is shocked by the venom in her mother's voice, and the expression on her face.

'What was her fault? What did she do?'

Diana sits back and closes her eyes. Anthony was right, she's behaved exactly how he said she would, throwing things about and now refusing to speak.

Helena waits for a while, tries to talk her mother round and then sees it's useless. She retrieves the two pieces of Bella's photo, and puts them in her pocket.

'I'll clear this mess up, and then later on maybe we can try again to get to the bottom of this. Because it's not going to go away, Mother.'

Diana is silent as Helena scoops the jigsaw pieces back into the box, gathering in those that ended up in the fireplace, and on the windowsill and sofa.

'Whatever the story is with Bella, it's going to come out one way or another. And I can't do anything to stop it, so you may as well tell me the truth.'

Helena bends down in front of her mother so she's at eye level with her.

'I mean it,' she says. 'Bella was always going to come back into your life, sooner or later, and now it seems that day has come. If I know the whole story I may be able to deflect people from getting too close to it, but all the time I'm in the dark there's really nothing I can do. Do you understand what I'm saying?'

Diana raises her eyes to Helena's and for a moment it looks as though she might be ready to talk, but then she looks away again.

'Put my television back on before you leave,' she says.

* * *

Anthony stops short of saying "I told you so", but is clearly not surprised by Diana's lack of co-operation in the matter of Bella.

'Well then, we'll have to find out without her help,' is all he says.

Helena pulls the two pieces of Bella's photo out of her pocket.

'Look at this,' she says. 'Lindsay will be terribly upset, I'll have to see if I can get it restored somewhere.'

'You obviously had her rattled,' says Anthony, 'so it seems like she may have something to hide after all.'

He can't shed any light on the new mystery, the sudden appearance of Douglas's photo on the corridor wall. The favourite, and only theory, is that it came down from the loft with other stuff and one of the volunteers put it outside the Douglas Memorial room, thinking that was the right place for it.

'Although I can't imagine which of them would take this upon themselves,' says Helena. 'If it were Reg, then maybe I could understand it although he would have wanted to put it in Douglas's room. But who else would do it without reference to us first? And where's the picture it replaced?'

Anthony shrugs.

'No idea,' he says. 'But as a mere man I can only concentrate on one problem at a time, and while you were busy with your mother I've come up with a plan for how to handle the Caroline lunch. I need to talk to you and Lindsay about it, but I think there's an obvious way forward there.'

LINDSAY

Gary's doing well. He's had a tough time of it but he seems to have turned a corner now and they've got him off all the machines he was wired up to, which is a huge relief to Rufus who found it really upsetting to see him like that. He's got by-pass surgery coming up at some later date but the specialist is completely sure he's strong enough to cope with that.

His mum's gone back to her place now, although she rings every day. I'm sure once he's out of hospital she'll be back, and Rufus will be glad of it because he'll need someone else around to take the pressure off him. It looks as if Gary's going to need quite a long period of recovery.

Deirdre has been marvellous. She calls one of us every few days to see how Gary's doing but curiously she hasn't been into hospital to see him. She says she's got a thing about hospital visiting. I think it's more that it would be very emotional for them both, and she thinks something like that is best handled away from the public arena of a hospital ward. It's been interesting getting to know more about Deirdre, I think we all misjudged her, just on the basis of the person we saw, and thought we knew, in the yoga studio.

I spoke to Nick yesterday about tomorrow's lunch with Caroline. He's completely confident that Anthony has it all under control – which he probably does have, although at first I did think it was a bit of a risky strategy. He'll do most of the talking to start with and Helena and I are just going to take our lead from him. I actually feel a bit sorry for Caroline, she'll be completely wrong-footed by Anthony and I feel mean colluding with him to put her in that position.

In a funny sort of way I've missed Caroline, daft bat that she is.

She's obviously out to catch Douglas. Imagine!
Who does she think she is?
Ruby Stanton's diary, July 9th 1936

STONEGROVE HALL

At the back of the Carriage Room Restaurant is an open-tread wooden staircase leading to what may have been a hay loft. Tucked up there under the huge beamed ceiling are a couple of long tables, usually reserved for large parties or for the Croft's business lunches, and it's to here that Anthony guides Caroline when he meets her at the restaurant entrance.

'It's a bit more private up here than down in the main room,' he says as he pulls out a chair for her. She's surprised to see that there are four places laid for lunch, one more than she was expecting, and a wary little voice in her head wonders if a legal eagle will be joining them. There's a bottle of red wine already opened in the centre of the table, and a vase of flowers, and the whole set-up looks very cosy and informal and not terribly business-like, which does not suit Caroline's purposes at all. She makes a mental note to go easy on the wine.

From her vantage point she can see through the wooden balustrade to where visitors are arriving downstairs. And then she spots two familiar people, chatting companionably as they come in through the door. It's Helena and Lindsay.

Oh bugger, she thinks.

* * *

Anthony gets straight to the point before their main courses arrive, first making sure that Caroline has a large glass of wine in front of her. He notices she only has a couple of sips though, which is somehow not what he's been expecting.

'Lindsay tells us you've found another relative who worked here?'

'I have. Her name is Betty and my great-aunt Elsie was her cousin. Their mothers were sisters, so they had different surnames and I suppose that's why the researchers didn't spot her. She told me a bit about what happened to Bella.'

'Yes... it's all terribly fascinating. So what did actually happen to Bella in the end?'

'Erm, I don't know exactly, not yet, but...'

Anthony nods vigorously. 'But you'd like to find out – and so would we. And once you've got the whole story, what then?'

'Well, there has to be a TV programme in this, maybe a docu-drama, maybe an investigative piece but it'll be something more exciting than *'Touching my Roots'*, that's for sure.'

Helena pipes up.

'If there's anything we can do to help...'

Caroline looks at her sharply. She hasn't been expecting this, and wonders if Helena is serious or just playing her along.

'Stonegrove is at your disposal,' says Anthony, leaning back in his chair. 'All we ask is that you keep us in the picture.'

'I... that's very good of you, I must say I didn't think...' Caroline is temporarily knocked off balance, and takes a large swig of her wine.

'You see Caroline,' says Anthony, 'it seems to me we're all looking for the same outcome here, which

144

is Bella's story and in particular the way it related to Stonegrove. It's just that our reasons for wanting it are different. Lindsay found her in the first place and simply wants to know where she ended up. Anything that went on in Stonegrove is of huge interest to Helena and myself both personally and from a business perspective. And you want to make a career-enhancing TV programme about Bella's fate. Am I right?'

Caroline nods slowly, wondering what Anthony is leading up to.

'I do want to find the truth, but it's not all about Bella,' she says. 'There are other players in this story.'

'Of course, we realise that,' says Helena.

'I'd like to talk to your mother, for a start,' says Caroline.

'Yes... that might be tricky,' says Anthony, fingering the cutlery in front of him.

'Oh? Why?'

'Well you saw her that day when you arrived to start filming. The problem with Diana is that she's... well frankly, she's barking.'

'I'm afraid you won't get very far with her,' says Helena, 'but you're welcome to try. Somebody should probably be with you though, she has a tendency to throw things about when she's put under pressure.'

Anthony leans forward.

'Look here Caroline, I think we can all get what we want from this situation if we work on it together, sharing our resources and our discoveries. You won't get very far without our cooperation, and we can't tap into the connections you have with your family and the TV research department unless we've got you on board. Basically, we need to become a team.'

Caroline stares at him for a moment, just to make sure he isn't having her on. She looks across at Helena who smiles encouragingly and then at Lindsay, who's been silent so far but now speaks up.

'Actually we worked together pretty well for a time,' she says, 'didn't we?'

Caroline picks up her wine glass, has another mouthful and considers her options. She's come here looking for a fight, ready to meet opposition head-on then go in with all guns blazing, and they've just taken the guns off her and emptied out all the ammunition.

'And what if we find something happened here that your family would rather leave undiscovered? You can't expect me to go all that way, find the answer and then just bury it... sorry, bad choice of wording,' she says.

'We're talking about an incident that happened around eighty years ago, but if something needs to be told and there's a case to answer then of course that should happen,' says Anthony. 'However we do have to bear in mind that Diana is still alive and at the moment we don't know how any revelations that come up might impact on her remaining years. So naturally we'll need to handle things sensitively, but I can assure you that we'll see this through.'

Anthony looks up as one of the waitresses appears at the top of the staircase. 'Ah good, lunch has arrived,' he says.

There's a lull whilst dishes of food are organised on the table, and then the waitress, after checking that they've got everything they need, leaves them again.

'You talked about "your cooperation", but since you don't seem to have any more information than I have I'm not completely clear about what it is you'll be bringing to the party,' says Caroline.

'We'll be bringing Stonegrove,' says Anthony. 'You'd almost certainly want to film here at some point, and your programme will lose its integrity if you're not allowed in and therefore can't get any footage of the location at the centre of the story. You *may*, and we don't know this although we might want to surmise it, you *may* want to poke around the grounds a bit. Dig things up, you know.'

Caroline blinks. Anthony's getting into a whole scenario here that she didn't think the Crofts would even contemplate.

'Well, I... I suppose that's a possibility...'

'And there are boxes and boxes of paperwork and other stuff up in the attics,' says Lindsay. 'None of us know what's there, but it must surely be worth a look. After all, that's where Bella came from in the first place, if that trunk of Douglas's things hadn't come down for Reg to sort through we'd never even have known of Bella's existence.'

'And we wouldn't be having this conversation now,' adds Helena.

There's a brief pause while vegetables and salad are passed around and social niceties temporarily override the Bella discussion. Helena glances first at Lindsay, then at Anthony. He is totally at ease, slipping into the familiar role of affable host. Lindsay catches Caroline's eye as she passes her the bread basket, and smiles. To her relief, and not a little surprise, Caroline smiles back. It's a small, rather tentative smile, but it's a start.

'OK,' she says. 'What happens next? How do we go about this?'

* * *

After lunch Anthony and Helena go back to work, leaving Lindsay and Caroline alone together to finish off the last of the wine.

As soon as they've gone Lindsay turns to Caroline and opens up a conversation before an awkward silence has a chance to develop.

'I was sorry things between us ended up the way they did. How have you been?'

Caroline sighs. 'Oh, you know, the usual disasters. I've had bits of work coming in but nothing much, just enough to keep me ticking over. I really need this story.'

'Yes, I realise that. They mean it you know, the Crofts – they really will work with you on this.'

'I wasn't expecting that. I thought they'd be completely up themselves and doing everything they could to prevent me from dragging the family name into disrepute. I even wondered if they'd try to buy me off.'

'Well at the moment we don't know there's anything here that will bring the family name crashing down. That's the trouble, it's all speculation.'

Caroline shrugs. 'No, we don't know – yet – but there's obviously something the mad old mother wants to keep quiet. Incidentally,' she adds, 'I was sorry too, and I know it was my fault so don't bother trying to tell me I'm wrong.'

'I wasn't going to.'

'Oh, good. Anyway, what shall we do now? Grab a couple of shovels and start digging up the grounds?'

Lindsay smiles, drains her glass and stands up.

'Did you actually see much of the house when you were here filming?'

'I saw everywhere the servants lived and worked, but only bits of the rest when I had a little wander round on my own. I went into Douglas's room and the main reception rooms – not the infamous conservatory though.'

'We could take a walk over there now if you like. But some time we really ought to sit down and trawl through those boxes of rubbish, just to satisfy ourselves that the answer isn't right under our noses.'

They leave the restaurant and follow a path round the gardens that will take them to the conservatory. It's devoid of visitors, and as they walk in through the garden entrance the volunteer whose duty it is to steward both this room and the one it leads from, hears them and steps in from the house. Lindsay has a little chat with her and Caroline stands to one side, looking around, until it's just the two of them again.

'What was it Betty said about the row in here the night Douglas died?' she asks.

'There were raised voices, one of the panes of glass got smashed and she had to clear up broken glass the next day. And someone had cut themselves.'

Caroline nods. 'Exactly. There was broken glass on one of the chairs and a table, and there was blood on the floor.' She turns around to face the garden. 'So that means the window must have been smashed...'

'...from the outside... of course! So they weren't all in here at the same time.'

'Or there was someone else involved we don't yet know about.'

They look at each other for a moment, picturing this new piece of the jigsaw, and then Lindsay speaks again.

'Er... has that helped us?'

Caroline considers for a moment.

'I'm buggered if I know.'

'I don't know why they're so unpleasant to Bella.'
**Douglas Stanton, to his friend Dickie Savage,
July 1936**

YOGA

In Cappuccino Blues Sergiu is setting out his stall, ready for the end of the yoga class. Since Gary's heart attack a camaraderie has sprung up between Janey's group, and now the whole lot go downstairs for coffee following their class. After the many times Rufus and Gary tried to encourage a bit of esprit de corps, and failed, it's ironic that it's taken a near-death experience to bring them together. This is of course good news for Sergiu, whose takings have gone up on Fridays, plus there's a knock-on effect. Some of the yoga people, having discovered Cappuccino Blues for the first time, now come in on other days and bring their friends, who pass the word on to their friends. If this keeps up Sergiu will have to get someone in to help him.

The numbers for the yoga class vary and today it's quite a small group, only five students plus Janey, and everyone is staying focused and working with their bodies. In Rufus's case this means lying down snoozing for most of the second half of the class, which nobody minds because they understand what he's been going through. If Rufus has been listening to his body, as Janey so often reminds them they should, he probably heard it telling him it's had enough stretching for one day and just needs a nap now. Janey lowers her voice even more so as not to disturb him and at the end of

150

the practice, as they come up into sitting, Lindsay gives him a very gentle nudge so that he can sit up just in time to murmur 'namaste'.

As they gather up their stuff and head for the door Rufus yawns loudly.

'I hope Sergiu's got a strong brew going,' he says to Lindsay. 'I didn't get much sleep last night.'

'I'm sure after tomorrow you'll just crash out. Sooner or later your body has to give in,' she replies.

Sergiu has the customary scones and Danish pastries ready, and these days he knows pretty much what coffee everyone will want. Deirdre takes charge of passing cups and plates across to the table they've all huddled around, the biggest one at the back of the cafe. It's busy in Cappuccino Blues, there are people occupying most of the other tables, and Lindsay's rather touched to see that Sergiu has put a reserved notice out for them. He's got some music playing, and it takes a while for her to realise it's the sort of thing he and Deirdre were dancing to up at the Hall.

'Is this the same band?' she asks Deirdre.

She nods. 'It's an old recording but probably some of the same guys you saw. We use it to practice to.'

Lindsay would like to have a look at the CD case to see if Nick's on the cover photo, but she knows that's ridiculous and in any case she can't think of a good enough reason to ask to see it.

Since reporting back on the lunch with Caroline, a week or so ago, she hasn't heard from Nick and she doesn't want to be the one to phone him again. He seems to work mostly in and around London, and the local band is just one of many that he plays with on a casual basis, so his trips to the area are by no means regular. Anthony rarely mentions Nick, and has stopped teasing her about him now – Lindsay suspects this is down to Helena – but they did let slip that Nick will be coming down to Stonegrove tomorrow morning. It's not one of her volunteering days, so she has no real reason to be there, but she's wondering if she could legitimately turn up on the pretext of sorting through some boxes of paperwork.

There are problems with this plan though. Firstly, Caroline is working away at the moment and they'd agreed to do it together so Lindsay doesn't feel entirely comfortable about getting started without her. Secondly, she has offered to do a big supermarket shop for Rufus, but in view of the fact that Gary will be in surgery tomorrow she's guessing that it won't matter much when she does this, since Rufus will be at the hospital all day anyway. Thirdly, and most importantly, she doesn't want to look desperate. She certainly isn't desperate.

'The band have booked us for some more dates, private parties and functions, that sort of thing,' says Deirdre, cutting in on Lindsay's thoughts.

In spite of all the speculation about Deirdre and Sergiu, it's become apparent that they really are just dance partners. Lindsay hasn't come right out and asked her, but now that she knows her better it's obvious that Deirdre is totally committed to her husband and children. Meanwhile, Sergiu has a string of adoring females in tow. One of them pops into the cafe now, sashaying up to the counter and flirting outrageously with him. She doesn't buy a coffee, just hangs around for a while, and blows him a kiss when she finally decides to leave.

'Fellow student?' asks Rufus, referring to the language class Sergiu attends.

Sergiu laughs. 'What could she learn?' he asks. 'Very smart girl.'

'Yes, I bet she is,' says Lindsay, handing Rufus' cup across for a refill.

'Maybe I give her some work here. Smart girls are not easy to find, good to keep holding on to.'

As he passes the coffee back, Sergiu lowers his voice.

'And how is Gary, my friend?' he asks Rufus.

'He's having his operation tomorrow. They keep telling me it's nothing to worry about but I'll be glad when it's over because after that it's just a case of resting up and getting his strength back.'

'We're all looking forward to seeing him again,' says Janey. 'He can sit in the studio and do a few chair exercises when he's ready.'

'Or sit down here with me,' adds Sergiu. 'I serve him black decaf coffee and special cake with low fat and low sugar. Maybe low flavour too.'

They all laugh. But Rufus looks at Lindsay and says quietly, 'Let's just get tomorrow out of the way first.'

She nods, and squeezes his hand. She's also thinking about tomorrow, mainly with Gary in mind but also, completely selfishly, Nick.

'She's an awfully good dancer, which is yet another reason for Ruby to dislike her.'

John Cecil Fellowes, to Douglas Stanton, August 1936

STONEGROVE HALL

It doesn't take long for Lindsay to navigate her way around the reasons not to go to Stonegrove on Saturday morning. A phone call to Caroline ('OK, but promise to let me know the minute you find anything useful...') and then another to Rufus to postpone the supermarket trip, and the first two are sorted out. Which just leaves it looking as if she's rushed over there the minute she hears that Nick is on his way.

I won't even mention his name, she thinks. I'll just go straight to the office when I get there, have a word with Helena and then settle down with a few boxes of paperwork. It's a big place. We probably won't even meet.

Lindsay is very persuasive with herself and quite soon she's convinced.

It's almost ten o'clock when she arrives at Stonegrove, too early for the first visitors to start arriving although the staff car park is already filling up. On her way up to the house Lindsay speaks to a number of other volunteers as they arrive for their shift, and marvels, with a little ping of pleasure, how quickly she has been absorbed into the life of the estate.

It's early June and the day promises to be a beautiful one. There will almost certainly be a number of groups from local gardening clubs visiting today, and the borders they will admire are studded with clumps of bright flowers and gently nodding shrubs. Snaking its way up the front elevation of the house is a wisteria, just going over now but with enough power left to transform the grey steps and gravel with a covering of tiny mauve petals, like wedding confetti. It's the bane of Marion's life, as visitors unwittingly tramp the flowers into the hallway and she struggles valiantly to sweep them back out again. But the wisteria problem is short-lived, and even she has to admit that when it's in flower it does lend a softness to the front of the building. Today is not one of Marion's volunteering days though, so wisteria petals will be collecting unchallenged in little mauve flurries around the front desks.

Beverley is alone in the office when Lindsay gets there.

'I haven't seen Helena yet but I'll give her a call,' she says, punching Helena's mobile number into her phone, 'You've just missed Anthony. He's gone into town with his brother.'

Ah. Thereby ensuring that neither of us looks desperate, thinks Lindsay. Excellent.

'She's already on her way over,' says Beverley.

And curiously, when she arrives in the office Helena doesn't seem all that surprised to see Lindsay there.

'I thought I'd make a start on some of those boxes.'

'What about Caroline?'

'I've squared it with her. She made me promise to call her if I find any leads.'

'There's a random selection in Ruby's old room, we put them in there because it's marginally more comfortable than up in the attics. I'll join you for a bit, I've got an hour to spare.'

The bedroom Ruby used is on the same corridor as Douglas's room and the Theatre Room, but further down beyond the rope and the 'no admittance' sign. Lindsay has never been along here, and it feels quite different, colder somehow, and that's not just the temperature.

Helena unlocks the door and pushes it open. Ruby's bedroom was clearly long since abandoned, leaving plenty of scope for dust and cobwebs to collect in the corners. Most of the furniture has been removed, although there's still a gigantic triple-door wardrobe with a silvery-patched mirror on the front, a spindly-legged side table and a couple of chairs the same as the ones in the Theatre Room.

And a stack of cardboard archive boxes.

Helena pushes the half-drawn curtains back further, releasing small puffs of dust in the process, and opens the windows. Ruby must have pulled rank on Douglas because her room faces the opposite way to his, overlooking the front drive, and the sun is streaming in.

'I suppose when we have the money we could open this room up, though there's nothing particularly interesting about it. Nice views though,' says Helena, leaning on the window ledge to look down. Clumps of wisteria hang just outside the open window, and a light breeze whisks a couple of flowers inside to land on the wooden floor.

'You're getting dust all over your sleeves,' says Lindsay, and Helena tuts and brushes her shirt sleeves as she turns back to the room.

'I expect we'll both be covered in dust after delving into this lot,' she says, looking down at the boxes. 'How shall we do it, one box at a time or one each?'

'Let's start on them one at a time, I think I'd rather do it together till I get into the swing.'

Lindsay lifts the first one onto the table and takes the lid off. It's full of papers; receipts, bills, an old book of maps, parish magazines – but everything is dated 1954 or 55, too recent for their purposes. So they close it up and put the box to one side. After half an hour they've moved about a dozen boxes to the same side, for the same reason. But then they creep closer to their target, when they open a box of miscellaneous papers from 1935.

They each take out random pieces. Lindsay finds a quote for replacing curtains in the dining room, and then a report torn from a newspaper about an art exhibition in London.

'Isn't this the chap who painted all those watercolours out in the corridor?'

She hands it to Helena.

'John Cecil Fellowes – yes, that's him. Maybe they bought the paintings at this exhibition. Or maybe they already knew him.' She skims the article and then places it on the pile next to the box.

'This is going to take forever,' says Lindsay, eyeing up the mound of boxes, which doesn't seem to have diminished much. 'The trouble is, it's all interesting stuff – I can't bring myself to just whizz through everything without a second glance.'

Halfway down the box they're currently working on they unearth some visitors' books and Helena starts to flick through them. On each page is the date, the menu for that evening and the signatures of the invited guests.

'You're right, it's still fascinating even when it's not what we want... here look at this!'

She passes one of the books across to Lindsay and points to a name halfway down the second page.

'Wallis Simpson,' she reads aloud. 'Obviously without the prince that night, or else he declined to sign.'

'Goodness, your family certainly moved amongst the rich and famous. I wonder how Wallis Simpson came to be down here in a Dorset backwater?'

'Probably because both she and my grandmother were from Baltimore,' says Helena, 'and the American society hostesses over in England all moved in the same circles – there was the Cunard woman, a garden designer whose name escapes me – Maud something I think – Lady Sackville, and quite a few others. I read something about them once, or maybe it was on television, probably to do with the abdication crisis. I expect Wallis was glad to escape to the country every so often and get away from the gossip in London.'

They pull their chairs closer to the table and pore over the visitors' book.

'Caroline's Betty said there were often famous people here.'

'And she wasn't wrong. Look – Evelyn Waugh... Emerald Cunard... Noel Coward...'

'Emerald? Really?'

'She liked wearing them, apparently they were her signature gem.'

'Wow. Imagine having a signature gem.'

Each turn of the page produces at least one name they both know. Wallis Simpson appears four times in 1935, but never with the Prince of Wales. And as they get towards the end of that particular year another name starts to appear, intermittently at first and then more and more often.

'They must definitely have liked John Cecil Fellowes.'

'Maybe he was doing them a special deal on the pictures.'

'Maybe he was American, too.'

'Possibly, I've no idea. We should look him up.'

They reach the end of the year, and start on the next visitors' book but they're not in chronological order and this one is dated 1933. And then at the bottom of the box they unearth the book for 1936.

Wallis Simpson appears twice, in March and again in July. John Cecil Fellowes continues to be a frequent visitor. But not at any time do they see Bella's name.

'But Betty said she was often here, I can't understand it.'

'Obviously not included in formal dinners, though. I don't know what the protocol was – would a girlfriend be invited to dine with other guests? Would the younger members of the family be present, come to that?'

They turn the pages until the entries come to an abrupt end in September. The last recorded dinner was quite a small affair – Fellowes was there, and two other couples, whose names are not known to either Helena or Lindsay. If the three Stanton children had been present that would still only make a party of ten.

'That was about the time that Douglas died,' says Helena. 'My grandparents moved out of the Hall and into the Lodge soon after, so that was the end of the grand entertaining they'd been used to.'

'Betty said something about that. But Ruby and your mother didn't go with them?'

'No, they stayed here. Can you imagine it? Two young girls living alone in this huge place. Well, alone apart from the servants, that is... And then after a while Ruby moved up to her parents' old flat on the second floor which left Mother down here on her own.'

'Where is the Lodge?'

'Long since gone. It was in a dreadful state of disrepair and Ruby had it pulled down years ago. It was roughly where the Welcome Centre is now.'

Lindsay looks back at the visitors' book.

'What was the date Douglas died?'

'I'd have to check with Reg but I think it was the nineteenth – oh I see, that could actually be the same night!'

'And Bella isn't on the guest list although we know she was here.'

'I wonder if Caroline's contacts in research can help us with this? There must be an expert who would know about the protocol of the day. It does seem strange that she was such a frequent visitor, according to Betty, yet never formally entertained.'

'I'll ask Caroline when I see her next weekend. What happened to Ruby and your mother in the war – where did they go?'

'Well as you know the Hall became a convalescent hospital, but the MoD couldn't get Ruby out, she simply refused to leave. So she just stayed put up in the flat and the military took over the rest of the Hall. The housekeeper and gardener were still in their estate cottage so she had some help.'

'George's parents...'

'Yes, that's right – he lives in the same cottage now. There were medical staff billeted in other estate cottages or with families in the town.'

'What about your grandparents?'

'They took themselves off to her home town of Baltimore and only came back for an occasional visit, till they got too old to even do that. Odd way of behaving isn't it, leaving your children behind? Mother went to stay with an aunt in Wales, where she met my father when he was home on leave.'

They keep the 1936 visitors' book to one side, and put everything else back in the box. Lindsay is just lifting another box onto the table when the door opens.

'Ah, here you are!' says Anthony, framed in the doorway. Helena frowns and glances at her watch.

'Good heavens, is that the time? I had no idea we'd been up here for so long. I'd better go Lindsay, but you can stay as long as you like, if you don't mind being on your own.'

'She won't be on her own, I'll stay and keep her company.'

This is when Lindsay realises that Nick is standing behind Anthony.

'Have you found anything interesting?' Anthony asks as Helena gathers up her bag and phone.

'Well, it's more a question of what we haven't found that's interesting,' she says as she ushers him out into the corridor. 'I'll tell you all about it on the way down... oh Lindsay, can you lock up when you leave and take the key back to the office?'

And then they're gone.

'So what is it that you haven't found?' asks Nick, and Lindsay explains about Bella's non-appearance on any guest lists.

'OK, well let's try and think about this without the benefit of twenty-first century political correctness,' he says. 'Back in the 1930s the class system in England was alive and well. If I'm right, and Bella was a girl educated in the state system, people like the Stantons wouldn't want her round the dining table displaying her ignorance and working class accent to their other guests. She might not even have washed her hands first.'

Nick crosses to the window and sits on the ledge.

'You'll have dust all over the seat of your jeans,' says Lindsay. 'Where could Douglas possibly have met such a lowly creature?'

Nick shrugs, and brushes the dust from his bottom. 'Where was he at university? Oxbridge I daresay – he might have run into her on his bicycle as she was crossing the road. Or maybe she was a barmaid in his favourite pub...'

'She looks a bit classier than that in the photo.'

'I'm probably being unfair to her, maybe she wasn't that low in the great scheme of things. She might have been a respectable girl from an aspiring family – maybe her father was a bank manager or something. Still not in the Stanton's league though.'

'But if you're right, what on earth could have possessed Douglas to think he could bring her down to Stonegrove to meet his parents? And presumably introduce her into the family as his girlfriend?'

'We don't know he did. We don't know they were a couple. Maybe they were just good friends and that was all.'

Lindsay gives him a sceptical frown.

'It does happen you know,' says Nick. 'Men and women can be friends without being in a relationship.'

'Yeah, yeah, I know. I saw "When Harry Met Sally" too.'

He laughs. 'And they ended up together.'

'Exactly.'

There's a pause.

'More boxes?' Nick asks. 'Or a coffee?'

'More boxes, and *then* a coffee,' says Lindsay.

The day is turning out quite nicely.

*'He won't listen to me or his father, but it seems
young people these days just won't be told. One can
only hope he sees sense soon.'*

Cecelia Stanton, to Emerald Cunard, August 1936

CHRISTCHURCH

It's the following Sunday morning and when Caroline opens her front door Lindsay holds a supermarket carrier out towards her.

'I brought lunch knowing what your supplies are like.'

Caroline takes the bag and looks inside.

'Great,' she says, 'real food. How on earth do you do it, I never seem to be able to find anything like this.'

'I think you're looking in the wrong aisles.'

In the kitchen they unpack pasta, vegetables and salad, bread and a bottle of Merlot, which Caroline immediately opens then reaches up to a top cupboard for glasses.

'I've got pudding,' says Caroline, and Lindsay looks up at her in surprise.

'Crunchies,' she says, 'or Snickers. Take your pick.'

Lindsay pulls a container from the bottom of the bag and holds it out.

'Or fresh fruit salad.'

'You'll be the death of me with all these bizarre health-food fads. Oh, is that pineapple in there? Lovely, my favourite.'

While Lindsay cooks, and Caroline drinks wine, they talk about the few days she's just been away gigging in Manchester.

'My mate Steve lives up there so I was able to stay with him. You'd love him, he's even more of a disaster than me, a much bigger challenge. You'd have to get used to him borrowing your clothes though.'

Lindsay is having trouble imagining what Caroline's working life is like. Lots of driving and eating in motorway services, she supposes.

'Do you ever get any local gigs?'

'Sometimes, most of the big towns are on the comedy circuit – there's plenty on offer in Southampton and Brighton. But it's really in London that you find the best comedy clubs and that's where the real money is.' Caroline dips the tip of her little finger in the tomato pasta sauce and licks it. 'Mmm, nice. Occasionally one of the bigger provincial theatres will put on a series of comedy gigs, I've done that in Bournemouth once or twice. You could come with me some time if you wanted.'

'That might be fun,' says Lindsay, wondering what she's letting herself in for.

'We can pretend you're my manager so you get in free.'

'Haven't you got a real manager?'

'No, they just take fifteen percent for doing stuff I can do myself. I've got an agent though,' she adds, topping-up her glass and moving across to Lindsay's, which doesn't need any topping-up as it's still full. 'She's pretty useless, half the time she doesn't earn her percentage either – most of my bookings are repeats.'

'Presumably she got you *Touching My Roots* though.'

'Yeah, and look what a disaster that turned out to be. I wanted *Strictly*.'

Lindsay looks at her in mild surprise.

'You? Sequins and high heels?'

'Why not? When you look at some of the people they get on there...'

'Anyway, *'Touching My Roots'* might serve you well in the end,' says Lindsay. 'This pasta is almost ready,' she adds, and Caroline plonks a handful of cutlery, the wrapped ciabatta loaf and an unopened bag of salad down in the middle of the kitchen table.

'It's fun cooking with you,' she says. 'I've learned so much.'

'You haven't even been watching,' says Lindsay, arranging the table and setting everything out. When Lindsay puts the dishes of pasta down Caroline's enthusiasm knows no bounds.

'Wow!' she says. 'This looks great, you're wonderful!'

'It's not difficult to cook pasta, you just have to follow the instructions on the packet. I bet you've never even tried.'

'I've thought about it once or twice.'

'I think you'll find you need to do a bit more than that. Bon appetit.'

They chink glasses. Although neither makes a thing of it, they're both glad that their relationship is back on an even footing. Caroline is so hopeless she makes Lindsay come over all motherly, a new experience for her, and Lindsay brings some much-needed structure to Caroline's chaotic lifestyle. Although she wouldn't admit to it, Caroline's fed-up with floating through life like a hapless teenager and yearns to be taken seriously as a grown-up at long last. Lindsay gives her that possibility. And so does the unfolding Bella story, if she can just grab hold of it and harness it into something worthwhile.

'So, did anything come to light when you were going through the boxes?'

'Not exactly. There are stacks more boxes though, we've only just started on them. We did find a visitors' book for 1936, but Bella wasn't mentioned at all. We know from Betty that she was a frequent visitor so it seemed odd that her name didn't appear. There were loads of well-known people though...' Lindsay reels off a list, and is faintly surprised that Caroline knows who these people were.

'Wallis Simpson! That must have been quite a coup getting her on their guest list.'

'Helena said all the American society hostesses in London stuck together and her grandmother Cecilia and Wallis came from the same town. I don't think there was any shortage of money in the Stanton family back then.'

Lindsay breaks off a piece of ciabatta bread and dips it in her pasta sauce.

'Do you still have access to the researchers on 'Touching My Roots'?'

'Probably, what do you need?'

'An insight into the etiquette of the day,' she says. 'Would it have been the done thing to include the young Stantons and their friends in formal dinners at the Hall, or did they have to reach a certain age before they were considered to be suitable for inclusion?'

Caroline nods. 'I can certainly ask. In theory my episode of 'Touching My Roots' is still on the drawing board, so there shouldn't be any problem with them helping. Why is it important to know this?'

'Because there has to be a reason why Bella was never formally entertained at Stonegrove.'

'Maybe they didn't like her,' says Caroline, with a shrug.

'Then why was she there so often?'

'Douglas must have liked her, maybe the parents just tolerated her for his sake.'

'The last recorded dinner party was in 1936 on the night Douglas died.'

Caroline's eyes widen. 'Really? Who was there?'

'Well not Bella, nor any of the Stanton children according to the guest list. There were four guests we hadn't come across before, seemingly two married couples, and an artist who seemed to be entertained at Stonegrove fairly often. He must have been a family friend, some of his paintings are hanging in the Hall and it's not exactly ground-breaking stuff so artistic merit probably wasn't their reason for buying them.'

'Relative?'

'Maybe, not a name that Helena knew though. John Cecil Fellowes – ever heard of him?'

Caroline shakes her head, and then reaches into her pocket and gets her almost brand new smart phone out.

'Did you get your lost phone numbers back?' Lindsay asks, remembering how Caroline's old phone was driven over by a lorry on the day they first met.

'Not all of them, I expect some have gone for good. Now what did you say his name was?'

Caroline taps it into Google and then scrolls down a bit.

'Here we are. Watercolour painter... blah, blah, blah... oh he wasn't very old then, I imagined him as an old fart... blah, blah... bloody hell!'

Caroline looks up at Lindsay, her mouth open.

'What? What about him?'

'He died in 1936,' says Caroline, 'in September 1936, so not long after Douglas.'

They sit and gape at each other.

'What have we just found?' asks Lindsay. 'A murderer?'

'Or maybe a victim?'

'A closet lover of Douglas's?'

Caroline shakes her head slowly. 'I don't know. But definitely something significant.'

'Does it say how he died?'

She scrolls down the page. 'Nope. Nothing here. You don't think he could have been on the back of that motorcycle and died later of his injuries?'

'The story has always been that Douglas was alone, but I suppose it's possible.'

'He was a member of the Royal Academy, they might have some more information. I could fish around there a bit.'

They read everything they can find on the Internet about Fellowes, which isn't a lot. The last link they click on is a short piece which featured in a society magazine of the day and was reprinted in an anniversary issue of the same publication a couple of years ago. And it's here that they find a nugget that might just get them a bit further.

March, 1936. Mr Charles and Mrs Cecilia Stanton, of Stonegrove Hall, Wareham, Dorset are pleased to announce the engagement of their eldest daughter Ruby Margaret, to Mr John Cecil Fellowes of Dulwich, South London, younger son of Lady Rose and the late Sir Basil Fellowes. The couple plan to marry next spring.

They sound like horrible people. Why do you go there if you don't like them?

Letter to Bella, from her sister Ada, September 1936

WAREHAM

It's almost the end of June, and Gary is coming home. The last seven weeks have been challenging for him and for Rufus, and he still needs a lot of rest and care, but at the hospital they're very pleased with his progress and if he follows their advice and behaves himself he should be fine.

Gary's return has been widely anticipated. Lindsay was at the house the day before to do a thorough clean, Iris has arranged to come and stay for the first few days – or until they feel confident enough to let her go – and in Cappuccino Blues Sergiu has been true to his word. He's put in a special order with the cake company he deals with for a low fat low sugar cake, and he plans to deliver it himself. Deirdre has promised to pop in as soon as Gary's feeling up to seeing her, and the regulars from the yoga class have organised a get well card and flowers. Rufus is expecting a succession of other friends to stop by in the first few days Gary is home.

'I'm a bit nervous, to be honest,' he told Lindsay, when they were drinking tea after she'd finished her cleaning stint.

'What about?'

'Well, everything I suppose. Suddenly there won't be that safety net of medical staff standing by and I'll be Gary's first line of support. I need to start cooking the right things, not the full-fat stuff we've been used to eating, he's been given loads of advice about diet.' He indicated the chocolate digestives on the coffee table. 'These will have to go – you'd better take the rest home with you. And I'll have to be patient but also firm, because at first he won't be allowed or able to do much but I just know he'll be pushing himself too hard all the time. And the trail of visitors will be relentless.'

'I can see that it's daunting,' said Lindsay, 'but you'll be fine, Iris will be here for a while and there are any number of people you know who'll be just a phone call away.'

'Yes but I don't want to bother people.'

'Well I for one will be cross if you need help and don't call me.'

And now it's the day, and Gary and Rufus are sitting side-by-side on his hospital bed waiting for the pharmacy to send up his medications, before he gets signed off and they can go home.

It seems to take forever, but eventually the ward sister comes round with several packets of tablets and some final instructions, then they're saying goodbye to the nursing staff and other patients and Gary's getting a bit emotional about it all and the nurses are saying jokily that they don't want to see him again – and then suddenly they're outside in the car park.

Gary blinks in the bright sunlight, and pulls his jacket closer around him. He's lost a lot of weight, and although it's a lovely warm day he feels chilly out in the fresh air, and as if that wasn't enough his shoes don't feel like the ones he went in with, or maybe it's his feet that don't seem to belong to him, and walking feels really odd. Rufus is nervous about all of this and lots of other things, but at that particular moment he's just very glad to be leaving the hospital with Gary beside him. What he doesn't fully realise is how nervous Gary is too. He's scared of having another heart attack, of going back to hospital, of living with restrictions, and whether his life with Rufus will ever be quite the same again. They don't talk about any of these things at the moment, because it's too soon and they aren't ready yet to put them into words. Instead they take refuge in a light-hearted banter to cover up their anxieties.

Rufus has parked as close to the hospital entrance as he was able to and it's only a few minutes before they're leaving the exit barrier and pulling out onto the road.

'Shall we stop and pick up some chips on the way home?' says Gary, and Rufus nearly swerves into a parked car before he adds, 'only joking!' and they both laugh, which seems to release some of the tension.

As they drive home Gary looks out at everything wide-eyed, like a new-born baby seeing things for the first time. It's as if he's been expecting their world to have changed in the time he was in hospital, but disappointingly it's all just the same except for some odd bits of roadworks that weren't there before. It seems the only thing that's different is him. By the time Rufus pulls up on their driveway Gary is feeling nervous all over again about his ability to cope post-heart attack but he knows he daren't let on or Rufus will get even more twitchy than he already is.

When they get in the house Gary makes his way straight into the lounge and sits down because he's already feeling exhausted, and that worries him even though he knows it's mostly an emotional response and to be expected. They've explained all this to him; his body is doing just fine, but his head needs a bit longer to catch up.

Rufus bustles about, making tea, telling Gary who's phoned, what's coming up in the garden, asking if he's warm enough, comfy enough, hungry, tired, thirsty... In the end it's a relief to them both when the doorbell rings and Iris arrives courtesy of her taxi-driving neighbour.

She's brought an overnight bag, a sturdy plastic carrier, and a cool bag full of provisions. Rufus has already stocked up with food but he knows Iris can't bear the thought of arriving empty handed, so he accepts her contributions gracefully and takes the bag into the kitchen to unpack.

While he's out of the room she pulls a jigsaw, puzzle books, a couple of DVDs, a paperback novel and an old biscuit tin from the carrier bag.

'This should keep you going for a bit,' she says, in her usual brisk manner.

Gary laughs but not unkindly, he's used to his mum and her gently interfering ways, and he can see that she's put a lot of thought into what to bring him. The DVDs are not the sort of thing she'd watch, nor is the book something he can imagine her reading, but she's chosen them carefully for him. He recognises that biscuit tin. It's been at home as long as he can remember, and he knows it's stuffed full of old photos.

'What are you hoping I'll do with this?' he says, indicating the tin.

'I thought you could help me to sort the photos out,' says Iris. 'There must be hundreds in there I can just throw away – some of your father's old army friends or people I've long since lost touch with. There's not much point in me keeping them, and those that we do want to hang on to should probably be put into albums.'

Gary's thinking that it couldn't possibly be worth all that effort, but he knows she means well, and it's just a scheme she's thought up to keep him from getting bored over the next few weeks.

'I've been meaning to turn this lot out for years,' adds Iris, 'and this seems like a good opportunity.'

Rufus comes in behind Iris as she's saying this, and he smiles at Gary over her shoulder and rolls his eyes.

'Not today, of course,' says Iris, oblivious of Rufus standing behind her. 'But there's a bit of rain forecast for later in the week and you'll have watched those films by then I expect.'

Gary wonders if his mum will produce a spreadsheet in a moment with his days all mapped out, colour-coded and timetabled in hourly blocks, but she puts everything to one side for now and seems content just to chat. The rest of the day passes quietly. Flowers arrive from the yoga class, they eat together and watch the television news, and then Gary goes off to bed early.

'He's lost so much weight,' Iris says softly to Rufus, once he's gone upstairs. She takes a tissue out from the sleeve of her cardigan and dabs at her eyes.

'He'll soon put some back on, hopefully not all of it,' says Rufus. He puts his arm around Iris's shoulders. 'They were very pleased with him at the hospital. He's going to be fine, you'll see,' he says.

And suddenly, surprisingly, he's now got to be the strong one for her, and convincing Iris helps him believe it himself and he starts to feel more confident.

* * *

The next days roll past quietly and without incident. Gary starts his exercise programme by taking a little walk each day, as he was advised to do. It's only a slow amble round the block, with plenty of stops, and the first time knocks him out for the rest of the afternoon, but little by little he's stopping less and managing a bit more. Usually Iris goes with him, and Rufus has a chance to chill out while they're gone.

Friends come by as and when, Lindsay pops in regularly, and on the fourth day home Sergiu turns up unexpectedly with the cake and they all have tea together. Gary is very touched by the gift, and Sergiu's concern for him.

'When they are in yoga class,' says Sergiu, nodding his head at Rufus and Lindsay, 'we will sit in cafe and chat, yes?'

'We certainly will,' says Gary, smiling. 'We'll put the world to rights.'

Sergiu looks a bit confused so Iris takes it upon herself to explain, which confuses him even more.

Deirdre has not visited yet. Everyone expects this to be a very emotional moment, and maybe she has been putting it off because of this, but after Gary's been home about a week she phones Rufus and says she'll come in the next morning after dropping the kids off at school.

When she walks into the lounge Gary is already out of his chair waiting to hug her. There's a long silence, and it seems as if they stay with their arms around each other for hours. Everyone waits for someone else to speak so nobody does, and they all hope they won't be the first to cry. In the end it's Gary, Deirdre, Lindsay and Rufus in that order.

'I don't know what I can possibly say to you,' says Gary, wiping a hand across his eyes.

'"Thank you" might be nice for a start,' says Iris, in her most mumsy way, 'remember your manners dear,' and Rufus gulps down a laugh but he needn't have worried because now they're all laughing including Iris, and the emotional awkwardness of the moment is broken.

'I'll tell you this Gary, I hope I never have to do that again,' says Deirdre, taking a tissue from the box Rufus offers her and blowing her nose.

'You're not the only one,' says Gary. 'I think once is enough for all of us.'

* * *

The following Wednesday Lindsay arrives for her regular cleaning stint. Rufus is cooking, with a recipe book open in front of him and utensils all over the worktops, meanwhile in the lounge Gary and Iris have made a start on the photos.

It's a bit tricky cleaning around all this activity – she's used to having the house to herself on Wednesdays – but Lindsay is making a go of it, dusting round the mirror above the fireplace, when she looks across at the photos spread out across the coffee table.

Iris has a plastic Sainsbury's bag into which she's dropping those that are destined for the bin, which at the moment seems like most of them.

'I have no idea where these were taken,' she says, flicking through a series of views in faded watery colours, and consigning them to the bag.

'My Mum's got a tin not unlike this,' says Lindsay. 'Some of them were pictures my grandparents took so the chances of us knowing who the people are is pretty remote.'

'You'll end up doing what we're doing,' says Gary. 'It's a bit sad really, these were all moments that somebody thought were worth capturing, and now they're just going to end up on a rubbish heap.'

Iris dips into the tin and brings out another batch, black and white, small rectangular prints. 'I can't get sentimental over things like this,' she says. 'Although I've got all of Gary's school reports and lots of stuff from when he was little. But that's different.'

Lindsay puts her duster down and picks one of the photos up.

'When were these taken?' she says, turning it over in case the answer is on the back. There's nothing.

'Oh, the early 1930s I suppose,' says Iris. 'This was our back garden in London when I was a kid. Whitstable Terrace, near the Oval in Kennington. I don't think the road exists now.'

She lays a few of them out on the table. 'That magnolia tree was my Dad's pride and joy. That, and the veg garden.'

And then a face comes into Lindsay's line of focus, and her heart thumps. She picks the photo up.

'This girl,' she says. 'Who was she?'

Iris squints at the picture, holding it arms-length away from her.

'One of the daughters of the family next door,' she says, 'they were all a lot older than us. The girls came round sometimes in the summer to lie in our garden because their back yard was full of junk. Their father used to repair things for other people and he just left the old bits in the garden to go rusty and clutter the place up. It drove my Dad wild.'

'It's Bella', says Lindsay to Gary. Her fingertips are tingling.

'Are you sure?'

'Bella?' says Iris, 'No that wasn't her name. The family were Coombs. There was Ada, Joyce, Edna and she was Mabel, the youngest daughter.'

Mabel, Bella, is wearing what looks like a knitted swimsuit, and is posing on something that could be a towel or a tablecloth laid on the lawn. Behind her three other girls in similar outfits are giggling.

'Do you know what happened to her?'

Iris shrugs. 'I've no idea. We moved out of London, probably not long after this was taken. Mum used to say that Mabel was the flighty one of the four girls, she had ambitions to be an actress and I thought she was terribly glamorous with her high heels and make-up. Once we came down to Dorset I don't remember hearing anything of them again. It was more difficult to keep in touch then, no email or Facebook and nobody had cars – well not people like us and the Coombs' anyway. So who's this Bella?'

Lindsay goes to the hallway and reaches into her handbag. Helena has had the photo of Bella restored, and it's back in the bureau in Reg's room, but Lindsay has a copy to carry around with her, and she brings it back into the lounge.

'This is her, isn't it?'

Iris considers the photo and then nods slowly. 'From what I can remember it certainly looks like Mabel, but you've got to remember I was only a little girl back then. How did you come by this?'

So Lindsay tells the story as succinctly as she can.

'Lunch is ready!' Rufus calls from the kitchen, and they wander into the dining room still talking about the connection they think they've just made. Lindsay has hold of both photos.

'Can I keep this?' she asks Iris.

'It was going in the chuck-out bag, so of course you can keep it. This afternoon we'll see if we can find any more pictures of her.'

Rufus bustles in with plates and dishes, stops suddenly and looks questioningly around the table. He can sense Lindsay's state of excitement.

'What's going on?'

Lindsay holds both photos up in front of him.

'I think we've just found Bella,' she says.

And then a particular penny suddenly drops, and although she loves these people she can't wait to finish lunch, get out and see if her theory is correct.

'I do think she's wonderful! And one day I'll win her over, you just see...'

Douglas Stanton, to his friend Dickie Savage, September 1936

WAREHAM

It's lovely and warm in the shelter of the walled kitchen garden and George has positioned the two old wooden chairs along the side of the potting shed, out of the breeze which is currently ruffling the silky ears of the sweetcorn Reg has just walked past. George hands Reg his mug of tea, and the sugar bag.

'Her doing alright up there?' he asks.

'Lindsay? Yes she's doing just fine. Still determined to find out more about that girl in the photo.'

'Ah. Thought so. She'll have a job, too far back now.'

They lapse into a comfortable silence which stretches into several minutes. George takes the sugar bag back from Reg and stirs a couple of spoonfuls into his tea.

'All daft, that family,' he observes.

'Mrs Croft too?'

'No not her, begging her pardon. The old ones.'

Reg unwraps his sandwiches. He eats the first one in silence and George does the same, throwing a crust down to a sparrow, who is immediately joined by his entire extended family and a couple of pigeons. Henry appears from nowhere and makes a dive at the sparrows, but they're much too quick for him. Feeling slightly foolish, he swishes his bushy tail about then wanders off to the shed, where George always leaves a saucer of cat biscuits for him.

'A photo of Mr Douglas has turned up. New to me.'

'He was a daft bugger.'

George gets up and moves into the potting shed. When he reappears he's carrying a small dark brown leather-bound book, which he holds out to Reg.

'What's this?'

'His diary, not much to it, only up to the end of February.'

Reg is astonished, takes the book and looks at the first page.

'Douglas Stanton's diary? How did you get this?'

'Dad found it in the garden. Fallen out of his pocket I expect.'

Reg flicks through it but the pages are small and the writing tiny and spidery, and in the glare of the sunlight it's hard to make much out.

'He didn't give it back?'

'He would've. I was sent with it to Mr Douglas, but I pinched it. Had it ever since.'

Reg turns the book over. He wants to show it to Lindsay but more than that he wants it for the Memorial Room. How to explain its sudden appearance though without involving George? It needs careful thought, does this.

'You'd better hang onto it,' he says.

George shrugs. 'Don't mind. No use to me.'

But he takes it back all the same and slips it into the pocket of his battered tweed jacket.

'She'd be interested,' says Reg, thinking he's probably blown it now and because he turned it down the diary will disappear again.

'Ah. You knows where it is.'

They finish their sandwiches and Reg drains the last of his tea before handing the mug back to George.

180

'Nothing much in it,' remarks George. 'All daft stuff.'

* * *

Lunch finally ends and when she leaves Rufus and Gary's house Lindsay drives straight to Stonegrove.

'Hello dear,' says Reg, 'I didn't expect to see you today.'

'I didn't expect to be here.'

She makes a beeline for the theatre programmes.

'I need to check something out, Reg.'

She flicks through each one, finding the cast credits, and way down at the bottom of every list she finds her.

Bella Coombs, in "*Love on the Dole*". Bella Coombs, in "*The Shining Hour*", in "*Eden End*", in "*Ways and Means*". She turns to a couple of musicals, and there she is again, appearing in "*The Cedar Tree*" and "*Anything Goes*". Mostly she's listed with a string of other girls, although occasionally she gets to play a named part.

Lindsay looks up at Reg. 'She was here all the time, Reg. Bella was an actress,' she says. 'Douglas kept the programmes from all the shows she was in... look...'

'Well I never! We didn't think of that, did we?'

'Not much more than a chorus girl, but she was a working actress – I bet that's how he met her.'

'Stage door Johnny?'

'Looks like it. No wonder the family didn't approve.'

Reg is wondering if the illicit diary would confirm any of this, but he can't say anything, not yet, not till he's figured out the right way to do it.

Lindsay tidies the programmes up again, though she's pretty sure Reg will move them into a better arrangement once she's gone.

'Now what?' asks Reg, a reasonable enough question.

Lindsay shakes her head. 'I don't know yet. But I feel that we're closing in on her.'

Reg shifts his weight from one foot to another. He feels a bit uncomfortable, knowing about the diary George has kept all those years and knowing how excited Lindsay would be to see it. But George had said there was nothing much in it, and he could see for himself that there were just a few entries at the beginning of the year. Probably not of any importance. And yet...

Lindsay looks across to where Reg has hung the picture of Douglas astride his motorcycle, having swapped it for a mediocre landscape, which is now hanging out in the corridor with the Fellowes watercolours.

'What on earth went on the night he died?' she says.

***

It's less than half an hour later when Lindsay calls Caroline's mobile and when she answers it's clear that she's only just woken up.

'I had a gig in Liverpool last night,' she says groggily, 'and there was stuff going on afterwards so I didn't get back till this morning.'

'Sorry to wake you up – it's gone two o'clock.'

'Is it really? Hang on.'

There's a clunk and then some rustling and Lindsay imagines Caroline hauling herself out of bed and into her dressing gown.

'This had better be good,' she says, 'I need my sleep.'

'I've found Bella.'

'Well obviously I wasn't expecting it to be that good. You want to tell me about it?'

So Lindsay does tell her, starting with Iris and her photos (Caroline yawns through this bit), and ending up with the theatre programmes in Douglas's room, by which time she can sense that she's got Caroline's full attention.

'We've got a name now, so we ought to be able to find her death certificate – if there *is* a death certificate, that is. It's a start.'

'I subscribe to The Stage,' says Caroline. 'I could see if they've got anything on her.'

'Under their radar, surely? I wouldn't have thought she was good enough for them to notice her, she only had bit parts in plays or in the chorus of musicals.'

'Up to 1936, but if she survived the fracas in the conservatory her career may have taken off later. Let me talk to them. I just need to have a cup of tea and some breakfast then I'm good to go.'

'Have you got any food?'

'Lindsay, don't be ridiculous. There's half a strawberry cheesecake in the fridge and it's only four days old.'

'Ah, then you'll be fine. Speak later.'

* * *

Nick has been on tour for more than two weeks, and Lindsay hasn't heard a peep out of him since the day they sorted through the boxes in Ruby's old room. But now there's something else to tell him she feels justified in giving him a call.

When he picks up it sounds as if he's in the middle of a field full of people, there's a lot of background chatter and occasional snatches of music drift past. Nick's having trouble hearing her, and Lindsay starts to think that phoning him was a very bad idea.

'I'll ring you back in five minutes,' he says, and then is gone.

Five minutes runs closer to ten, and Lindsay knows this for sure because she's watched most of those minutes tick past on the clock in her kitchen. In the meantime she tries to keep busy doing mostly unnecessary things. When her phone finally rings it makes her jump. She lets it go for a while before answering, and then is in for a surprise.

'I was going to call you a bit later anyway,' says Nick. 'I'm just on my way down – I thought I'd impose myself on Helena and Anthony again seeing as I haven't seen any of you for a few weeks.'

'... *any of you...*'? It sounded promising, Nick linking Lindsay with the Crofts in the same sentence.

'There was an awful lot of noise around you when I called.'

'Yeah, sorry about that, motorway services,' he says. 'I'm ready to set off again now and I reckon I'm about an hour and a half away. Are you in for the rest of today?'

'Erm, I could be,' says Lindsay, although there's nothing else on her agenda and she had absolutely no plans that would be taking her out. 'You'll go straight to Stonegrove I suppose?'

'I don't have to, they know I'll be there at some point but I have a fairly flexible arrangement with them. What did you have in mind?'

Lindsay doesn't want to let on exactly what she had in mind, so instead she goes for a less racy scenario.

'Well, it's a lovely day. If you came here first we could go for a walk along the river – I've got some interesting things to tell you, a lot's been happening this last week.'

She's only suggesting a walk, but even so it feels quite daring. Nick sounds rather pleased with the idea.

'Great, I should be in Wareham by about four-fifteen.'

Well, she thinks, this is a turn-up for the books.

And then half an hour later the phone rings again and it's Caroline.

'I'm coming over to you,' she says. 'The Stage weren't terribly helpful but I just spoke to a very nice man at the Royal Academy about John Cecil Fellowes. He told me something you've just got to hear.'

'Tell me now,' says Lindsay, because if Caroline pitches up on her doorstep any time soon she's going to ruin a nice riverside walk.

'No, I need to get out of the house for a bit. We could have a walk along the river, that would be nice wouldn't it?'

It'd be nicer without you, Lindsay's thinking. She knows that's mean, but knowing it doesn't stop her from thinking it. Quite how this walk is going to work as a threesome – especially this threesome – is beyond her imagining.

'I'll be there in about an hour,' says Caroline and then she rings off.

They're going to arrive at the same time, Lindsay thinks. Damn.

She calls Nick back to forewarn him but he's driving and doesn't pick up so she leaves him a text message. After that there's nothing else she can do, so she gets changed, fixes her make-up, and sits down to wait.

Caroline is the first to arrive at the flat. When Lindsay opens the door she's got her phone clamped to her ear and is having a loud conversation with someone who is making her laugh a good deal. She lifts a hand in greeting then walks ahead of Lindsay into the living room and flops down on the sofa, and just as she's got herself settled the doorbell goes again. Caroline looks up at Lindsay, who smiles weakly and disappears out into the hall.

Nick opens his mouth to speak but before he can do so Lindsay whispers that Caroline is there. He looks mildly surprised but is undeterred and follows her through, taking a seat opposite Caroline. She looks at him, and then falters slightly in her flow of chat.

'I think I'll have to go now, talk more later,' she says, letting her caller evaporate suddenly into thin air with the press of a button.

'Hello,' says Nick.

'Erm... Anthony?' she says, not entirely convinced but not entirely sure why.

'No! This is Anthony's brother, Nick!' says Lindsay, gaily. 'Almost identical aren't they? Nick, this is Caroline!'

Caroline narrows her eyes slightly. 'Weren't you... erm... didn't we...?'

'I'd have remembered if we had,' says Nick extending his hand across the coffee table. 'Very nice to meet you.'

'TEA?' asks Lindsay, a little too loudly.

'I thought we were going for a walk,' says Caroline.

'So did I – excellent, we can all go together in that case,' says Nick.

Lindsay groans to herself.

They set off towards the river, Nick at his funniest and most charming, Caroline at her funniest and loudest, and Lindsay silently trailing along ever-so-slightly behind.

'Anyway, Caroline,' she says brightly, when a gap in the witticisms opens up, 'what did you find out about Fellowes?'

Caroline is momentarily thrown. 'Now?'

'Of course... Nick knows pretty well everything to date so he'll understand where you're coming from.'

'Fascinating story,' says Nick, 'I can't wait to hear the next instalment.'

'Oh, well OK. The man I spoke to at the Royal Academy knew of Fellowes, said he belonged to a certain group of watercolour painters based near Wincanton, I can't remember the name of them offhand but I wrote it all down.'

'The Somerset School?' Nick suggests.

'Yes, actually I think it could have been that. How did you know?'

Nick shrugs. 'A lucky guess.'

Lindsay ignores him. 'Go on.'

'So, Fellowes and some of the others in this group spent a lot of time around here which is probably why there are so many local views of his in Stonegrove Hall, and probably explains how he came to meet Ruby. But that's not the really interesting bit.'

Caroline stops walking and starts checking things off on her fingers.

'One: he was only twenty-nine years old when he died, seemingly healthy up to that point. Two: it was on September the twenty-third, exactly four days after Douglas Stanton died. And three: he killed himself.'

'What?'

'Yep, suicide. Now don't tell me those two deaths are not related in some way.'

There's a silence. They find a bench to sit on, and look out over the river.

'Related in what way?' asks Nick.

Caroline shrugs. 'That's what we're going to find out.'

'Oh, I can't put all this together,' says Lindsay, frustrated by not being able to join up the dots. She runs a hand through her hair. 'All these facts are telling us something, but for the life of me I can't see what. Can you?'

Caroline shakes her head. 'Not yet, but soon we will, I really think we're getting there. Oh, and the research team got back to me about the formal dinner thing,' she adds. 'They think it unlikely that the Stanton children would have been included until they were older – unless like Ruby they were engaged to one of the guests, in which case she'd be there when he was, but of course not listed on the visitors' book.'

'And Bella?' asks Nick.

'Boyfriends and girlfriends probably not invited to dine with the grown-ups. They said it would have varied from one family to another though.'

'So Bella was left out in the cold,' says Nick, 'not welcome at the table.'

'Ah yes, you don't know this bit yet,' says Lindsay. 'Her real name was Mabel Coombs, and she was an actress, just an ordinary south London girl with ambition who seems to have caught Douglas's eye.'

'How did you find that out?'

'Oh... I'll explain it all later. It's a long story – why don't we get a take-away supper and...'

And then Caroline's mobile rings and she's off again, embarking on another loud conversation with hoots of laughter.

Nick nods in her direction and raises an eyebrow.

'I don't know what her plans are,' Lindsay says, with a shrug.

'I could give Anthony a ring, see what they're up to?'

But then Caroline winds up her call and glances at her watch.

'I should be going,' she says. So they stand up together and say all the right things and Caroline shakes Nick's hand.

'Must be great, having a twin,' she says, 'all those opportunities to wrong-foot people. Have fun, you two.' And then she's gone, back up the path the way they came.

'She knew,' says Lindsay. Nick laughs.

'Most people work it out in the end. Anyway, no harm done, it just gave Anthony a bit of breathing space. Do you want to see if they're up for a take-away?'

Lindsay gets a mental picture of her little flat with the Crofts in it. It's hardly what they're used to, living up at the manor, but then she remembers what nice, normal people they are and knows they wouldn't give a fig about that.

'Why not? Tell them to come down here, I can run to four sets of everything.'

But the plan is thwarted, because Anthony and Helena have the twins overnight and are therefore stuck at Stonegrove on babysitting duties.

'They said we were welcome to go to them but I could hear the sound of little girls acting-up in the background, so I declined.'

'Well done. I'm not really comfortable around small children, it's bad enough being with Caroline.'

'She's quite a character isn't she? I think if she can actually get this programme off the ground she'd be very good at fronting it. Let's face it, she can't be a stand-up comedian all her life.'

'No, and that's what's driving her on. I really hope there will be something in it for her, she seems to have mellowed a bit just recently.'

'That'll be your influence,' says Nick, 'plus she knows everyone's pulling in the same direction now so she hasn't got to fight her corner.'

They carry on walking for a while and Lindsay lists the take-away options in Wareham for Nick's benefit. They settle on fish and chips, and once they feel they've walked far enough to have earned their supper Lindsay takes him to the best chippy in town, which is luckily only two minutes away from her flat and even better, next door to an off licence.

There's still late afternoon sun on her balcony, and Nick puts the table and chairs out there – something Lindsay has never thought of doing in all the time she's lived in the flat. The view may not be the best in the world, or even in the town, but the communal gardens are neat, and eating outside in the warmth of an early evening does have a certain Mediterranean feel to it. And maybe a chilled bottle of Sauvignon Blanc helps with that too, it certainly doesn't hurt.

Nick tells her about the tour he's been on for the last couple of weeks, hardly the glamorous lifestyle she'd imagined, and how in typical freelance style his diary is now completely blank for the next ten days.

'Something will come in,' he says, 'but in the meantime I may as well be down here as back in London on my own.'

He's still a bit of an enigma to Lindsay and there's a lot she'd like to know, but every time just as she feels herself getting close to asking, the pendulum swings away from her again. Which is exactly what happens now, too.

'How's the job-hunting going?'

Lindsay is ashamed to have to admit to herself, and then to Nick, that she hasn't been doing any.

'I seem to have let things slide a bit, what with my friend Gary in hospital, and Bella...' she says weakly. It makes her feel a bit pathetic.

'Ah yes, you haven't explained how you made the breakthrough with Bella,' he says and then she's off on that track again. She places the two photos side by side on the table in front of him.

'Clever you, spotting her, I'm not sure I would have done.' he says, picking up the one from Iris's tin and then comparing it to the other. 'But it's definitely the same girl.'

'I wasn't even looking especially closely, she just kind of pushed herself forward.'

'Well maybe Bella wants this cleared up as much as you do.'

It's a fanciful notion and he doesn't intend it to be taken seriously, but somehow that's exactly how Lindsay does take it.

'Then I can't just drop her now,' she says, looking at Bella. 'If she's waited eighty years for me to come along and take an interest the least I can do is see it through.'

When she glances up she expects Nick to be looking at her as if she's mad, but he isn't.

'And the least I can do is pitch in and help, although you seem to be doing just fine on your own. You and Caroline are quite a formidable team.'

'There's room for another one,' she says. 'and I'd like your help.'

They finish off the wine and at about nine o'clock Nick decides the twins will be in bed by then and it's safe to head up to Stonegrove.

'It's my volunteering day tomorrow,' says Lindsay.

'Oh good, so I'll see you there. I could trawl through some more boxes if you like.'

At the front door, Nick drops a kiss on the top of Lindsay's head, and then is gone.

His offer of help is a nice idea, although by the morning Stonegrove finds itself having a bit of a crisis, and the archive boxes in Ruby's bedroom remain undisturbed for quite a bit longer.

'John? Oh no, you don't have to worry about him, he's much more sensible than Douglas. He'd never be taken in like that. Douglas is a complete fool where she's concerned.'

Ruby Stanton, to her sister Diana, September 1936

STONEGROVE HALL

When Lindsay arrives in the staff car park there's an ambulance there, parked as close as possible to the door. Her heart does a little flip at the sight of it, and she thinks back to the day Gary was stretchered down from the yoga studio. It's too early for visitors so it can only be there for one of the staff, or one of the Croft family.

She goes straight to the estate office and finds Beverley opening the post.

'It's George,' she tells Lindsay, 'one of the apprentices found him in his cottage, lying on the flagstones in the kitchen with a wooden stepladder on top of him. One of the legs of the ladder had got wedged under a cupboard and he'd been trapped there all night.'

It's hard to imagine what eighty-six year old George was doing with a stepladder in his kitchen in the first place, but frighteningly easy to picture him missing his footing and falling off, pulling it down with him.

'How bad is he?'

'We think he's broken his arm for starters, maybe something else. The paramedics are over there with him now.'

Anthony comes into the office behind Lindsay.

'Either way he won't be doing any gardening for some time,' he says. 'He's lucky that lad found him when he did, and had the good sense to break in and raise the alarm.'

'Poor George, at his age something like that might have finished him off,' says Lindsay.

'It still might,' says Anthony, 'but he's a strong old chap, and this may be the one thing that will force him to retire and start to take life a little more gently.'

'But the gardens...?'

'Those lads do most of the work anyway, and they're almost at the end of their apprenticeships so they know what they're doing. If they struggle with the workload then we'll have to take someone else on.'

Beverley turns to look out of the window. The ambulance driver is just starting up the engine and they watch as he backs out of the staff car park and turns off towards the cottages.

'Helena went to gather up some of his things and take them over to the hospital,' says Beverley.

Lindsay is early for her shift so she has time to spare. 'I'll pop across and see if she needs a hand,' she says.

The ambulance is pulling away from the front of George's cottage as she approaches it, with the paramedics car following. The front door is open, and she calls out to Helena as she goes in. It's gloomy in the hallway, and it takes a few minutes for her eyes to adjust.

'Oh Lindsay, bless you, I'm just trying to find some basic things he might be glad of in hospital. They've taken him to Poole and at his age I'm pretty sure they'll keep him in at least overnight, especially if he really has broken a bone.'

They stand together in George's bedroom, and feel like interlopers. For an old man, he keeps his cottage quite neat and tidy and it won't be difficult to find the things they need, but neither of them feels quite right about opening drawers.

'Do you think this was his parents' room?' asks Lindsay, indicating the big double bed and dark, old furniture.

'I expect so, there's a box room too that was probably his. I don't suppose that's the original bed though... it looks too modern to me. Now, let's see, what will he need?'

Then they do have to start opening drawers, where they find everything neatly folded away and in order. They sort through some clothes in the wardrobe and chest and put the most useful things into a soft cabin bag Helena has brought with her, then add a clean pair of pyjamas and his slippers. After that they move into the bathroom.

It's a weirdly personal thing to be doing, especially for someone neither of them really knows well. Even Helena, who has known George all her life, can't claim to actually know him. Toothpaste and toothbrush, shave foam and razor, soap and flannel – they all go into the bag, wrapped in a towel.

'We'll just check the living room, in case there's a magazine or something he's reading – we could take that in to keep him occupied.'

They find a puzzle book on the coffee table, a bulb catalogue alongside it and a trade magazine that's unopened and still in its plastic wrapper. Helena picks these up and flicks through the catalogue before adding them all to the bag.

'I've got *Dorset Life* coming in this morning,' she says. 'They're planning a feature on us – still I'm sure Anthony can see to them.'

Lindsay glances at her watch. She was going to offer to do the hospital run so that Helena can be there to see the magazine people, but there won't be time now before the house opens to visitors. Then she has an idea.

'Can't Nick go to the hospital? Then you'll be here for the '*Dorset Life*' interview.'

'What a good idea – I'll ask him.'

They turn to leave the room and just as they get to the door Helena stops so abruptly that Lindsay, who is zipping up the bag, crashes straight into her.

'Well, well,' says Helena. 'Just look at this.'

She's looking at a picture on the wall, and Lindsay peers over her shoulder to see the now familiar signature of John Cecil Fellowes at the bottom.

'He certainly got everywhere,' she comments.

'This is a picture of Maiden Castle, which is exactly what's missing from the landing outside Douglas's room. I wonder if it's the same one?'

Helena peels the frame carefully away from the wall and finds that underneath it there's a smaller rectangular patch showing dark against the faded wallpaper.

'That photo of Douglas on his motorbike, it came from here.'

'George did the swap?' says Lindsay. 'But why would he do that?'

'And how would he do it? George hasn't been in the house for as far back as I can remember. How would he know where to put it? And when? He couldn't just wander about in his gardening clothes without being noticed.'

They stand and look at each other, and then back at the painting. From the back kitchen there's a hammering sound where the apprentice gardener is busy boarding up the window he broke earlier to get in to George.

'He had help,' says Lindsay, and they both turn their heads towards the sound of the hammering.

The lad at the kitchen window finally buckles under Helena's relentless interrogation.

'Hello Darren,' she says as she walks round the back of the house, the painting tucked under one arm, 'thank you, you're doing a very good job there. Thank goodness you had the sense to come round here and look for George, or he might have been lying on the kitchen floor for many more hours.'

'I hope he'll be OK, Mrs Croft. I didn't move him, just lifted that stepladder off and put a blanket over him. If only he'd asked me I would have changed the light bulb for him.'

'You're very good to him and I'm sure George appreciates your help. Was it you that swapped this painting for him?'

Helena holds the picture up for Darren to see. He puts the hammer down and wipes his hands on the back of his jeans.

'Yes, that's right. He said the photograph needed to go into the house and told me to swap it with one of the pictures on the landing outside the Douglas room.'

'He didn't say why?'

'No, and I didn't think to ask him. It was OK to do it, wasn't it?'

'Yes of course. We just wondered where the photo had suddenly come from.'

'Oh, I thought he'd spoken to you about it already.'

'It's fine, no harm done, Darren. I'll let you know how George is getting on.'

Back in the cottage Helena replaces the painting on the wall. 'That photo of Douglas may have been hanging in this room since George's parents lived here, so I wonder why he suddenly felt the need to move it into the house?'

Lindsay shakes her head. 'I can't begin to guess at that. Let's hope George gets well soon so we can ask him.'

* * *

George has a small fracture in his wrist, two cracked ribs and a fair bit of bruising so although it's bad enough, it's not as bad as it might have been. It's mid-afternoon before Nick gets back to Stonegrove, having sat with him through A&E and the fracture clinic, before finally seeing him settled in a temporary bed. Once he's reported back to Anthony he wanders up to the Theatre Room.

'It's not a bad break on his wrist but they're keeping him in overnight, mainly because of his age and the fact that he lives alone. I'll go and get him tomorrow once they've phoned to say he can come home.'

'That's good of you. Poor George, he'll be very frustrated until he can get back in the garden,' says Lindsay.

'I doubt if he'll be doing any more gardening,' says Nick, 'and that's probably not a bad thing at his age. It gives Anthony and Helena the chance to pension him off and let those two boys show what they're worth, but they'll need someone else in as well I expect. You any good at gardening?' Nick jokes with her.

'Nope, not a clue. Will George be able to stay in his cottage do you think?'

'I don't think they'd turn him out, Helena will probably be rushing over there each day with home made soup.' Nick is not far off the beam as Helena is already organising with the kitchen staff for meals to be sent over to George on a regular basis.

'We found something out when we were getting the bag ready for the hospital,' says Lindsay, and she tells Nick about the picture swap.

'How bizarre. Where's the photo now?'

'Reg has got it next door.'

There's nobody around just at that time so they go together to see Reg, who's pleased to get an update on George.

'Not a man of many words,' he says, 'but I've got a lot of time for him. Very loyal to Stonegrove and the Crofts – it'll be a sad day for George when he has to give up caring for this garden.'

'His broken bones will heal but it'll take time, and given his age...' Lindsay trails off.

'He'll always be on hand even if he can't manage the garden any more. You couldn't replace the wealth of knowledge George has about this place,' says Nick.

'Quite,' says Reg. 'He knows more about Stonegrove than we'll ever get to hear him tell. Anyway, you wanted to see this photograph?'

Back in steward mode, Reg is delighted to show Nick and Lindsay the photo.

'It all adds to the atmosphere,' he says, 'and helps to build up a more rounded picture of Douglas. And I don't think the landscape it replaces in here was any great loss, rather a gloomy thing if you ask me.'

Nick peers closely at the photo and Lindsay hopes he'll spot something they've all missed so far, but he doesn't. Unless...

'It must have taken him ages to get all those wrecks of motorbikes arranged so perfectly around him,' he says, 'most of them are still in pieces, it doesn't look as if they're even bolted together so the bits must be propped up on stands of some sort. If he was also setting up the shot he can't have done it alone, surely someone must have helped him.'

'George's dad?' suggests Lindsay.

'Maybe. Or any of the other estate workers, I'm guessing there were more then than there are now.'

Reg has an idea. He takes the frame off the wall, extracts a small case of miniature tools from his briefcase and selects a screwdriver. Only Reg, Lindsay thinks, would carry a piece of kit like this around with him. She glances up at Nick and smiles and he winks at her, obviously thinking the same thing.

Reg carefully prises the back off the frame and takes out two layers of corrugated cardboard holding the photo in place. He's hoping, as with Bella's photograph, for an inscription on the back. Disappointingly, there's nothing there.

'It was worth a try,' he says as he puts the frame back together and replaces the photo on the wall. 'You'll just have to ask George about it.'

***

Nick collects George from hospital the following morning, gets him settled in his cottage with a cup of tea and books within easy reach, empties the cabin bag and puts back in the wardrobe and chest all the clothes Helena and Lindsay had carefully selected the previous day. George is in a good deal of discomfort from his cracked ribs and cross with himself for doing something so silly.

'You were just trying to be independent,' says Nick.

'Ah,' says George, and he winces as he tries to get more comfortable in his armchair. 'Daft bugger.'

The two apprentices look in to give him an update on what they're up to in the garden, and Nick uses that as an opportunity to leave, telling George on his way out that lunch will be sent over from the restaurant.

The apprentices do most of the talking, but Darren doesn't mention the conversation he had with Helena about the photograph because as far as he can see it isn't important.

'He's an idiot, that's what he is.'
**Mrs Legg, Stonegrove Hall housekeeper, to her
husband Ernest. September 1936**

CHRISTCHURCH

Caroline is having a dreadful night. She woke first
in the early hours, sweat pouring off her as she cried
hysterically, and the nightmare of the hit-and-run kept
her company for a long time afterwards. She got up
and made herself a cup of hot chocolate and finally,
because she was so tired, she broke her own rule and
went back to bed to try and get some more sleep.

It's less than an hour later when she wakes again,
but this time she feels perfectly calm. Later, when
she thinks about it, she will wonder if her eyes were
actually open, if she really was awake, but right now
it certainly feels like it. The sky is just beginning to
lighten, and in the bedroom doorway Caroline sees
her mother. She isn't afraid, nor even surprised. Her
mother is wearing an outfit she remembers, a navy and
white striped cotton dress and a white lacy cardigan
that she knitted herself.

Caroline sits up in bed and tries to speak but nothing
comes out. Then she hears her mother's voice, so soft
that it's no more than a breath.

'Let it go, sweetheart.'

Caroline would like to get out of bed and go to her
mother, but she finds she's unable to move her legs. It
takes a while to even summon the energy to speak, her

throat is dry and her tongue seems to be swollen and too fat for her mouth.

Eventually she manages a hoarse whisper.

'I can't.'

'Yes you can, just let it all go. Everything.'

A sob catches in Caroline's throat, she reaches for a tissue under her pillow, and when she looks up again her mother's gone, and the bedroom door is closed.

* * *

By midday, Caroline has showered and is sitting at her kitchen table with a coffee and a packet of chocolate biscuits in front of her. She feels quite rested which is surprising, considering the night she's had, even though she did manage to get a few hours sleep in the morning.

For a while she does nothing but stare into space, munching her way through the biscuits, one hand cupped around the coffee mug. Since waking up over two hours ago her mind has been in a turmoil, going over the events of last night again and again, and now she's weary of it. Finally she makes a decision, gets up from the table with a sigh, and fetches her phone.

It doesn't take long to find what she's looking for on Google, and her subsequent call is answered on the second ring. Once that's done she calls the only person she knows who won't ask questions but will just come round because she needs her.

Disappointingly, Lindsay's mobile goes to answerphone, so she has to leave a message. This is particularly frustrating because she can't remember if it's one of her volunteering days at Stonegrove, in which case she might not get a callback till much later. Caroline needs to see a bit of action quickly before she loses her nerve.

But she's in luck because it's Friday, and yoga. A little more than an hour after she made the call, Caroline's phone rings and it's Lindsay speaking against a combination of voices, laughter and a Gaggia machine hissing away in the background.

'Are you OK? You sounded rather stressed in your message.'

'I could do with a bit of help, this afternoon if you're not busy,' and Caroline goes on to tell Lindsay what she's got in mind. She sounds fired up and raring to go.

'Are you sure about this?'

'Absolutely. Bring some boxes if you can, or a couple of suitcases would do.'

* * *

In less than an hour Lindsay is ringing Caroline's doorbell. At her feet are a stack of three large, empty cardboard boxes, previously holding bags of crisps, which Sergiu had put aside for recycling.

Caroline scoops up the boxes and ushers Lindsay inside.

'What I'm going to tell you you'll never believe, but you've just got to suspend disbelief and go with it. I may be going bonkers but I don't think so.'

Lindsay tries very hard to suspend disbelief, but as she listens to Caroline what she's really thinking is that she's had a particularly vivid dream, one that has stayed with her into the day. She doesn't say that though.

'I think your mum's right. It *is* time to move on.'

Caroline nods and sighs, looking down at her hands in her lap.

'I know. I've known it for a long time but it's just so hard to do, and when you're on your own there's nobody else around to bounce things off and get a different perspective.'

'But you're really sure now you want to do this?'

'Yes I am. Let's get started.'

Caroline stands up. Lindsay stands too, but then reaches out and takes Caroline's hand.

'Look, I can do it on my own if you don't want to – why don't you go for a walk?' she asks.

Lindsay watches her weighing this up. First yes, than a hesitation, and finally no.

'No, I'll help. I'd kind of like to say goodbye.'

They take the boxes into the small bedroom. The amount of toys they'll get into them won't even dent the collection as a whole, but it's a huge step for Caroline and after this it'll be easy. That's her theory anyway.

'The lady at the toy museum was really sweet, she said they'd be a great addition and I can go in free and see them any time I like.'

'And will you?'

'Probably not. No, I don't think so.' She gives herself a little shake and then snaps into action. 'Right, dolls and soft toys first, then whatever else we can fit in.'

Now that it's come to it Caroline's quite brisk, although as they pack and she handles each of her precious toys for the last time it's almost as if they were valuable pieces of porcelain. They don't talk as they work – there's nothing to say and although conversation might be a diversion the occasion seems to demand more respect than that.

It doesn't take them long to fill all three boxes, even packing them with such care.

'I don't know when I'll be able to get them over to the museum,' says Lindsay as they carry the boxes through the front door, 'hopefully one day next week.'

'It doesn't matter, we've made a start and that's the important thing. I'm going to hire a van in the next couple of weeks and take all the rest in one go. It's just that... well I couldn't go straight into that...'

For the first time it looks as if Caroline might cry.

'Don't know how to thank you, Lindsay...'

'There's really no need. Maybe you could just open the front door though before these boxes break my arms.'

Caroline gulps and shifts up a gear.

'Oh sorry, yes of course. Did you get the heaviest ones?'

'You know I did. Your box is full of teddies.'

'Yeah, just lucky I guess.'

'Ha! Lucky my arse.'

They put the boxes in the back of Lindsay's car and she's just wondering whether to suggest staying for a while or maybe going together for a coffee, but then Caroline takes charge of the situation.

'OK, off you go before I change my mind and make you bring them all back in.'

Lindsay hesitates for a split second, and then gives her a quick hug.

'Well done,' she says. 'You're a brave girl.'

* * *

Caroline sleeps right through the night, the first time for ages. She wakes refreshed, and makes herself go into the spare room as soon as she gets up to survey the progress they made yesterday in clearing it. It's very little, nobody else would notice that anything had gone, but to Caroline it's significant.

'Good,' she says out loud, tightening the belt on her dressing gown. 'Good work Caroline.'

Two nights later the dream wakes her again, but this time it's different. She doesn't see her parents or the collision. All she sees is the car heading towards her, the driver's face no longer that of the terrified, spotty youth she's used to seeing behind the steering wheel. This driver is older, and he's grinning at her through the windscreen.

It takes her a few seconds after she's woken up properly to realise that it's the face of Douglas Stanton. She's not frightened, or upset, but she is puzzled. The nightmare has moved on, and she supposes that she has too, but this direction of change has taken her by surprise and she has no idea what to make of it.

One of these days she'll go too far, all that flirting and shimmying in front of the chaps. Diana and I think she's terribly coarse.

Ruby Stanton's diary, September 12th 1936

STONEGROVE

On the following Monday Helena takes George's lunch over to him so she can see for herself how he's doing, now that he's had a few days to settle back home. She doesn't have to step far beyond the front gate to hear the row going on inside.

'How dare you! If it went anywhere it should have come to me!' yells Diana.

'It's gone back where it belongs.'

'Where it belongs? He was my brother! It belongs with me!'

Helena pushes the front door open and heads for the kitchen and the sound of her mother's slightly hysterical voice. She plonks the tray down on the hall table and barges in on them. Diana is leaning on the kitchen table with her back to the door, hands gripping the edge, face pushed towards George, unaware that Helena is behind her. George, sitting opposite, looks up as she steps forward. He seems to be completely unfazed by Diana's verbal attack.

'Mother! What on earth is going on?'

Diana is in such a fury that she doesn't hear Helena, even though she's shouting.

'My brother,' she continues, 'and merely your parents' employer. Don't ever forget that. The picture should have been mine.'

'Ah. But it wasn't, was it?'

Helena walks around the table and into Diana's line of sight.

'Mother, just calm down. Whatever is this about?' she asks, although of course she already knows.

Diana looks up and is clearly surprised to find that Helena is in the room. She immediately backs off.

'Nothing for you to get involved in.'

'Fine, have it your own way, but in any case I don't think you should come in here and start shouting at George like that.'

Diana glares at Helena, but the fight has gone out of her.

'You have no idea,' she says.

'Then maybe you'd better tell me,' says Helena.

Diana takes hold of her stick and pulls herself up straight. Then she turns and stomps out without another word.

Helena sighs.

'I'm sorry, George, she's quite impossible sometimes. I can guess what she was referring to – do you want to tell me about it?'

And so George does, and his lunch is forgotten and goes cold out on the hall table.

***

It's a busy day at Stonegrove, and the house is bustling all afternoon with families, young and old couples, and a party from one of the local schools. It's almost half past five by the time the last visitors have left the house (via the shop, clutching their purchases), and the last car has driven out of the car park. And suddenly Stonegrove is still and quiet again, the only voices those of the volunteers as they gather up their things and say their goodbyes. In the front hall Marion tidies the leaflets and slips the clicker back into the desk drawer. She picks up her bag and jacket and takes a last look around before heading for the back corridor, and at just that moment Helena walks through the hall towards the stairs.

'You haven't seen Lindsay come down yet, have you?' she asks Marion.

'No, nor Reg, but everyone else from upstairs has gone I think.'

Helena finds them having a natter in the Theatre Room, Reg with his briefcase in his hand, Lindsay her bag slung over her shoulder.

'I thought I might have missed you, I got held up on the phone,' she says, 'but I'm glad you're both still here because I wanted to tell you that I found out about that photo, George told me the story.'

Reg puts his briefcase down and Lindsay slips her car keys back into her bag.

'We might as well sit down,' says Helena, and they turn around three of the audience chairs in the back row. Reg and Lindsay get themselves settled, waiting for Helena to explain.

'Douglas gave the photo to George's dad because he'd helped him set up the shot with the motorbikes, apparently it took them hours to get it right. George was just a small boy at the time so he doesn't remember anything of this himself, only what his parents told him later.'

Reg, nodding, comes in with an observation. 'Yes, we thought that might be the case, in view of the fact that his father was the gardener at the time and living on site so to speak.'

'And his mother of course was the housekeeper, which is also relevant.'

Lindsay thinks back to the day she and Caroline visited Betty in the Shady Pines home and she suddenly came out with the revelation about washing blood off the conservatory floor. *Mrs Legg the housekeeper said we wasn't to talk of it again.* That had been Betty's parting shot as Lindsay hustled Caroline out of her room.

'George said his mother had no time at all for Douglas and never wanted the photo on their living room wall in the first place, but Mr Legg insisted it should be hung there. It became a real bone of contention and whenever there was a disagreement between them that photo was brought into the argument. Mrs Legg used to tell George that the day his father died she'd take it down and put it back in the Hall.'

'But obviously she never did.'

'She died first, so Mr Legg got his way and the photo stayed where it was.'

Lindsay frowns. 'But he must have died years ago – how come George has only just thought to remove it?' she asks.

'I got the impression it was for you, Lindsay. He heard you'd been taking an interest in Douglas and he probably thought that now was the right time to do what his mother wanted. Clearly it would be of more use to you than it was to him.'

'I've hardly ever exchanged more than 'good morning' with George so I don't know how he could know I was interested in Douglas.'

Reg shifts in his chair. 'I think that might be my doing,' he says, and explains about the sandwiches and the lunchtime chats by the potting shed.

'He could have just given me the photo,' says Lindsay, 'it would have been much simpler.'

'I don't think that's George's style,' says Helena. 'I've known him all my life but today was the first time he's said more than a few words to me.'

There's a bit of a pause. In the end, George's revelations have come as something of an anticlimax.

'So that's it,' says Lindsay, 'no big mystery after all.'

'Well, that's not quite all. But we've got to remember that George was only five years old when Douglas died, so anything he says about the incident in the conservatory came from his parents – mostly his mother as far as I can make out, I suspect George takes after his father in terms of communication skills. But it does get a bit more interesting...'

From downstairs, they hear two of the room stewards calling out goodbye to someone else, and then the bang of the door taking them out of the back corridor.

'According to what Mrs Legg told him, and this must have been years after the event, the argument in the conservatory ended up with one of the party getting a shotgun from the tack room and firing it through the conservatory window.'

'Oh my goodness, so Caroline may be right after all – Bella *might* actually be under one of the flowerbeds...'

'Well now we're back in the land of make-believe, Lindsay,' says Helena, with a shrug. 'That may just have been servant's gossip, and even if it wasn't we don't know that anyone was killed or even seriously injured.'

Reg can't quite get his head around this. 'Why was Mrs Legg so set against Douglas, I wonder?' he says, unable to let the Douglas he thought he understood have his reputation damaged without anyone weighing in on his side. Reg has never thought there was anything particularly interesting about Douglas, in spite of the dashing picture he paints for visitors. But he's never considered him to be a villain, either.

'She thought he was spoilt, arrogant and feckless, apparently. The girls were the strong sensible ones but everyone rushed around after the young heir and pandered to his every whim. That's pretty much George's assessment anyway.'

'Filtered down through his mother.'

'Quite.'

'Except where Bella was concerned,' says Lindsay, 'that was one whim they didn't pander to since she obviously wasn't welcome at the Stanton table.'

'No, I suppose that was just a step too far for them to go. Bella must have come as quite a shock, a working class girl and an actress to boot.'

There's a collective sigh, as they all assimilate George's evidence.

'Is there any point in trying to talk to your mother again, Helena? She's really the only one who can tell us.'

Helena grimaces. 'I can try. But she's a very stubborn old lady.'

* * *

Nick has been in London after getting a last-minute call for a gig, so it's not till the following day that he comes back to Stonegrove. Helena has (thoughtfully) kept Lindsay informed about his whereabouts, and as she has something positive to tell him she doesn't feel awkward about phoning. In the event though, Nick rings Lindsay before she can get to the phone.

'We know the story behind the motorbike photo now,' she says. 'And Caroline had a great idea! She's put a message up on Facebook, to see if anyone out there has any information about Bella.'

'Yes, I know,' says Nick.

'You do? How come?' This has taken the wind out of Lindsay's sails.

'Because I saw it. We're Facebook friends.'

'You are?'

'Yes, aren't you?'

'Erm, I don't really do Facebook, actually.'

'Oh, you mean you don't look very often?'

'No, I mean I don't actually do it at all. I'm not on Facebook.'

'Ah, that would explain why I couldn't find you. I thought maybe you used a different surname, your married name or something.'

'Oh no, I wouldn't do that. I'm not on there under any name.'

Nick takes this in for a second or two.

'Well, if you were you'd have seen what a brilliant post it was. If all her friends share it, and then their friends share it, there's a reasonable chance she may turn something up.'

There's something about knowing that Nick and Caroline are Facebook friends that has irritated Lindsay, and she's been caught on the back foot by it.

'Yes, well let's just hope that the virtual world succeeds where the real world has failed miserably so far.'

There's a bit of a pause. Lindsay has not been able to keep the irritation out of her voice, and she knows it.

'Are you OK?' asks Nick, genuinely not realising what's going on.

'Fine. Probably just a bit tired,' she says, spikily.

'Do you fancy a drink later?'

Lindsay takes her time over replying. It's just hit her that Nick said he'd been looking for her on Facebook, which is quite nice to know.

'Erm... OK, but I don't want to be too late.'

'I could get you on Facebook, if you like. I mean, you don't have to but sometimes it's useful – like with Caroline asking for information about Bella, for example.'

'Maybe. You'd have to explain more about the benefits to me, I'm not really convinced.'

'Well, for a start you could follow any comments about Bella as they come in, then you'd be up to speed without me or Caroline having to let you know.'

Lindsay umms in a sceptical way, but Nick is undeterred.

'I can see you'll be a hard nut to crack, but I like a challenge. How about The Old Granary, seven-ish?'

* * *

It's three days later, and Lindsay is hooked on Facebook.

She's amazed at the amount of time she's wasted on it, but there's no going back now as her virtual world expands before her eyes. She's gathering in friends at an alarming rate, has shared Caroline's post to them all and watched as they've shared it with their friends.

Slowly, slowly, the ripples edge a little further out.

But there have been no positive sightings so far and it's too slow for Lindsay, as she complains to Rufus a couple of weeks later in Cappuccino Blues.

'You have to be patient, not everyone checks their Facebook page every day,' he says.

'Don't they really? How strange...'

'No, they don't. And you might not when you've been doing this for a while.'

Lindsay shrugs. She can't explain the little frisson of expectation she gets every time she logs on to see what's awaiting her. It's disappointing that there haven't been any further clues in the search for Bella, but many other interesting, bizarre and just plain crazy things have cropped up from her new online family. It's been an education.

Deirdre has become a Facebook friend, but Rufus tired of the whole thing a long time ago and has resisted Lindsay's repeated attempts to befriend him. Anxious to move the conversation on he tells them about Gary's rehabilitation in the real world.

'He's walking a little further each day, and is much less anxious now. He had a check-up last week, all fine, and they don't want to see him for three months so that's good.'

'Will he come back to yoga?' asks Deirdre. 'Janey said he could do it from a chair.'

'I doubt it,' says Rufus. 'It was never really his thing, to be honest.'

'He'll find something else,' says Lindsay.

'I think he already has, he's taken up swimming,' says Rufus, leaning back and folding his arms across his chest. 'He'd been going to the pool each week for water aerobics and a bit of gentle swimming and now he's stepping it up to every few days. And we're both keeping the weight off by eating more healthily.'

'It was a wake-up call,' says Deirdre, 'and you've responded to it. Not everyone does, you know.'

It's at precisely that moment that Lindsay's phone rings. It's Caroline, squeaking with excitement, her voice several notches higher than usual. Lindsay listens for a moment and then gasps, her hand flying to her mouth.

'Sergiu, I need to look on your computer!' she calls out, scraping her chair back and rushing forward, phone in hand, the high pitch of Caroline's voice still audible to the rest of the room as Lindsay lifts the flap on the counter. Sergiu steps aside and ushers her through to the back room.

'Sure, sure,' he says. 'Now I am internet café too, huh? Maybe I get some computers here, make more money that way.'

And while Lindsay disappears into the store room Rufus and Sergiu embark on a discussion about the practicalities of starting up a new business venture.

Lindsay is all fingers and thumbs as she tries to access the comment on Caroline's Facebook page, not helped by having Caroline, now on speaker phone, screeching her excitement down the line.

When she finds it, it's pleasingly succinct.

My mother worked with Bella during the war and I met her once or twice afterwards. How can I help?

Lindsay leans back in her chair. Caroline continues to squeak, and after a moment she lifts the phone to her ear again.

'She lived through the war, Caroline... she's not under the herbaceous border...'

'Whoever was shot that night, it wasn't her... at least not fatally...'

Then they both fall silent. Lindsay is elated because Bella survived both the conservatory and the war. Caroline's elated because her TV programme has just moved one step closer to reality.

'I've sent her a message,' says Caroline, using her normal voice again.

Lindsay looks back at the screen.

'Anne Carpenter. What else do we know about her?'

'Not much. She lives in Hertfordshire. She was a teacher. She's got kids and grandkids from the look of it. Doesn't matter, she's got information, that's the important thing.'

It seems a bit cruel to relegate Anne Carpenter to the margins in this way, but Lindsay is used to Caroline now. She's so focused on this story that she just sees Anne as a necessary step on the way, and nothing more than that. She's useful, that's all.

'Where are you?' asks Lindsay.

'Taking a break on the drive from the Cardiff Comedy Festival, heading towards Coventry. I won't be back until really late Sunday night.'

'OK, I'll come over to yours on Monday, after I finish at Stonegrove.'

'Ermm... that's when I pick up the van for, you know, moving the stuff to the museum. I'll be loading it all on Monday afternoon to take over there on Tuesday.'

'Then I'll help you.'

'Well... I don't know. I might be better doing it on my own.'

Lindsay sighs. Caroline's not quite there yet.

'OK, let me know on Monday. I can be with you around five-thirty if you like. Or not, it's your call. But in the meantime ring me if you hear back from Anne.'

She leaves the storeroom, lifts the flap on the counter and goes through to the cafe, where she finds that Deirdre, Rufus and Sergiu have their heads together over what turns out to be, literally, the back of an envelope.

'Breakthrough!' she calls out.

'Here too,' says Sergiu. 'Compuccinno Blues!' he adds triumphantly.

There's a silence.

'That's dreadful,' says Lindsay.

Rufus looks a bit sheepish, so clearly the name was his idea.

'Look upon it as work in progress,' he says. 'I accept it might need a bit of tweaking.'

'Does anyone know first-aid?'
*'Oh don't be ridiculous Diana. Just get her out of
here and away from Stonegrove – now!'*
**Ruby and Diana Stanton at Stonegrove Hall,
the night of September 19th**

CHRISTCHURCH

Caroline has backed the hire van up as close as possible
to the front door, but it's still quite a walk each time to
go to and from the spare bedroom, and especially tricky
on the outward trip when she's carrying a loaded box.
In the end she'd bought a pack of fold down cardboard
boxes from a local furniture remover and they hold
a lot of stuff, but for safety's sake the bottoms need
taping and the width of them means she keeps bashing
her hands on door frames. She's already got sticking
plasters on a couple of fingers and a growing collection
of bruises along her knuckles. This hasn't turned out
to be the straightforward job she was hoping for, and
it's taking up much more time than she'd originally
thought.

It wasn't easy to get started. She put it off until
almost lunchtime and then had to give herself a good
talking or the van rental would have been completely
wasted. The first few boxes were particularly painful
and took ages, partly because Caroline had to keep
stopping to soak up the tears that were dripping off
her chin, but mostly because she couldn't let anything
go into a box without close examination, as if she were
trying to imprint every little detail on her mind. She

kept coming across things she'd almost forgotten about – jigsaws and boxed games that they'd played together as a family, each one of which had to be opened and the pieces handled before she could put the lids back on and consign them to a packing carton. Then she found an old shoe box containing doll's clothes, all of which had been hand made by her mother. It was a complete wardrobe for her favourite doll, and she remembered the excitement of opening the box one Christmas morning, and insisting on trying everything on the doll before any of them could have breakfast. Indulged in this as in so many other things, Caroline has never forgotten how it felt to be so loved. She hasn't felt that way for such a long time it makes her ache with sadness. She would ring her brother, but the house in Boston will be empty, Mike and Lori both at work and the kids in school. She has his mobile number but this doesn't feel like an emergency to Caroline, and it definitely won't to Mike.

And then there are all the photo albums – no good sending these off to a toy museum, so what does she do with them? It takes more than an hour, with a coffee and a multi-pack of chocolate bars, just to look through each page of each album. Caroline as a new-born baby, Caroline at her christening, taking her first steps – she's seen them all before of course but not for a long time and never on a day like this when her past is slowly loosening its grip on her present. In the end she puts them to one side in the living room, and decides they can go up in the loft next time she has to get up there for something. Then it's back to it.

The job gets easier as the day goes on and whereas the first box took a couple of hours to fill, she's becoming quicker and more efficient by the end of the afternoon. At around five o'clock she takes a break, looks around at the items still left to clear, and decides to stop being independent and send out a call for help. What started out as a very personal, emotionally draining exercise has now turned into nothing more than a job that needs an extra pair of hands, and she's wishing that she'd taken Lindsay up on her offer to help. But then she checks her watch and decides it's not too late.

As Caroline punches the digits into her phone Lindsay is just leaving Stonegrove and walking towards her car. It's been a busy day and she's looking forward to a quiet evening in. And then her phone rings.

'It'll only take an hour or so, with both of us on the job,' says Caroline, sensing Lindsay's reluctance. 'I can get some pizzas in for us later, save you cooking when you get home. It's such a fag doing all that just for one, isn't it?'

'How would you know? You never cook a meal for yourself, or anyone else as far as I can see.'

'Well, it stands to reason. The pizzas will be my treat,' she adds, 'as a thank you.'

There's a pause. 'Oh go on Lindsay, be a pal. You did offer...'

She's right, of course. And so there's not much Lindsay can do about it but point her car in the opposite direction to home, and head over to Caroline's place.

The driveway at the front of the bungalow is blocked by the hire van, and as she squeezes between this and the gate post Caroline emerges from her front door carrying a pink scooter.

'You took your time!' she calls out breezily.

Lindsay bristles at this.

'It's rush hour – you know, people heading home after work?'

'OK, OK, only joking. Do you need a drink of anything first?'

'Yes,' mutters Lindsay crossly, 'a very large, very cold Chablis would do it.'

Caroline has disappeared into the van so she misses this.

'Kettle's on as it happens,' she says with a cheery smile as she steps out again. 'Tea or coffee?'

Once they're both on the job it actually takes less than an hour to clear the room. The last remaining item is a large doll's house – more like a doll's mansion – and it's as well Lindsay's there because Caroline could never have managed it on her own. It's a wooden masterpiece, with two floors plus an attic, leaded light bay windows with miniature curtains, and a full complement of furniture inside. Above the front door hangs a tiny, handpainted sign. 'Villa Caro' it says.

'My Dad made it,' says Caroline, as they stand looking down at the doll's house in the spare bedroom, deciding how best to lift and then carry it out. 'Mum made the curtains and all the bed covers – look...' She opens the front and lifts a bed out from one of the first floor bedrooms, complete with a tiny hand-stitched patchwork cover.

Lindsay peers into the rooms. 'This is beautiful,' she says. 'Your mum and dad must have spent ages making all this stuff.'

'They bought some of the furniture, or at least put it together from kits. It's got electric light but there aren't any batteries in it now so I can't demonstrate.'

Lindsay's thinking that if she owned this wonderful doll's house there is no way she'd want to part with it.

'You don't have to get rid of everything...' she starts.

'Oh, I do. I've come this far and anyway, look how much room this takes up. No, it's got to go with all the rest.'

Now it's come to it Lindsay isn't quite so sure this is the right thing to do. What if Caroline regrets it later? She might not be able to get anything back.

'Don't you want to hang onto one or two little things though? Lots of people have stuff they've kept from their childhood.'

'Not for the reason I've kept mine. And how would I decide what to keep? I can't choose one special item, because... because it's all special to me.'

Caroline's voice cracks, and Lindsay pulls her into a hug. They stand for a moment like this, Caroline gulping a bit, hiccupping and trying not to cry, Lindsay wishing that she would because after all it can only help.

'OK. Let's get it over with,' says Caroline, pulling away and fishing out a tissue from her sleeve to blot her eyes.

The doll's house is heavy and cumbersome and once they've managed to get it out of the room they still have to keep stopping and putting it down, and every so often one of them loses her grip because there's nothing much to hold onto, but finally they make it out to the van. Lifting it inside is the next challenge but they're beginning to get the measure of it now and it only takes a couple of attempts before they manage it and close the doors.

'Thank goodness that's over,' says Caroline, 'I'm exhausted. Come on, I've got a bottle of wine in the fridge and a dial-a-pizza menu by the phone. What more could a girl want?'

Monday is obviously a popular night for avoiding cooking because the pizza place is really busy, so while they wait Caroline pours them each a large glass of wine. It's not Chablis, but it's not bad either, and anyway Lindsay has calmed down and isn't quite so fussy now.

'What will you do with the spare room now it's empty?'

'I've got a decorator coming first thing tomorrow morning to give me a quote, and then I'll get new carpet and curtains because they're the same ones that were here when I moved in, and frankly they're pretty revolting. I'm going to get some decent office furniture and move my computer and files and other stuff in there. Which reminds me...'

Caroline puts her glass down and disappears into her bedroom, where the computer currently lives.

'I sent that Anne a message and asked her to email me with anything she knows about Bella...' she calls back to Lindsay. 'Oh, nothing yet,' she adds after a few minutes.

But by the time they've finished off their pizzas and most of the bottle of wine, there is something.

Anne's email pings into Caroline's inbox and both their heads lift at the same time.

Caroline dashes into the bedroom to check. 'It's from her,' she says. Lindsay joins her and they read it together.

Bella and my mother were in ENSA together...

'What's ENSA?' asks Caroline.

Lindsay frowns. 'Not sure,' she says.

..first in London and then abroad, certainly France and North Africa and probably other places I've forgotten.

'Ah, I think it was entertainment for the troops. We can look it up.'

They joined as dancers in 1939, the very first days of ENSA. My mother left in 1944, married my father shortly afterwards and they set up house in north

London. I don't know if Bella was still in ENSA by then or if she'd already left. But I know she married a Canadian captain she'd met in France and after he was demobbed they lived in Montreal.

'Ha! No wonder she slipped off our radar, we've been looking in the wrong bloody country.'

Every few years she came back to the UK because she still had family here, and usually she visited my Mum too. That's how I met her, although I was only a child at the time. Mum often used to talk about her and the fun they had working with ENSA.

'C'mon Anne, what did she tell you?' mutters Caroline, impatiently.

Their son was a year older than me but I only saw him once. I can't remember what he was called, nor Bella's married name I'm afraid.

'Bugger.'

I've got some pictures of her and Mum in their stage costumes. I could send you copies if you like.

Anne's email ends, having thrown up another load of questions and none of the answers they want.

'She must have told her mum something. They were mates for years,' says Caroline.

'Ask her some specific questions. Or maybe go and see her, perhaps that would be better. If she thinks she might get onto a TV programme she'll be only too pleased to help.'

'Well,' says Caroline, 'I suppose we just moved a bit closer. Bella certainly had a colourful life, one way and another.'

'Maybe there's a way of checking the ENSA records, find out when she left?'

'Probably, but I'm not sure it would get us much further. You're right, I really need to have a chat with Anne Carpenter.'

'Well go easy on her,' says Lindsay, recalling the time Caroline 'had a chat' with Betty in the Shady Pines Care Home. 'She's all we've got and we don't want to upset her.'

Caroline rolls her eyes.

'Yeah yeah yeah, I'll tread carefully. I'll just send her a quick reply now and ask if I can call her tomorrow, before I head off again for a few days. Best to get her while she's hot. So, we may as well polish off the rest of that bottle of wine, don't you think?'

* * *

Lindsay's just finishing breakfast the next morning when her phone goes, and it's Helena.

'We were wondering if you could pop in and see us later this morning, if you're free that is. It won't take too long.'

She doesn't say any more, so it's all a bit mysterious. Lindsay wonders if they're having second thoughts about getting involved with the Bella story, especially now that things are starting to move – but then she remembers that Helena and Anthony don't even know the latest developments yet. Or maybe, she thinks, Diana has had a change of heart and spilt the beans. Worst case scenario, Nick has just added to the string of wives she still doesn't know anything about. Best case scenario, he's just added to the ex-wives.

Anyway Lindsay's free of course, so they fix a time to meet in the restaurant, not the Stables Tearoom as she would have expected. Eleven o'clock is much too early for the restaurant to have started serving lunch and they don't do coffee there as a rule, which would make it a more private meeting place than the Stables but also makes her feel slightly uneasy. It's clearly not a casual meeting if they've gone for privacy – and Lindsay can't imagine for one moment what they would need to say to her in private.

She hasn't been inside the restaurant since the day of the lunch with Caroline, and as she pushes the door open she sees Helena and Anthony at the back of the room. Anthony stands up and Helena waves at her. It doesn't look as if they're just about to tell her Nick has met with a ghastly accident, or acquired yet another wife, nor that they're going to ask her to leave if she persists in chasing Bella and her story, so she sends them back a cheery smile and starts to feel more positive.

Anthony steps forward and takes her arm, guiding her to the seat next to Helena.

'Bang on time as always, just as we expected. Coffee?'

They've already got a large cafetière on the table, and a plateful of fancy biscuits – presumably supplied by the tearoom since this is not the usual fare of the restaurant. Anthony pours the coffee and they spend a few minutes in jolly small talk before Helena pitches in.

'We've come up against a bit of a problem,' she starts. 'And we think you might be just the person to help us with it. If you want to, of course.'

'*Whatever are we going to tell the parents?*'

'*We'll blame it on Bella. We'll say she got the shotgun from the tack room, and then Douglas was upset and stormed off. After tonight she certainly won't be coming back here to tell them anything different.*'

'*But where is Douglas?*'

'*How should I know Diana? Just remember, when they ask what happened we say Bella was to blame. It was all her fault, do you understand? Bella fired the gun.*'

**Ruby and Diana Stanton,
the night of September 19th 1936**

YOGA

When Lindsay gets to yoga on Friday morning there's a reception committee waiting for her and a cheer goes up as she comes through the door.

'Rufus told you!' she says, laughing.

'We're just so pleased for you,' says Deirdre. 'You really deserve this.'

'Let's give it a few minutes just to make sure there are no new arrivals this morning,' says Janey, 'and if not we decided we'd cut the class short by fifteen minutes and then go down to Sergiu. Are you OK with that?'

Lindsay certainly hadn't expected this, in fact she's completely overwhelmed by all the attention she's getting.

'And then you can tell us the whole story,' says Deirdre.

When they crowd into Cappuccino Blues later Gary is already there and Sergiu is in the process of opening a bottle of Prosecco.

'Congratulations lovely lady!' says Sergiu. 'I should have been quicker, now is too late for me.'

Lindsay can't imagine what he's talking about.

'Soon I go home to Romania for one week, my cousin she gets married. But I try to think how I can go and not close my café... and I think of you.'

'Just like buses,' says Rufus. 'You wait for a job offer for months and then two come along together.'

Sergiu passes the glasses of Prosecco around. 'So now I can't have you in café I think I must close. Is only one week.'

Rufus and Gary exchange a look.

'Actually we've been thinking about that,' Gary says quietly to Sergiu. 'Talk to you later.'

But this is Lindsay's moment, and they're determined to keep her centre stage.

'So how did this come about?' asks Janey.

'Beverley, the Croft's office angel, is leaving. Her husband's being transferred to Birmingham with his work, and they asked me if I'd like to take her job on.'

It sounds unexciting when just the bare facts are presented, but at the time it was such a thrilling moment that Lindsay could hardly speak.

'Me?' she'd squeaked. 'But how could I... Beverley knows everything there is to know about Stonegrove...'

'And so will you after a while,' said Anthony. 'Look, we'll never find anyone who can hit the ground running, but you're about as close as it gets. Besides, we know you'll do a great job.'

Lindsay can hardly believe her luck. 'I'd like to keep one of my days in the Theatre Room if possible...' she says.

'Yes, we thought you'd say that,' Helena said with a smile, 'but we think you could probably fit in almost the same hours as Beverley, just spread out differently across the week, and still keep a volunteering day.'

Every time she tells the story, it sounds a little more real to Lindsay.

'So, I'm going to do three full days and a half day in the office, plus Mondays as a volunteer. The good news is that I should still be able to make it to yoga on a Friday.'

As she says this she looks across at Rufus and Gary, because there's something she needs to talk to them about. Rufus gets there first.

'We'll soon find someone else for Wednesdays,' he says. 'Don't even give that a second thought.'

'I'm good for the next four weeks anyway,' she says. 'Beverley goes in six weeks time, and we're doing a two week handover.'

Lindsay can't quite believe she's back in the world of work, and in such a wonderful place, which she's grown to love. True, the money's not great, nowhere near as much as she'd been earning before, but it's enough for her now that her lifestyle has adapted to living on benefits – and Anthony had hinted at a raise in pay once she's served her probationary period.

'Does Caroline know?' asks Gary, who has of course never met Caroline but heard a good deal about her and knows everything there is to know about their Bella partnership.

'Not yet. She's been on tour this week, back tonight.'

'I was just thinking that once you're working this will clip your wings a bit in terms of other activities, such as, er... searching for mystery women...'

'You know what, I think this whole Bella thing is starting to take on a life of its own since Caroline put it out on Facebook,' says Lindsay. 'We've had one positive sighting already. But I somehow doubt we'll ever know the whole story.'

Sergiu comes out with a tray of cheese straws, and lays a hand on Gary's shoulder.

'Maybe, as is special day, you can have one,' he says, sternly.

'He's stricter with you than I am,' Rufus says, adding 'don't get carried away by this.'

'I won't, I promise.'

'I was talking to Sergiu, actually.'

After a while the group starts to break up and head off home until there's just Lindsay, Gary and Rufus left.

'Sergiu, we've been thinking,' says Rufus. 'While you're away Gary and I could take over the café. If you want us to, that is.'

'We'd need a bit of tuition, I've no idea how that Gaggia machine works...'

Sergiu claps his hands together and comes out with a stream of Romanian. None of them have a clue what he's saying but it must be good because he's got a huge smile on his face and he enfolds each of them in turn in a bear hug.

'You are very good friends to me,' he says, 'and I trust you to take care of Cappuccino Blues. Maybe I take ten days holiday instead of week? Yes?'

'Well, yes I suppose so,' says Gary. 'Once we're up and running what's a few more days?'

'But you must take it softly, Gary. Let Rufus do everything on the feet. You sit down at counter, take money, talk to customers.'

Lindsay chips in. 'I could probably help on Saturdays.'

'No you won't, you'll have more than enough to do as it is. We'll look after the café. At least, Rufus will,' says Gary. 'I'll encourage him from my seat behind the counter.'

'Yes, I can see this is going to be loads of fun,' says Rufus.

***

Caroline gets home at about two thirty in the morning. It's been a challenging few days out on tour, followed by a long drive home from her last gig in Essex that found her caught up in the tail-back from an accident. Eventually, she's massively relieved to be pulling onto her drive, and for once can't be bothered to put the car in the garage.

The house feels chilly, even though the last few days have been sunny and warm. Without consciously heading in that direction, Caroline does what she usually does when she comes home, she goes straight to the spare bedroom.

She flicks the light switch and her heart gives a little lurch as she sees the empty room, even though she already knows what to expect and she's been faced with the emptiness before. She's quite proud of herself for getting rid of everything, but over many years she's become used to the comforting sight of all her old toys, and now she misses them. No teddies to pick up and hug, no baby doll's dresses to straighten. Maybe Lindsay was right, she should have kept something back.

She sighs, and switches the light off again. Once the decorator's been, she thinks, and I've smartened the room up and got my computer in there, then it'll be OK.

But it's late, she's tired, her spirits are low, and in spite of her brave face she finds herself starting to well up.

Last week's Cardiff Comedy Festival wasn't her finest hour. In spite of being billed as a headliner, she didn't get large crowds in to her gigs. There were plenty of people milling around the festival but it seemed the people they were queuing up to hear were the new kids on the block. Caroline struggled to perform to her usual standard, and fell short of her own expectations. Basically, faced with the decline in her audiences and the growing realisation that she's yesterday's woman, it was hard to be funny.

With her confidence knocked slightly askew by Cardiff, she'd been looking to the last few days out on tour to build it back up. But although she got a good house in Coventry the last two venues were nowhere near full and it was hard to ignore the gaps in the front few rows – especially those where people didn't come back after the interval.

On the long drive home from Essex she tried to think what to do next. She knows she's not the first comedian to find themselves in this position and Caroline did a quick assessment of how other people got over it. In every case she can think of they re-invented themselves into a different kind of entertainer (well, except for the ones who got so depressed they topped themselves, she thought. Caroline's not up for that.) She could try to get on the after-dinner speaker list, even though it's notoriously difficult to break into by all accounts. She could tell Polly to have another go at *Strictly* or one of the other many reality shows on the go, but her recent experience with '*Touching My Roots*' has put her off that kind of thing. She could have another crack at sitcom, but Miranda Hart and others have set that particular bar very high and all the signs are that TV companies have had their day with celebrity shows like that.

No, the most obvious solution for Caroline is to keep on the track of the Bella story, especially since she's already invested quite a lot of time in this. And that's another reason why she was dissatisfied with Cardiff and the gigs since. All the material she was working with was old, she hadn't written any new routines, thanks to this obsession with the past and the television programme she hopes will finally emerge.

The trouble is, it's not emerging. She followed up Anne Carpenter's message, but it didn't get her any further. The photos Anne had promised to send have arrived, judging from the look of the envelope she's just picked up off her doormat. She turns the brown envelope over and opens it up. There are half a dozen photos in there, and a hand-written note from Anne to say that these are copies of the originals, so Caroline can keep them. In spite of a vague hope that some nugget of information would suddenly have flashed into Anne's memory, there's nothing else to go on. The pictures show chorus girls in various different costumes, with a multitude of feathers and sequins, and she has to look carefully to pick Bella out of the line-ups. There's one close-up photo of two of them, Bella and presumably Anne's mother, looking glamorous in typically 1940s style, with their wide-shouldered frocks, waved hair and bright lipstick.

They're interesting and they help to flesh out the story – but with no ending, and no answers to the lingering questions about what happened that night in the conservatory at Stonegrove, the programme Caroline envisages falls flat on its face.

She sighs, pushes the photos back in the envelope and abandons them on the hall table. And then she puts out the lights and heads towards her bedroom.

In the corner her computer screen flashes at her. In her hurry to get on the road a week ago she forgot to turn it off and now as she moves the mouse the screen springs into life. There are a string of emails that will need to be dealt with in the morning. And there's one that catches her eye, which just might need dealing with now. Someone, a name she doesn't recognise, has messaged her on Facebook.

She's dog-tired and longing for her bed, but she knows it will just niggle and keep her awake if she doesn't take a look at this one now. The message, when she gets it up on screen, sends a little shock wave pinging through her body.

I think I can help you with your research into Mabel Coombs, it says. I'm her grandson.

'They're all completely mad down there. Last night those awful sisters provoked a huge row and then Douglas went quite potty and charged off with Ruby chasing after him. The next thing I knew a bullet came crashing through the conservatory window. I got a cut on my arm from flying glass.'

'But didn't the parents come down to see what was going on?'

'It's a huge house Joyce, and they'd have been asleep for hours by then. They probably didn't hear a thing. I think all the servants had gone to bed too, I didn't see any of them around when it all broke out. Douglas got panicked by what he'd done, jumped on his motorbike and roared off into the night, and Ruby and Diana started shouting at me as if it was all my fault.'

'Well, they've never liked you... what had been going on to set all this off?'

'Oh, nothing much, I was just trying to teach Ruby's fiancé to dance. Let's face it, she's such a lump she can't dance for toffees, far less teach him.'

'Mabel, you were flirting with him!'

'Perhaps I was, just a little, but it was only a bit of fun.'

'That's not how they saw it, obviously.'

'Anyway, the sisters told me to leave Stonegrove at once, so I got my bag and the fiancé drove me to the local station. Then I sat there for a couple of hours until the milk train came through.'

'On your own? With a cut to your arm?'

'No, John stayed with me. He's the most sane out of all of them, can't think why he got involved with Ruby. The cut had stopped bleeding by then anyway.'

'Too much money, that's the trouble with posh people like that. We're better off without their money. At least we care about other people.'

Bella and her sister Joyce, September 20th 1936

CHRISTCHURCH

Lindsay waits until almost midday before she phones Caroline, knowing she'll have had a late night. But when she answers she sounds surprisingly chirpy, as if she's been up and about for hours.

'I've got some great news to tell you,' Lindsay says, and Caroline can hear the smile in her voice.

'I've got some great news to tell you, too.'

'You go first.'

'No, you go first.'

'Oh, OK. Well. I've got a job! Helena and Anthony have offered me a real, paid, almost full-time job up at Stonegrove! Isn't that great?'

'It certainly is, well done, I'm really pleased for you. Why don't you come over and tell me all about it? Maybe we could go out to lunch – if you want to, that is?'

Lindsay immediately thinks about her finances. It's a long time since she's done things like lunching out and she's got to remember that she hasn't actually earned any money yet.

'Erm, I'm not...'

'I'll pay,' says Caroline, jumping in as soon as she realises. 'My treat.'

'In that case I'd... oh, what was your great news?'

Caroline pauses for a few seconds. Her routines might be a bit creaky but there's nothing wrong with her timing.

'I was talking to Bella's grandson this morning,' she says.

***

It's almost one o'clock when Lindsay arrives in Christchurch. Caroline's all ready to go when she opens the door, looking bright and smiley and in a thoroughly good mood.

'There's a new Italian restaurant in town,' she says, before Lindsay can a get a word in edgeways. 'Let's go there.' And she grabs Lindsay's arm and wheels her off in the direction of the town centre.

On the way Caroline makes Lindsay tell her all about the job at Stonegrove, even though Lindsay would much rather be hearing what Bella's grandson had to say. But Caroline made it clear at the start that the grandson conversation will keep until they've got a glass of Prosecco in front of them and a plateful of pasta on the way, and she refuses to be drawn any further.

'You'll love it, Lin, this job is just perfect for you. Plus you'll be able to see more of Nick.'

'Will I? How do you work that one out?'

'He's often hanging around Stonegrove, isn't he? You'll be able to have cosy chats in the tearoom over a lunchtime sandwich.'

'I don't think he's the least bit interested in having cosy chats, or indeed anything else, with me,' says Lindsay. 'More's the pity.'

'That's not how it looked to me,' says Caroline. 'And you like him, don't you?'

Lindsay considers this. Yes, she does like him. He's a very attractive man and it's not as if she's got anybody else beating a path to her door, nobody else to stand in the way – at least not on her side of the equation.

'I do like him. I'm not sure if he can manage a proper, grown up relationship though.'

'What makes you say that? He seemed perfectly normal to me.'

'I think he's normal enough. He just doesn't have a very good track record with women, that's all.'

And she repeats Anthony's comment about the ex-wives and girlfriends club.

'He was probably joking,' says Caroline.

'Maybe, I can't always tell with Anthony.'

'We could find out,' says Caroline, 'we're good at finding things out.'

'Don't you dare put it on Facebook,' says Lindsay, 'I'll kill you.'

Caroline laughs. 'No, not Facebook. But what about the Records Office? Marriage certificates? Divorce papers?'

'I would feel pretty sneaky, doing that.'

'Then you'll just have to ask him, won't you?'

Caroline yanks the restaurant door open, and breezes in. Lindsay, trailing behind in her wake, catches hold of the door as it bounces back and wonders if she could live with feeling sneaky in such a good cause.

The menus arrive. The Prosecco arrives.

'Well? Time's up. It's your turn now.'

Caroline picks up her glass. 'Cheers,' she says, and takes a sip.

'Come on, Caroline, I've played the game your way. Now just tell me before I have to resort to violence and stab you with this fork.'

'He messaged me on Facebook. I messaged him back. He said he'd call this morning, and he did.'

'Is Bella still alive?'

Caroline puts her glass down and sighs, because she knows Lindsay doesn't want to hear this. 'No, she died a couple of years ago, when she was ninety-five. But it sounds as if she'd had a happy and full life – she married the Canadian that Anne told us about, and after the war she went to live in Montreal, so she was right about that too. They only had the one son, and he died about twelve years ago.'

'Before her, how sad. Must be awful to have to attend your own child's funeral.'

'As it must have been for the Stanton parents when Douglas died.'

'That's an unfortunate parallel,' says Lindsay. 'Just about the only thing her life and theirs had in common.'

They're both quiet, absorbing this thought. Then their pasta arrives, and there's a pause while they go through the process of having the Parmesan sprinkled on and the pepper ground over their plates before the waiter leaves them alone again.

'And the husband?'

'Also dead, but only last year, he outlived Bella.'

Caroline tucks into her pasta with enthusiasm but Lindsay puts her fork down quietly and leans back in her chair. Caroline looks up at her.

'What's wrong?'

'I was just thinking about the day Douglas took that photo of Bella and how everything was ahead of them and they had no idea then of what was going to happen.'

Caroline shrugs. 'Same for all of us, Lin. Nobody knows what life's going to throw at them. I certainly didn't.'

Lindsay sighs. 'Yes, you're right of course, sorry that was insensitive of me. It's just that I've got a bit hung up on young Bella, never thinking really about what the years might bring her as she got older. I never even pictured her as an old lady, probably because until recently we didn't think she'd made it into old age.'

Caroline reaches across the table and takes Lindsay's hand.

'Look, what we're doing here is putting one life, and not an especially unusual one given the times she lived through, under the spotlight. Biographers do it all the time to famous and important people, but we're doing it for the common man – or at least woman, in this case. And I think there's something rather special about that, and maybe also something to be proud of. Everyone has a story to tell, and we're going to tell hers.'

Caroline lets go of Lindsay's hand.

'Now eat your pasta before it gets cold, and drink your Prosecco before it gets warm.'

Lindsay nods. Caroline's right of course. It's a good thing they're doing, and if the television programme comes off, and if she gets it just right, ordinary people throughout the land with a story to tell will have found a champion. There are a lot of 'ifs' there, but who knows what other tales might come to light, given the chance.

'What else did he tell you?'

'Nothing.' Caroline picks up her glass again and takes a mouthful of Prosecco. 'We'll find out tomorrow if he knows anything else. We're meeting him in London.'

* * *

After she leaves Caroline, Lindsay goes straight over to Stonegrove. The first person she runs into is Anthony. It's the end of the afternoon, and there are the usual loose ends to sort out before closing, but as always he's pleased to see her.

'Lindsay! How lovely that you dropped by, did you want to see Nick?' he asks, with a little twinkle in his eye.

'Not especially, well what I mean is, I was actually hoping to see you all. I've got some news on the Bella front.'

'Excellent! Well Helena and I are a bit tied up at present, but if you head up to the flat Nick's there and he can keep you company for an hour till we get back.'

Lindsay's a bit taken aback by this. She's never been up to the Crofts' apartment, and as far as she knows none of the other volunteers have either. Maybe Beverley has been invited up there, and maybe the imminent shift in Lindsay's status at Stonegrove is what's prompted this. She doesn't know, but it does make her feel slightly off-balance.

'Perhaps you'd better warn him... or I could meet him in the tearoom...'

'Nonsense, he'll be delighted to see you. Just go on up.'

She knows where the staircase is because of the cord across it with the 'Private' sign attached. Apparently there's a lift somewhere too, but up to now she hasn't come across that. She unhooks the cord and then follows the curving stairs until they come out halfway along a corridor that is substantially different to the one below, where the Theatre Room and the Douglas Memorial Room are. For a start there are no varnished floorboards up here, instead her feet sink into a thick-piled cream carpet that must worry the life out of Helena when the twins are visiting. The wallpaper is a geometric Art Deco print in turquoise and gold, and Lindsay can only guess at what it must have cost. Last year she put a couple of rolls of wallpaper from B&Q on her bedroom walls and was staggered at how much that set her back, and clearly this is in a different league completely. There are doors along the length of the corridor, in both directions and on both sides, so she starts on the left and tiptoes along – pointlessly since this is a carpet that deadens every footstep – listening for a sound from behind one of them.

She's about halfway along when the nearest door to her swings open suddenly and Nick comes striding out. They're both startled.

'Hello stranger,' he says, 'I didn't expect to see you here.'

'Anthony told me to come straight up, he and Helena will be here in about an hour, once they've done the closing up. Sorry to have taken you by surprise...'

'No need to apologise. I was just going to make a coffee, but now that you're here I might go completely mad and have a biscuit too.'

She follows Nick into the room opposite, which turns out to be a massive kitchen with startlingly white units, a black and white tiled floor and lots of chrome. In the centre of the room hangs a huge glass chandelier with opaque glass shades.

In spite of its opulence, the room doesn't feel at all sterile, rather it's just a posh version of most people's kitchens and clearly the hub of the flat. Underneath the chandelier is a white table and chairs, the table top cluttered with a discarded newspaper, somebody's reading glasses, opened letters stuffed back into their envelopes, a cereal packet and a couple of mugs with coffee dregs still in the bottom. Beyond the kitchen units, on the far side of the room, are two squishy black leather sofas with a sprinkling of books and magazines spread across them. Underneath the small television in the corner lies a cuddly pink bunny, an escapee from the overflowing plastic toy box nearby.

Nick fills the kettle and starts to organise sugar, milk and mugs. There's no sign of a clever espresso machine, just a couple of cafetières in different sizes. It all feels refreshingly normal, considering they're in such a grand house.

'You can carry the biscuits,' he says, handing her a tin of chocolate biscuits, which she recognises as being currently on sale in the Stonegrove shop. Then he holds the door open with his foot and off they go, back across the hallway. Since Lindsay is ahead of him she pushes the door open and steps inside first.

'Wow!'

It's certainly a beautiful room, and feels rather like walking onto the set of a Noel Coward play with its all-cream décor. It's actually two rooms connected by triple glass doors, but as these are opened right back it just seems as if it goes on forever. Lindsay's thinking that her entire flat would probably fit into this one area.

'You're allowed to go right in,' says Nick, because she has stopped just inside the doorway and is therefore blocking the way for him to get in.

'Oh, sorry, just a bit overwhelmed. This room is amazing.'

Nick puts the mugs down on a coffee table and moves his laptop aside so she can get the biscuit tin on there too.

'I could sit in the kitchen and do this but it always feels a bit gloomy in there to me. Something to do with the light.'

Lindsay walks across to the windows, which overlook the front of the house. The kitchen is probably above Douglas's room or the adjoining bathroom, on the back of the house, whereas this room overlooks the front.

'We must be over Ruby's bedroom,' she says. 'Fabulous views from up here.'

'I think the dining room is actually directly above her room,' he says, wandering past the glass doors into the other half of the room. 'I'd say the view is pretty much the same from here as from Ruby's room, wouldn't you?'

Lindsay edges up to Nick at the window, and looks out over the front drive. It's empty of visitors now, although Henry has sat down smack in the middle of the gravelled strip and is cleaning himself, one tabby leg delicately pointing skywards.

'So this is where Helena's grandparents lived? Such a strange arrangement, their children were all downstairs and they left them in favour of living up here.'

No wonder, she's thinking, that they didn't hear what had gone on in the conservatory – two floors up and on the opposite side of the house.

'And the attic rooms above us were where the servants lived I guess.'

'Yep, and it was fairly basic accommodation too. Look...' Nick leads her out into the corridor again. 'There's a staircase behind that door right at the end, and that takes you up to the attics. And there's another staircase at the opposite end of that corridor which goes down directly into the old kitchens. I imagine that was the usual route for the servants, unless specifically summoned to the Stanton's living quarters.'

Lindsay nods. 'It's another world, isn't it?' she says.

'Well it was, but if we went up there now you'd see it's just a string of rooms with paint peeling off the walls that are either completely empty or full of junk. Those boxes we stacked in Ruby's bedroom came from one of the attic rooms, and God knows what else is lurking there, apart from whole colonies of spiders. It's been a real job for Helena and Anthony just clearing the few rooms they have done so far.'

'Don't tell me they've done it all themselves?'

'Who else do you think? I've helped a bit when I've been down here but there aren't estate workers to call on any more, you know. If they want something like that done they have to get on and do it themselves. Their kids haven't been much use either, too busy sorting out their own lives.'

Lindsay would love to have a look up in the attic rooms but doesn't want to seem pushy. For now it's enough that she's been allowed onto the hallowed ground of the Croft's private accommodation.

Back in the sitting room they sit opposite each other on matching cream sofas. Lindsay is terrified she'll spill her coffee and doesn't dare have a biscuit in case she leaves any crumbs or, heaven forbid, a splinter of chocolate, on the cream carpet. Nick apparently has no such reservations, casually brushing crumbs from his lap.

'Congratulations on the job, by the way. I'm very pleased for you – and for them too, I think you'll do a great job.'

'Thanks, I think I'm still in shock actually. I've been unemployed for such a long time, and after a while with absolutely nothing on the horizon you do start to think that you'll never work again.'

Nick lifts his coffee cup to hers in salute. 'Cheers – sorry we haven't got anything stronger, maybe Anthony can be persuaded to break out the sherry when they get home.'

'I've got news.'

'Bella news?'

Lindsay nods. 'Better wait till Helena and Anthony get here, or I'll be saying the same thing twice over.'

'Now you're teasing me.'

Lindsay feels the start of a blush creep up her neck. 'Wouldn't dream of it,' she mutters.

'I'm glad to hear it.' Nick smiles and leans back, folding his arms. Exactly like Anthony, thinks Lindsay, no wonder Caroline was taken in.

'What are you working on?' Lindsay asks, indicating the laptop. It's the first thing she can think of to divert Nick's attention away from her.

'Some band arrangements,' he says, shifting the laptop back in front of him. 'Do you play anything?'

Lindsay shakes her head. 'Not any more. I played piano when I was a kid, and guitar for a bit as a teenager. I can read music, at least I could. How can you write it on a computer?'

'Well, I'll show you.'

And so when Helena and Anthony arrive twenty minutes later they find Lindsay and Nick sitting on the same sofa, with their heads together.

'Aha,' says Anthony, 'you two look very cosy.'

Helena flashes a warning look at him.

'How about we open a bottle of wine,' she says brightly, 'then we can all relax for a bit and you can tell us your news, Lindsay.'

* * *

'So what do we know about this grandson?' asks Anthony, as he settles down opposite Lindsay and Nick, glass of red wine in hand.

'Not much so far. His name's Matthew Gerritsen, he's a Canadian national working in London for a couple of years. He's an architect. And he's her only grandchild. That's it really.'

Lindsay picks up her glass and sips. 'His father was Bella's son, and he died about twelve years ago. Bella made it to ninety-five and her husband survived her by almost a year.'

'And you're going with Caroline to meet this Matthew?'

'Tomorrow morning, yes.'

'Good. Wouldn't want you doing this on your own, we don't know yet if he's genuine.'

'You've got a very suspicious mind, Anthony,' says Nick.

'I must admit it hadn't occurred to me that he might not be the real thing,' Lindsay says. 'Why would someone claim to be somebody they're not in this situation?'

Anthony shrugs. 'He might think there's money to be made from it, you never know. I'm sure it's all completely above board, I would just like you to be cautious, that's all I'm saying.'

'He's bringing photos with him, apparently his mother has sent a load of them to his iPad so if old Bella looks anything like young Bella then I guess he's genuine.'

Helena leaves temporarily to fetch dishes of nibbles from the kitchen, and picks up the biscuit tin from the table as she goes.

'Did you complete your quality control on the chocolate shortbread?' she asks Nick.

'Not quite,' he says. 'But I think it's safe to keep that line on sale for the time being.'

'So what are you hoping to get from this meeting with Matthew Gerritsen?' Anthony asks.

Lindsay has a feeling he's putting her through her paces, making sure she has an agenda and will be in control of the meeting. Lindsay knows this is ridiculous. Caroline will be in control and working from her own agenda.

'We don't yet know what he knows. Maybe Bella left diaries, which would be handy, or letters. At the very least he'll be be able to give us an insight into what sort of person she was.'

'This really is going to happen, isn't it?' Helena asks as she breezes back in, places some dishes on the table and sits down alongside Anthony. 'Caroline's programme I mean.'

Lindsay nods. 'As long as the TV company want to go ahead, and she's been talking to them already about it. It's all looking good in principle.'

'I must admit I didn't think it would get this far. You two have been very tenacious,' says Nick. 'All credit to you both.'

'Caroline's career is on the line with this. She's desperate to break out of stand-up and into something new, and this looks like being her best bet. She's determined to make it happen.'

'Then we must hope she does,' says Anthony. 'For us it can only be a good thing.'

'But not for Diana,' adds Nick.

Helena sighs. 'No, not for her. But she doesn't have to know too much about it, and she doesn't have to see it when it eventually makes the screen. I could engineer that.'

'She hasn't said any more then?' says Lindsay.

'No, I did have another go but she was completely tight-lipped. And I can't push her too far, we've had the doctor out to her twice in the last couple of weeks as it is.'

They all know it takes many months to make a television programme happen, and at ninety-four time is not on Diana's side. Helena says what nobody else can.

'Realistically, she might not be around by the time the programme's made anyway. And when she goes, whatever it is that she knows will go with her.'

'Why is John to blame? I thought it was all Bella's fault...'

'Yes, of course it was at the start, but you saw the way he was egging her on last night. In the end he was as much to blame as her. She was out to make both me and Douglas jealous by behaving like that and John was too stupid to see what was happening. And now Douglas is dead and poor Mother is beside herself with grief and it's all because Bella set off this chain of events and drove him to go off like that.'

'Oh Ruby, everything's beastly. Whatever can we do?'

'Do? We can't do anything. It's too late now to help Douglas and telling the parents the truth about what happened didn't do any good at all. You heard Mother – nobody's to know anything of it, they don't want the slightest hint of a scandal or for Douglas's name to be tarnished in any way. All they want is to keep his reputation safe, they're not interested in the rest. And we made them a promise, remember? Nothing untoward happened last night.'

'But the police might want to ask us and then what will we say?'

'Diana – nothing happened. That's all we have to say. Anyway they won't ask us, Father will make sure of that.'

'It's as if the parents are pretending it's all over – Mother won't speak to anyone, Father hasn't come out of his study since the police were here first thing this morning... but it's not over is it?'

'I've written to him.'

'Father?'

'*Don't be an idiot, Diana. I've written to John. I don't think I could ever forgive him. I've told him it's all over between us and I never want to see him again.*'

'*Oh, I see. Ruby?*'

'*What?*'

'*Do you think John saw that it was you with the gun?*'

Ruby and Diana Stanton, September 20th, 1936

LONDON

Their train leaves Christchurch a little late, and because they don't have to make any changes they settle down for the couple of hours it will take to get to Waterloo. Caroline has brought chocolate, naturally. Lindsay has brought fruit and water.

The meeting place – Caroline's choice – is a newly converted gastro-pub a few minutes walk from the station. The last time Caroline was there it was called the Horse and Groom and it was a typical Victorian London pub, but now it's had a makeover and the name has been changed to the Old Grey Horse, although neither of them notice this on their way in. Caroline stops in the doorway and looks around at the unfamiliar interior.

'They've shaken this old place up a bit,' she says, wandering into the main bar area. 'I think I preferred it the way it was.'

But then she picks up a menu and gets more enthusiastic, telling Lindsay that if it's going well they could all have lunch together there. Lindsay's hoping Caroline will be paying for that, after all it's her programme that's at stake.

They'd planned to arrive well before the agreed meeting time, thinking that they might need a chance to calm down and prepare themselves, but their train was late coming in and so they've ended up getting there almost exactly on time. They practically jogged from the station and so a breathless last-minute entrance, the one thing they'd been hoping to avoid, is now exactly what they've got. Caroline is twitchy because she wants to be the one running this scene, not the other way around.

'I'll get in some drinks,' she says, heading off towards the bar.

Lindsay makes herself comfortable at an empty table and looks up to see Caroline paying for their drinks. There's a man seated at the bar, and he's looking at Caroline intently, although she doesn't appear to have noticed him.

'You're Caroline van Dell, aren't you?' the man asks, causing Caroline to turn sharply in his direction.

'Yes! How lovely to meet you! We're just over there, please come and join us – I see you've already got yourself a drink,' she says, and they walk together between the tables to where Lindsay is sitting.

'This is very exciting for us,' says Lindsay, extending her hand.

'Really? Well it's exciting for me too,' he replies, with a twinkly smile. 'An absolute pleasure.'

Caroline smiles at him and Lindsay pauses for a second before tugging at her arm.

'Erm, could I have a quick word, Caroline?'

Caroline turns and looks at her as if she's gone completely mad.

Lindsay lowers her voice and leans in towards her. 'He's got...'

She's interrupted by a ping from Caroline's phone as a text comes in, and she tuts a bit then pulls it from her bag.

'Sorry,' she says, 'I'll just make sure this isn't important.'

She reads the text and her mouth freezes into a tight little smile, then she snaps the cover back on the phone, puts it on the table and turns to face Lindsay.

'… a London accent,' Lindsay finishes, lamely. They both turn to look at their companion, who flashes them an engaging smile.

'Is there another pub near here with the same name?' Caroline asks him.

'This is the only Old Grey Horse. But there's a Horse and Groom in the next road,' he says. 'It used to be The King's Head but then they…'

'… did it up. Yes, I see.'

Caroline reaches behind her for her jacket.

'We're in the wrong pub,' she says to Lindsay. 'With the wrong man,' she adds.

They all stand up and then Lindsay feels a bit awkward although Caroline doesn't seem the least bit fazed by the way things have worked out.

'Very nice to have met you,' she says, shaking the stranger's hand. 'Enjoy the rest of your day.'

And then they walk away with as much dignity as they can muster, and the man watches them go, a huge smile breaking out on his face.

Once they get outside Lindsay can't hold her laughter in any longer. Caroline doesn't join in.

'Disaster,' she says, striding ahead so that Lindsay has to rush to catch up with her. 'Complete disaster, and we haven't even got started yet.'

'Oh come on Caroline, it's not that bad. Look on the bright side – you're a comedian, you must be able to make something out of a situation like this. You could start it off with "a man walks into a pub"…'

'Yes, well thank you for that, I'd never have come up with such a sizzling opener by myself.'

It seems that Caroline's sense of humour has deserted her, but then as they scuttle off in search of the Horse and Groom she suddenly bursts out laughing.

By the time they push open the door to the pub they're struggling to stop. It's not quite the business-like entrance they'd had in mind and they haven't even made it to the bar when a man, this time one with a Canadian accent, steps forward to greet them.

'You must be Caroline and Lindsay,' he says. 'I'm Matt, it's very good to meet you.'

'Sorry about the mix-up with the pubs,' says Caroline, but Matt doesn't seem too bothered.

'I got us a bottle of wine,' he says, and gestures to a cosy table in the corner where they settle down. Matt pours them both wine and indicates his own almost-empty glass.

'Dutch courage,' he says. 'I've been feeling a tiny bit nervous about meeting you, to be honest, I've never been interviewed by a television film-maker before. So I didn't want to be late, and then I ended up getting here much too early. It's something I've inherited from my Mom. That, and talking too much when I'm anxious...'

An admission like that to two complete strangers is quite endearing and Lindsay warms to Matt immediately. He looks very much like Bella, same high cheekbones, same smile. Dark auburn hair, which could have come from either side, thinks Lindsay.

'You're so much like your grandma,' she says, and she can't quite believe that they've actually connected with Bella's family and it's her flesh and blood sitting next to them.

'Yeah, my Dad was the image of her and I've taken after him. Seems my Mom didn't get her fair share where looks were concerned.'

'Did you get your mother's hair colour?'

'No, this was Grandma's too.'

'Our photos are all black and white so we didn't know that.'

Caroline brings a folder out of her bag. In it are all the photos from Anne, plus the one taken in Iris's back garden and the original Stonegrove picture. Matt has seen some of the ENSA photos before, but not the earlier ones.

'This is what started the whole thing off,' says Lindsay, picking up the girl in the garden photo. 'I work as a volunteer at the house where this picture first came to light. Nobody knew who she was, except that on the back of the photo she'd signed it *'Love Bella'*. And I started wondering about her.'

They've brought with them the Visitor Guide to Stonegrove, and Lindsay is able to point out the side of the house where the dining room windows are. Matt peers closely at the brochure, and then compares the view to the picture of Bella. He's clearly impressed by the house, and surprised that his grandma was once a part of life there.

'She never mentioned this to me,' he says. 'Did she live there? Or was she on the staff?'

'Neither, but it seems she was a frequent visitor.'

'Well frankly I'm amazed. She and I talked a lot about everything and you'd think this would be something quite important in her life, but it certainly never came up.'

'That's a shame because we were hoping you might be able to shed some light on what went on at Stonegrove,' says Lindsay, catching Caroline's eye.

'You see there's a bit of a mystery and a few unanswered questions there,' says Caroline, 'and pretty well all the people around at that time are dead now so there's nobody else to ask. Did Bella keep any diaries or letters? There may have been things that she wrote down at the time but didn't want to discuss with anybody afterwards.'

Matt shakes his head slowly. 'I don't know of any diaries and I've never seen any letters. There are a couple of boxes of her stuff still in my attic at home but probably nothing of any significance, I did go through them after she died but I don't remember seeing any paperwork in there. I wish I could be more help – how would you even start to unravel an eighty-year-old mystery?' says Matt.

'With a lot of difficulty, and a fair bit of luck,' says Caroline.

'Facebook was the real breakthrough,' says Lindsay. 'But right from the start there was no way we were going to let Bella go without a fight.'

'So, tell me what you do know about this mystery. And how you got involved, Caroline.'

It takes a while to explain how they reached this point, and once they get to the stage where the bottle of wine is empty someone suggests lunch and they gather up all the photos and other bits and move into the dining area.

'You know, Grandma was a pretty down to earth lady, it doesn't sound as if she would have fitted in very well with the folks there,' Matt observes while they wait for their lunch to arrive.

'Probably not,' says Caroline. 'They were a strange crowd from what we can make out, but they had impressive connections. Some very famous people were visitors at Stonegrove,' she adds, and reels off a few of the names they found.

'She certainly never said anything about meeting people like that.'

'We don't think she did meet them. She was never formally entertained there so their paths probably didn't cross.'

Something is niggling at Lindsay.

'Did Bella ever mention an artist called John Cecil Fellowes?'

Matt leans back in his chair and nods his head slowly.

'I believe so, she certainly spoke about a painter and I'm pretty sure that was his name. I didn't think much about it at the time, but she did say she'd known him briefly before the war. Is he significant to the story?'

'He was a regular visitor to Stonegrove during the period she was also there. He was engaged to one of the Stanton girls.'

'How did his name come up?' Caroline asks.

Matt runs a hand through his hair and they can see him calling back to mind the occasion.

'We'd gone to an auction in Montreal, it was for some charity or other, the sort of thing Grandma enjoyed doing at weekends. It amused her to see what people were getting rid of – she used to say most of it wasn't good enough for a flea-market and people were just desperate to get the stuff out of their cellars. Anyway on this occasion there were some pictures being auctioned, and when this particular one came up she was quite shocked and told me she'd once known him and never expected to see one of his paintings in a sale like that. It was the one and only time she ever bought anything from an auction. I think she paid over the odds for it actually, but she was determined it was going home with her.'

Lindsay nods her head. 'I have a hunch about him,' she says. 'I think he played a bigger part in this story than we've given him credit for up to now.'

'Really? His paintings were pretty drab,' Caroline observes.

'Well yeah, if they were all like Grandma's, it was a fairly colourless landscape – she told me the name of the place but I can't recall it now.'

'What happened to it?'

'I don't know, maybe my mother still has it. I'll find out.'

The food arrives, and the conversation moves on. Matt shows them photos of Bella on his iPad, including the last one taken of her shortly before she died. Lindsay looks at it and gets all teary. He promises to send them on to Caroline.

'Bella had three sisters,' says Lindsay. Do you have any idea what happened to them, or their children? I believe she was the youngest.'

Matt nods. 'I know of them though I can't remember their names offhand. I think two of them had children and for all I know they also had children, so they would be my generation – second cousins, isn't that right? But I don't think any of them ever came over to Canada, and as far as I know nobody has had any contact with them since Grandma died.'

'Somebody might just come forward after seeing the programme,' Lindsay says.

'Would you come on the programme?' Caroline asks Matt, adding, 'not that we've reached that point yet, but when we get there, would you?'

Matt seems immensely flattered.

'Sure, if you think I can contribute anything worthwhile. And in the meantime if I come up with anything else to help you... I'll ask my Mom what she knows. It's really a pity Dad or my Grandad aren't alive, they would have had much more to offer than me.'

They assure Matt he's been very helpful, but in truth the meeting has been a disappointment because they haven't learned much they didn't already know. He was their big breakthrough, and for all that they are no further forward. Matt will be going home with far more to think about than they will.

On the journey back to Christchurch their spirits are very much lower than when they set off that same morning, full of anticipation and excitement. They sit opposite each other, with little to say. Caroline dozes a bit. Lindsay watches the landscape go by, and doesn't really see any of it as she turns things over in her mind.

They're just approaching Southampton when Lindsay leans forward and taps Caroline on the arm, waking her up. She yawns and runs both hands through her hair, making it stand up in peaks.

'Where are we?'

'About forty minutes away. Listen Caroline, I think we've missed a trick along the way.'

Caroline yawns and blinks a few times. 'Go on.'

'Well we've checked out the Stantons as far as we can, given that Diana knows the answer but hasn't been any help whatsoever. So mostly we've concentrated all our efforts on Bella, and because of that we haven't really tried to follow up on the only other person who we can be certain was there that night.'

'Fellowes.'

'Exactly.'

'But he died four days later, we do know that much.'

'In those four days he might have talked to someone, he might have written something in a letter, or in a diary – he was the younger son, so he must have had at least one sibling. And they may have had children. And they...'

'... may have something relevant.'

Caroline sighs. The fight has gone out of her.

'I don't know Lin. I wonder if we've gone as far as we can. Maybe we just have to settle for not knowing. Maybe we're not meant to find out what happened. We set out to find Bella, and we have. Maybe it's enough.'

But Lindsay's not ready to give up that easily.

'No, come on Caroline. They were a high profile family, there may even be another artist or two in the fold. We could go back to the Royal Academy and see if they know anything.'

Caroline shakes her head.

'Another dead end,' she says.

'OK, how about this? There must have been an inquest on Fellowes, if we can find out where coroners records are stored...'

But it's no good, because Caroline's given up on taking that line of enquiry any further. By the time the train pulls in to Christchurch station it's no longer up for discussion and Lindsay can tell that she's on her own from here on.

'Mr Farrow, please tell us in your own words what happened on the morning of Wednesday September the twenty-third. How did the incident occur?'

'I pulled away from the bus stop at the far end of Angmering Road, and then picked up speed as I drove out into the traffic lane. And then suddenly, I don't rightly know, a man came from nowhere and walked straight in front of me. There wasn't time to avoid him I … I'm sorry... I can't...'

'Please take your time Mr Farrow. I know how difficult this is for you but I do need to ask you this. Did the deceased look up at you in your cab?'

'No... no I'm sure he didn't, he was just looking straight ahead. I braked as hard as I could, I heard the passengers shout out and some of their bags and parcels went flying. I saw him for a split second before he disappeared under the bus. I had the impression he was holding something in his hand, a piece of paper I think. There was nothing I could do, you see...'

'Nobody blames you in the least, Mr Farrow. This was an unfortunate accident that could not have been prevented, or foreseen. I thank you for giving your evidence in such a clear manner .You're free to stand down, and this inquest will now take evidence from Miss Rose Potter.'

* * *

'Miss Potter, please tell us what you saw in Angmering Road on the morning of September the twenty-third.'

'I was on my way to work, I was a bit late that morning and I saw that I'd just missed my bus – I usually pick it up at the end of Angmering Road. So *there was no point in running any more, I slowed down and walked in the direction of the bus stop to wait for the next bus. And suddenly this man rushed down the front steps of number sixteen, leaving the door wide open for anyone to walk in, and brushed past me because I was right at his gate at that moment. And he just kept on walking, almost a run, as if he needed to get somewhere or do something really quickly. He carried on across the pavement and out into the road without looking to see if there was anything coming. I shouted out to him but he mustn't have heard me because he never even turned his head, he just kept heading across the road. It all happened so fast... the bus driver sounded his horn but he couldn't possibly have missed him.'*

'And did you see anything in the man's hand?'

'Oh yes, he had a letter in his hand. He was looking at it as he came down the front steps.'

'How did you know it was a letter and not just a shop receipt or some other piece of paper?'

'I'd just passed the postman further down the road. And the man dropped the envelope as he went past me, but he held onto the letter. I picked the envelope up and it had his name and address on it, handwritten. There were two or three taxi cabs parked opposite and the drivers got out when the accident happened and rushed forward, and then a policeman arrived so I gave the envelope to him.'

'Quite so, we have the envelope here, addressed to Mr John Cecil Fellowes, sixteen Angmering Road, London, west eleven. Did you see what happened to the letter?'

'I never saw the letter again, your honour. It was a very windy day, it probably got blown away.'

***

'Mr Greening, will you please tell the court what you saw on the morning of the accident.'

'I'd parked my taxi in Angmering Road and was sitting in the cab, it's usually a good place to pick up fares. There were three of us there on that morning. And I looked up and saw a man hurrying across the road in my direction and a number fifty bus heading straight for him. The driver braked and tried to avoid hitting him but the man never turned around, even when he sounded his horn, he just kept going straight into his path. He must have heard the horn but it didn't stop him. The bus driver never had a chance, it all happened too fast.'

Inquest into the death of John Cecil Fellowes,
October 5th 1936

WAREHAM

Lindsay makes phone calls. She starts with the Royal Academy, moves on to the coroner's office, and ends up with a local historian. She goes down to the library and looks in Who's Who, and then with the help of a friendly librarian scours the town directories for 1936. Records from that far back are hard to locate and none of this activity gets her anything but a headache and a growing realisation that Caroline is probably right. It's just too distant now, and out of their grasp. There are of course still boxes and boxes of paperwork up in the loft that might hold the key, but it's a long shot and it would take months to go through them. Caroline doesn't have the luxury of time on her side any longer – if she's going to get her programme together she has to do it very soon and then pitch it convincingly to the television company. They won't wait forever and once the moment's gone it probably won't come again.

In another week Lindsay will start her new job at Stonegrove, and she knows her time will be limited then. Caroline has already run out of time and enthusiasm to keep up the search for some elusive remaining details, her theory is that Bella's story is so colourful it won't suffer if the ending is left hanging. For Lindsay though this is an unsatisfactory conclusion and not the one she'd been hoping for.

Nick, back in Wareham between gigs, is sympathetic and cheers Lindsay up by putting a positive spin on the outcome.

'OK, it's frustrating for you,' he says, 'I get that. But just look how far you've come. Who would ever have thought that you could end up knowing as much as you do about a woman nobody even knew existed.'

They're chatting in the Theatre Room. It's ten minutes to closing, the visitors have almost all left, and Nick has dropped by on a mission, so far undisclosed.

'Until that picture turned up Bella was completely unknown to everyone here – well, except to Diana of course but we pretty quickly established that you weren't going to get very far with her,' he adds.

Lindsay nods. 'I know you're right,' she says, 'and so is Caroline when she says she's uncovered enough. I'm just a bit disappointed, I guess I'd hoped for more than was realistic. I assumed there'd be someone somewhere who still knew a bit more about Bella, I didn't think Diana would be the only one.'

'Mrs Stanton-Lewis may not be the only one.'

Lindsay and Nick both turn to see Reg standing in the doorway. He's looking a bit sheepish, not his usual confident, forthright self.

'I couldn't help but hear you from next door,' he says. 'And there's something I should have told you about before, Lindsay. It might not be of much help, but it does indicate that someone else did know Bella, even if only by association.'

Lindsay is so surprised that she just stares at Reg, her mind whirling through the possibilities. It's left to Nick to step into the growing silence.

'Why don't we sit down for a bit and you can tell us which piece of the jigsaw you've just turned up,' he says amiably, pulling out one of the theatre chairs for Reg and then turning a couple of others round.

'It's George, isn't it?' says Lindsay as she sits down.

'Correct. The only other person alive who was at Stonegrove at the time, although he was only a small boy.'

'But he remembers Bella?' asks Nick.

Reg shrugs. 'I don't know the answer to that, but he does have something that might interest you, Lindsay. And I'm guessing that he must have seen Bella around the place. With George...' Reg sighs, '... you see, it's not easy to get anything out of him unless you know the right questions to ask. He doesn't usually volunteer much.'

'Reg, what if you and I went together to see him, and asked the right questions?' says Lindsay.

'Well then we might get somewhere.'

There doesn't seem to be much point in saving it for another day, so Reg and Lindsay make their way out of the Hall and over towards George's cottage. Nick leaves them at the main entrance and heads for the staff car park.

'What was it you came over to say?' Lindsay asks him.

'Oh, it'll wait till later. I'm just going into town – call me when you're finished with George, I'll probably be back here by then.'

* * *

Still recovering from his fall, and having to take things easy, George is frustrated and bored. He's never been one for sitting around and isn't mentally ready for an armchair and slippers yet it seems, even though his body is telling him otherwise. So visitors are very welcome and he cheers up when Reg and Lindsay tap on his door and let themselves in with a breezy greeting. They join him in the kitchen, where he's sitting at the old scrubbed pine table reading the local paper. Henry, usually chased out of George's kitchen, is making the most of what is currently a more relaxed regime, and is stretched out on an ancient rag rug in front of the range.

'How are you, my friend?' asks Reg, patting him on the shoulder. This is much more effusive than their previous meetings have ever been – down there at the potting shed there were few social niceties observed, nor any need for any. George seems to welcome this new level of friendship though, and a rare smile crosses his face.

'Ah, not so dusty,' he says, folding the paper and laying it to one side. The tray brought across from the restaurant earlier is still on George's kitchen table, although there are no traces left of the lunch it arrived with.

'Nothing wrong with your appetite, anyway,' Reg observes, indicating the empty plate. 'That's good, and they're feeding you well?'

'Ah, twice a day they come over. Mrs Croft's a good woman.'

'She worries about you, George,' says Lindsay. 'We all want to see you back out there in the garden, it's not the same without you.'

'Them apprentices, they're good lads,' says George. 'They pop in for a cuppa sometimes so I know what's going on. Put them right a couple o' times.'

Lindsay can well imagine that. He's not about to let go of Stonegrove's gardens without a fight.

'George...' Reg starts, but he doesn't get any further because George is there before him.

'You wants that diary now?' he says.

'I think Lindsay would like to read it. You know she's been trying to find out about Mr Douglas's young lady friend?'

Lindsay whips Bella's photo out of her bag and holds it up for George to see.

'Ah. I heard you was interested.'

'You might have seen her around here when she came for weekends.' George nods. 'Did you ever get to speak to her?'

George settles back in his chair and considers for a moment. In his mind he's travelling back to his childhood, revisiting a time when his life at least was simple, the cottage his home then as it is now, his parents always working, working their fingers to the bone as his mother often said. And none of it being appreciated at all by the Stanton family, that was their common complaint when they thought he was asleep and not ear-wigging on their conversations as he often did from the landing upstairs. Mr Douglas and his motorbikes ('those bloomin' motorbikes' according to Ma), Miss Ruby and Miss Diana and their endless selfish demands, Mr and Mrs Stanton standing aloof from all of this and everyone, probably not even noticing George's parents, who worked so hard day after day to keep Stonegrove ticking over nicely for them to enjoy and show off to their posh high-and-mighty friends.

And then one spring day Bella arrived, and brightened the place up just by being there. Bella with her red hair and bubbly laughter, her energy and uncomplicated sense of fun. Bella, who came across a lonely little five-year-old boy digging for worms in the kitchen garden, and ended up playing a game of tag with him around the greenhouses.

'She'd come and find me when she was here. Brought me a bat and ball so's we could play cricket, and a wooden train another time.' George breaks off, as his mind wanders back to seemingly endless summer days and Bella stealing away from the big house for half an hour, calling out his name as she came near to the cottages.

Reg glances across at Lindsay, who sits with her hand to her mouth and a pucker across her brow. For a moment he thinks she might cry, and very much hopes she won't because he's not very good at coping with tears.

'And then one day off she went and didn't come back. I kept looking out for her but I never saw her again. Don't know what happened to her after that...'

In all the years they've known each other Reg has never heard George talk so much. And now he's got started it seems there's no stopping him.

'Ma said it were a disgrace how they treated her. But that were years later.'

Lindsay realises she's been holding her breath, and lets it go with a sigh.

'Did your mum say any more about what happened with Bella? As far as we can tell she disappeared from Stonegrove straight after Douglas died, there'd been an incident in the conservatory that night and we think that may have had something to do with it.'

George shakes his head. 'No not really, I know a bit about that business though. Told Mrs Croft, t'other day, the party got out of hand, like. Someone fired a shotgun, but if Ma knew proper what went on she never told me. She didn't have a lot of time for the young Stantons. Dad got on alright with Mr Douglas but he couldn't be doing with them two girls.'

Reg leans forward.

'That picture of Douglas with the motorbikes – why did you get young Darren to move it into the house? After all this time?'

'I knew her was interested,' says George, indicating Lindsay,' and I thought it might be useful, help her a bit, like. Never see it in here, would she? Same as I thought that old diary might be useful. Here Reg, get my jacket will you?'

Reg gets up, takes George's tweed gardening jacket off the hook on the back door, and passes it across to him. Lindsay's wondering how many years the jacket's been in service, it must take an awful lot of use to wear heavy-duty tweed down to threadbare. The elbows have been patched with leather at some point and now need replacement patches, although she's thinking that the fabric probably couldn't stand the strain of being repaired yet again. George reaches into the left-hand pocket with his good hand, pulls the diary out and passes it across the table to Lindsay.

'Thank you George. I'll be very careful with it and then give it back to you once I've had a look,' she says.

'No no, you keep it. T'ain't no good to me. Only goes up to February anyway, so nothing much to read.'

She turns it over in her hand. Bound in dark brown leather, it's smaller than a postcard and about a centimetre thick, with gold edges to the pages. She opens it carefully to the first page, where Douglas had written his name and address in a scratchy, untidy hand on January the first, 1936. He'd used blue-black ink, which has faded over the years although it's still legible, and she imagines him writing with the black fountain pen she and Reg found with his dinner jacket all those weeks ago. The pen is currently on display in the Memorial Room alongside the Rolex watch and the other items that were in his pockets, except of course for the photo of Bella. There's something about this thought and the connecting strands that sends a shiver down her spine.

'I'll read it later George,' she says, closing the little book and putting it in her bag. As an afterthought she picks Bella's picture up from the kitchen table and slips it between the pages of the diary.

'And I can tell you what happened later on in Bella's life. We found out quite a lot about her.'

George nods his head slowly. 'I'd like to know she was happy. That'd be good enough for me.'

'I think she was, George. She had a long and happy life.'

Reg stands up and pushes his chair in under the table, startling Henry, whose head shoots up and then sinks down again as soon as he realises he's not in any danger. 'I think I'm going to leave you two to it now. Lindsay's got a lot to tell you and if I don't get home soon my wife will think I've run off.'

Reg shakes George's hand and heads for the door.

'It's quite a story,' he adds on his way out, lifting a hand to wave goodbye.

* * *

It's more than half an hour later when Lindsay leaves George's cottage and heads back towards the Hall. The main front door is locked by then so she makes her way round to the back and the estate office entrance. When she gets there she finds Nick and Anthony standing in the corridor chatting.

'How did it go with old George?' Anthony asks.

'Oh... it was interesting. He remembers Bella, she used to play with him and he was obviously fond of her. I feel I finally got close to her today, talking to George, even more so than when we met her grandson.'

'So does this signal the end of her story?' asks Nick.

'Not quite, but maybe it's near enough.' Lindsay sighs. 'I think I've achieved what I wanted to – actually far more than I ever expected, if I'm honest.'

'An excellent outcome then!' says Anthony. He makes as if to go, then stops and turns towards them.

'I should think a celebration is called for, wouldn't you Nick? A bottle of Prosecco at the very least...'

Lindsay looks from one to the other and it's left to Nick to pick this up and run with it.

'That's uncanny, just what I was thinking. There's a new Spanish tapas bar in town...'

Anthony wanders away from them, whistling. When he reaches the end of the corridor he calls back, 'If you don't go Lindsay, I just might. Helena's out this evening and I'm faced with cooking my own supper... Actually even if you do go I might tag along...'

'No you won't,' says Nick. 'I only booked for two.'

Anthony laughs and leaves them to it.

'You already booked a table?'

'Yeah, this afternoon. I was going to ask you and then this thing with George came up – but I figured I might as well book anyway. I mean, what's the worst that could happen?'

'I could agree to come.'

'The inquest report is in the Times. They say he walked in front of a bus and it couldn't stop in time.'

'Yes, I know.'

'And he was reading something, a witness said it was a letter. Ruby, you don't think it could have been your letter, do you? It probably arrived just that morning, I mean if he was upset... Ruby?'

'Bella's got a lot to answer for, if it wasn't for her none of this would have happened and there wouldn't have been a letter. We're never going to talk about this again Diana, I mean it, and just remember the promise you made to the parents. It's all over, and you must never, ever speak of it again.'

Diana and Ruby Stanton, October 6th, 1936

STONEGROVE, THE FOLLOWING YEAR

'I wonder how Caroline's feeling at the moment?'

It's Nick who says it, although they're all thinking the same thing.

The four of them are sitting in Helena and Anthony's beautiful cream sitting room, all ready for the television awards programme, many months since Caroline's show was finally completed and aired, much longer since she first pitched the idea to the television company. Lindsay & Nick arrived an hour ago with a take-away and Helena and Anthony have provided champagne, so now they're all set.

It's been an exhausting few months for the Stonegrove team, what with the increased foot-fall thanks to the Bella effect, plus the conversion of two of the estate cottages as holiday lets, a project which is now nearing completion. Anthony took on the major part of this workload but some of it has still fallen on Helena, mainly for decisions on interior décor and fittings, and administratively there's been a knock-on effect on Lindsay too.

One of the cottages undergoing a make-over is Diana's. Helena's anxiety about her mother watching the screening of 'Finding Bella' was not warranted after all. Diana suffered a stroke before filming had even started at Stonegrove, and she died in a private hospital room only a few days later, with her daughter and grandchildren at her side. The funeral was a quiet affair, with just the immediate family present, although the local paper did send a photographer along to the house to capture the moment when the hearse took Diana away from Stonegrove for the last time.

Helena had arranged for a florist to use some flowers from the gardens in a wreath, but as a matter of courtesy she mentioned this to George first.

'You tell her to take whatever she wants,' he said, although when Helena asked him for guidance as to which plants Diana was particularly fond of he just shrugged. In the end and with nothing to go on, the florist had a walk round the gardens and snipped lots of buds that were just opening, plus plenty of greenery. The resulting wreath had a pleasant rustic look to it, which Helena thought her mother would have liked.

It took many months to clear Diana's cottage. For a start, this had to be fitted in around the ordinary work load at Stonegrove, plus Helena didn't want to miss anything important so she sifted through each drawer, chest, box and suitcase painstakingly. Lindsay offered to help, but really it was something that only Helena could do and be sure that the search was as thorough as she wanted it to be. She wasn't looking for anything in particular, but living somewhere like Stonegrove does place certain responsibilities on the incumbents. Helena has known this since she was little, and her family history is more important to her than she lets on. Anything of interest that she found was archived in the hopes of making it available to the public one day, in a form that hasn't yet been decided.

Anthony had suggested moving everything up to the Hall so that work on the cottage could begin, but Helena kicked against that idea.

'We're already overrun by Ruby's boxes, which I don't often have time to go through. If I add Mother's stuff to the pile we'll never see an end to it. All the time it's in her cottage and I know I've got a deadline to meet it'll get done,' she said. She was right, of course. It did get done.

Since then, Helena's working days have returned to normal and now she can enjoy granny-duties again without feeling she ought to be up at the cottage working her way through yet more memorabilia. Disappointingly, although some interesting family paperwork did come to light, there were no diaries, letters or anything else relating to the period around Douglas's death, and no mention of Bella. Caroline's story was left hanging in the air, and it's a moot point whether that wasn't actually the best outcome. Diana remained true to her parents and Ruby right to the end; she never did speak of the incident in the conservatory again, so there was no deathbed revelation. In a funny sort of way, Helena is quite proud of her mother for that.

So now here they are, the four of them, with a bottle of champagne on ice, the awards programme just about to start and a feeling of celebration in the air.

'You should be there, not here,' Anthony says to Lindsay as he pops the cork on the bottle and passes glasses around.

'Caroline asked me to go as her guest, but I don't have a posh evening dress and anyway it's not really my sort of thing. I'd rather be here with you three – I wonder what that says about me?'

'It says you've got your feet on the ground,' says Nick, 'and you're hopeless at spotting a good thing when you see it.'

Lindsay feels nervous on Caroline's behalf, although most of the pundits and everyone involved in the programme seem to think she'll walk away with the award. Caroline doesn't.

'Can't compete with cute fluffy animals,' she says to Lindsay before setting off for London.

Reg had been invited up to the flat to watch the programme, but in spite of really wanting to get up there and have a look round he declined, saying he'd watch it at home with his wife. George was also invited but clearly felt uncomfortable with the idea. In the end his faithful apprentice Darren has heroically offered to keep him company through the evening and watch the awards ceremony on George's small, ancient television. Across town, Rufus, Gary and Iris are also watching, although there's no champagne on their coffee table, just sparkling water. Since his heart attack Gary has become quite a fitness freak, something Rufus encourages but generally resists joining in with.

The public loved *'Finding Bella'*, the critics were a little more subdued in their enthusiasm, although it was universally agreed that Caroline had found her niche, tackling the people she interviewed and the issues raised with just the right blend of humour and sensitivity. With a hit on their hands the television company have signed her up for a series of six programmes, and are now casting about looking for other 'ordinary' men and women whose stories were lost and waiting to be found.

Nobody is more surprised at this success than Caroline herself. Although she never lost faith in Bella's story, she is overwhelmed by the response it's had with the general public. As she once said to Lindsay, they found their champion, and there is seemingly no shortage of candidates for subsequent investigations. From soldiers who went AWOL in the First World War to start new lives with new identities, to people who simply disappeared from cruise ships on a port stop in the middle of their holidays, the suggestions keep rolling in. Caroline reads them all through herself, if she's going to take something on it needs to strike a chord with her at the very start. The process of discovery will never again be as difficult as Bella's story was though – from here on Caroline has a dedicated team of researchers at her disposal who have unlimited access to people and archives she would have struggled to tap into on her own. The process will be fast and slick, and it won't be nearly as much fun, but now it's become a job of work rather than a consuming interest with hopes of a pot of gold at the end of it.

Filming at Stonegrove went rather better than the last time she was involved there for '*Touching My Roots*'. From the outset she insisted that the Hall should have as much prominence as possible, her side of the deal with the Crofts, with the result that visitor numbers have soared. Reg, Matthew Gerritsen, Anne Carpenter, Gary's mum Iris and even George all had their moment before the camera, filmed in different locations at Stonegrove. Lindsay didn't, at her own insistence.

'Whatever I did, we did together,' she says. 'I don't need to take any of the credit, it's all yours.'

So now the television awards have got their hands on Bella, along with three other notable documentaries from the last year and right now they're all gathered in a swanky London hotel with a whole swathe of celebrities from the television world showing off their tuxedos and designer evening gowns. The camera pans round and picks up the four presenters whose documentaries are up for the award. Caroline is done up to the nines in a bright pink silk dress, and she looks uncharacteristically sophisticated and remarkably relaxed. After the nominees have been introduced and the host of the award ceremony has given a short resumé of each programme, snippets of each one are screened. For 'Finding Bella' they've chosen to show the scene where Caroline's talking to camera, with the original photo of Bella in her hand and the dining room windows behind her. She holds the photo up and the camera zooms in, then merges the image with the scene beyond so that the two melt together. As she watches, Lindsay remembers doing something rather similar herself, with Helena at her side. It seems like a very long time ago.

And then you can hear a pin drop in Helena and Anthony's lounge and Lindsay's palms suddenly get very sweaty as that moment of maximum tension arrives, and the flap on the golden envelope is lifted.

AND THE AWARD GOES TO...

'Are you disappointed?' Lindsay asks Caroline. It's a couple of hours later and she's on her mobile, being taxied back to Christchurch. The first person she wants to speak to is Lindsay, her brother and Steve can wait till the next morning.

'No, not really. I never actually expected to win, I told you the bear cubs would get it. And anyway they haven't been offered a six show series – what's to be disappointed about?'

Lindsay is glad she's taking this on the chin. The offer of a series of programmes has definitely made up for missing out on a gong that she'd only need to dust regularly – or knowing Caroline, not dust at all. And plenty of other work has been coming in.

'Guess what, I've been offered another reality show.'

'Fantastic! Please tell me it's '*Strictly*', I've always wanted to see it live and you could get me a ticket.'

'It's not '*Strictly*'.'

'Oh. Not...'

'Yeah, it's the cooking one.'

Lindsay laughs so much tears start to leak from her eyes.

'Well obviously I'm not doing it, I'd be a complete disaster. But I know someone on the production team and I told him they'd be mad if they didn't get Steve on there.'

'Would he do it?'

'Oh yes, Steve'll do anything. It'll be hilarious – I'll get us into the recording.'

Lindsay has seen him on a programme recorded at a comedy festival – plus she's heard a lot about him from Caroline. The prospect of Steve on the cooking show is certainly an interesting one and while Lindsay tries to imagine how he would pull it off Caroline fills the gap by suggesting they meet for breakfast the next day.

'You mean you want me to come to your place and cook breakfast, or you want to go out and get someone else to cook it for us?' asks Lindsay.

'Out, of course. I suppose it'd better be brunch actually...' says Caroline, glancing at her watch. 'Bring Nick if you like.'

'He'll be on his way to Chester for a gig.'

'Just us then. My treat.'

And so the following morning at around eleven o'clock they meet up in a café in Christchurch where Caroline assures Lindsay they make the best all-day breakfast in town.

'I really hoped you'd get that award,' says Lindsay, once they've ordered. 'We all did. There was a cloud of disappointment hanging over Stonegrove last night, I can tell you.'

Caroline shrugs.

'Maybe next time. It doesn't matter, 'Finding Bella' was a great success with the public, and that's what's really important to me. Plus the work that's come in since off the back of the show.'

Breakfast arrives, and Lindsay has to admit Caroline's right about this place. She'd have been hard pressed to make it better, and Nick is always telling her she cooks a mean breakfast.

'Remember the first time we had breakfast together?' Caroline asks, diving in to her full English.

'Yeah, I'd just rescued you from spending the night in a hospital bed. I thought you were really odd.'

'I thought you were really bossy.'

'Ha! We were both right in a way, weren't we?'

Lindsay puts her knife and fork down and reaches into her bag for something.

'If you don't want to keep this I can easily take it away again.'

She places a small teddy on the table in front of Caroline, who looks at it open-mouthed with astonishment, then puts a hand out towards it.

'You kept him back from that first lot.'

Lindsay nods. 'Just in case he was needed.'

Caroline picks up the teddy. He's got a blue ribbon around his neck and a knitted beret perched at an angle on his head.

'I didn't know which one to rescue... hope I made a good choice.'

Caroline gets to her feet, comes around the table to Lindsay's side and gives her a big hug.

'You made the best choice,' she says, and wipes at her eyes with the napkin that's still in her hand. 'The absolute best. Thank you.'

There's a moment of silence which neither of them seem able to fill.

'Your breakfast's getting cold,' Lindsay says finally.

Caroline sits down again and puts the little teddy back on the table, propped up by the salt and pepper pots.

'As it happens, I've got something for you as well,' she says, taking an elaborately wrapped parcel from her bag and handing it across the table to Lindsay.

'Wow, this looks too good to unwrap.'

'That's what I admire most about you, Lin, you've got such amazing self-control. I'd have ripped the paper off already.'

It takes a while to get through the ribbon and gift-wrap, and Lindsay is careful about doing it, but finally the last layer of tissue paper comes away. Inside is a replica of the award that Caroline didn't quite get. Lindsay turns it over in her hand. Caroline watches her, sees the moment when she spots the engraving at the bottom, and the small gulp in her throat as she reads it.

Awarded to Lindsay Walton
In the category:
Best Friend

'You're a daft bat,' she says to Caroline, with a smile.

'Yeah, I thought you'd say that. I want to see this on your mantelpiece every time I'm round at your place.'

'What makes you think you're coming round to my place on a regular basis?'

'You never finished teaching me how to cook.'

'I never even started.'

'Exactly.'

Not quite The End...

Dear John

What happened between us last night wasn't love, as you seemed to be thinking. After the shock of hearing about Douglas we both needed some comfort, and that's what we found together. You have to understand that it was really nothing more than that.

I've decided to take that job in Scotland. By the time you get this letter I'll probably be on my way to Euston station to catch the Edinburgh train, so I don't think we'll be seeing each other again. I'm sorry, but that's how it has to be, better by far for both of us to leave Stonegrove and all that went on there behind us. We would just be a constant reminder to each other of what happened. But I hope you'll remember me fondly, as I will you.

You're a good man, John. Too good for me and far too good for Ruby. Let her down gently if you can, though goodness knows she doesn't deserve your kindness.

With love from Bella.

Letter from Bella to John Cecil Fellowes, received on the morning of Monday September 23rd 1936

Annette Keen lives on the south coast with her musician partner Andy, where she spends her non-writing time running a jazz club, making quilts and theatrical costumes, practising yoga and walking the seafront.

Finding Bella is her third novel. *The Generation Club* and *Distant Cousins* are also published by Sunbird Publishing and both are available in Kindle format from Amazon UK, or as paperbacks via the contact form on her website.

www.annettekeen.co.uk